Fleeing Owen Sound

STEVEN PERSEN

ISBN 979-8-89309-068-0 (Paperback)
ISBN 979-8-89309-069-7 (Digital)

Copyright © 2024 Steven Persen
All rights reserved
First Edition

This book is a work of historical fiction. All names, characters, places, businesses, and events are either the products of the author's imagination or are used fictitiously. Any resemblance to actual persons, living or dead, events, businesses, or locales is entirely coincidental.

All rights reserved. No part of this publication may be reproduced, distributed, or transmitted in any form or by any means, including photocopying, recording, or other electronic or mechanical methods without the prior written permission of the publisher. For permission requests, solicit the publisher via the address below.

Covenant Books
11661 Hwy 707
Murrells Inlet, SC 29576
www.covenantbooks.com

PREFACE

I find that history is an unlimited resource from which an author can use their imagination to fill in the gaps and weave a fictional tale that continues to bounce against and through the framework of what has actually happened. The challenge I found was to find a piece of history that had not already been done hundreds of times before but was new, fresh, and compelling to the reader.

I found that unicorn while I was researching shipwrecks upon the Great Lakes. For the reader to fully appreciate the story that follows, it is important that the reader first knows the unique history that actually occurred. Below is a brief outline of the history from which this story came to life.

Isle Royale is an archipelago in the northwest corner of Lake Superior. At the treaty of Versailles in 1783, which drew the boundaries of our new nation after the conclusion of the revolutionary war, Benjamin Franklin moved the proposed northern boundary between Canada and the United States north so that Isle Royal would fall into the territory of the United States. He did this because he had heard about the vast amount of copper that had been reported on the island, as he learned that it had been mined for hundreds of years prior by the Ojibwe Indians. In fact, as time passed, it was discovered that Isle Royale had one of the world's largest deposits of copper.

The Silver Islet Mine was founded in 1863 when silver was found on a rocky island a mile off the southern edge the Sibley Peninsula into Lake Superior, roughly fifteen miles northwest of Isle Royale. The Silver Islet was at that time only about eight feet above the level of the lake, so the miners built wooden seawalls around the opening of the mine to keep the waves generated by the fierce storms the lake spawned from flooding the mines. The mine shafts extended 1,250 feet below the surface of the lake. They used a lot of the crushed rock from the excavation of the tunnels to enlarge the size of the tiny island to almost ten times its original size. Unfortunately, in 1884, the mines flooded as a shipment of coal was delayed in reaching them, which caused the pumps to stop during the winter storms. The mines flooded and have never been reopened.

Canada was behind the US in forming their new nation. In fact, it wasn't until 1867, with the signing of the Canadian confederation, that the provinces united to form a country that went sea to sea like the US. A major condition of this signing was the promise of a Canadian transcontinental railroad. They had seen that America had already undertaken this task, which would eventually be completed in Promontory Utah in 1869, and didn't want to be left behind.

The *Canadian Pacific Railway Company* (CPR) was formed in 1880 to take over the uncompleted Canadian railroad project and fast track it to completion. This company was given twenty-five million acres of land, a huge revolving line of credit from the government, plus other considerations to complete the project.

The town of *Owen Sound* was chosen to be the CPR headquarters for both their railroad and shipping operations. On a side note, Owen Sound became the counterfeit capital in the world for US currency by 1875.

The *Algoma*, the first of three new ships the CPR had built in Scotland, had arrived for service on the Great Lakes in 1883. It and her sister ships were built too big to pass through the Welland canal on their journey to Lake Superior and had to be cut in half, floated through the canal on barges, and then rejoined on the other side.

On November 7, 1885, two important events occurred: the CPR railroad finished the transcontinental railroad project, and the *Algoma* sunk off Isle Royale in a winter storm.

These are some of the basic facts recorded in history. Everything else written in this book is fiction, created by me to entertain the reader and weave a tale that ties all this history together in a neat, thrilling package.

FLEEING OWEN SOUND

Map of the Region

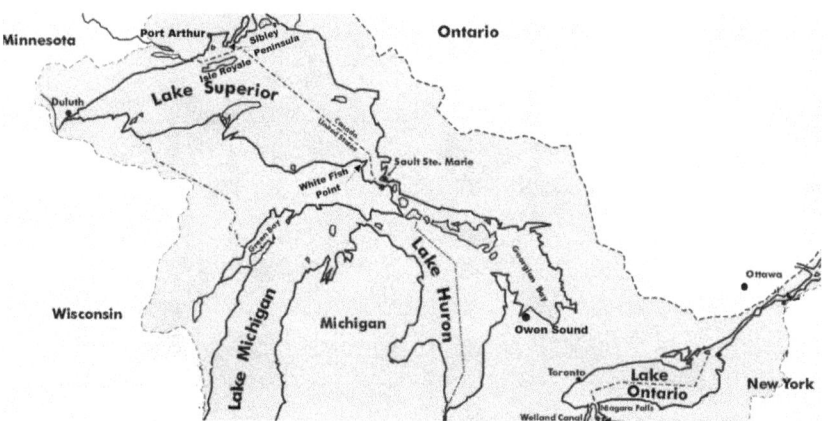

CHAPTER 1

Up North

I didn't yet know who was sent to track me down, but I was sure that they were coming, and I worried that they were not the type of men to be reasoned with.

—Winston Hawes, reporter, *Owen Sound Times*, November 1885

The arctic wind was blowing from across the Georgian Bay causing each breath to sting as I gasped, struggling to keep up my hurried pace. I pushed on to the waterfront as fast as I could go into the darkness, frantically looking for a train or ship to board. It did not matter which one or where it was headed, I just needed to put some distance between this town and myself. I quickly glanced at my surroundings and noticed that several of the gas street lamps were not lit, which was a mixed blessing. It would help to conceal me; unfortunately, it would also help to conceal anyone that might be chasing after me. I darted a few more steps until my fatigued and numb legs caused me to stumble. I fell down against a wooden fence near Damnation Corner. It was so named because it had a rowdy tavern on each corner of the intersection of Tenth Street and Third Avenue. I cursed at my legs for staging a rebellion against me. I guess that's what I get for not putting on the thicker wool pants. Rubbing my legs to get some feeling back into them, I leaned against the fence in the darkness and strained to see or hear whistles, or shouting men, or even running footsteps but to no avail. All I could hear was the rowdy crowd a half a block farther down the street on my right. My eyes confirmed this upon seeing the faint but soft glow of light from the taverns, as men satisfied their desires inside them. My pounding chest was the only sign of immediate danger my ears could detect; however, I couldn't do anything about that now. I needed to push on, staying here was not an option. The only person I trusted in this town was dead, and I was to blame. I slapped my legs one final time, when I noticed that I was injured and there was blood on my hand from my pants leg.

Funny, my legs do not hurt, I thought. *Must be too cold.*

Forcing myself to stand up, I tentatively looked down at the gash in my pants leg, and I felt the hairs on my neck stand up in fear. A dark thought washed over my consciousness like a tidal wave crashing down with absolute authority, as I began to sense that death itself was pursuing me! Now don't get me wrong, death was no stranger in this Canadian port town of forty-five hundred mostly miserable souls, which was still more frontier than civilized. Life here was hard, and the people here lived a hardscrabble life, where they had to claw and fight year round just to survive. Winters brought a whole nother level of desperation and misery, especially for the unprepared, unlucky, or injured. I just never expected to be one of them. My attempt to escape Owen Sound with my life intact was probably being done in vain, as I was now all three. I was unprepared, unlucky, and, now, injured. The trifecta of bad news. More importantly, I was to blame for another person's death, which is a hanging offense in these parts. Come morning, I was going to be the only suspect—that is, if I lived until morning.

Face it, my mind whispered, *it's almost certain that you will not make it through the night alive. Look at the odds. It's inevitable. Who are you to escape death? Are you immortal? Death from this wretched place or death at the hands of your pursuers. Does it really matter which one wins at this point? Besides, now you are injured too.*

"Death is coming, and I am unable to outrun it," I mumbled to myself out loud.

That's right, the voice whispered inside my head. *You're going to die. Death is the cost of living, so you might as well accept it. Your only choice now is how you get to die, and whether your man enough to go out on your own terms.*

I looked over at the Georgian Bay just a few blocks away pondering my mortality when my will to live showed up and joined the fight in my head.

This is not just about you… many others will be hurt if you give up. You have a job to finish. You have got to try to make it, even if the odds are remote. Be a man and choose life. Go out on your own terms, on your own time… just not here, not now!

As if the space inside my head wasn't crowded enough, a voice from my past joined the conversation.

Are you going to sit here all day like a statue?

"What was that?" I mumbled audibly again. "Where have I heard that before?"

I thought for a moment, trying to quiet my mind. Then after a few moments, the present was lost, and I found myself reliving a scene from my past.

*****

Four years ago, I had taken a job at the *Owen Sound Times* as a reporter. It was my first job after graduating from college, and I was eager to start my new life. I took the job with the hopes that it would give me the experience I needed to eventually return home and secure a job with one of my hometown newspapers. I still find it hard to believe that all three newspapers had no interest in me, especially the *Duluth Evening Herald*, which had just started publishing a month before I graduated and had been actively hiring new reporters. But that is beside the point.

A few months into my job at the *Times*, I started a series of articles on the Canadian Pacific Railroad. They were the biggest thing happening in all of Canada, and they were headquartered right here in Owen Sound. This recently formed company had undertaken the task of finishing the transcontinental railway project for Canada.

The project was a source of great controversy due to the delays and cost overruns already incurred, as well as a source of conflict and consternation over which towns the final route would go through as it spanned the Atlantic and Pacific oceans. Even with that said, the project also stirred up great national pride and was helping to unite the provinces. It had actually been the key condition for British Columbia to enter the Canadian Confederation in 1871, which solidified the new nation of Canada. A nation that now would span from sea to sea, just like America.

My first article in the series focused on the difficult challenges that had already been overcome during the construction of the railway and included some interviews with a few workers involved with the project. Soon after it was printed, I found an anonymous threat left on my desk, warning me I would be endangering myself if I continued. I should have heeded the warning, but I was taught to expect criticism as a reporter and dismissed it.

The second warning was delivered a few months later after an article I had written was published, focusing on the great cost of this project, both in money spent and lives lost. It was attached to a brick flying through my office window.

"Get out of town now, while you still can," the attached note said.

I was still sitting there almost in a trance, completely surrounded by broken shards of glass, the note clutched tightly in my hands, when my editor entered the room. Mr. Fontaine was a French Canadian who had taken me under his wing in the newspaper reporting business. He was like a second father figure to me, which was something I needed, as my father and I had not been close. He had always been consumed by the family business and had little time for me. Then while I was away at college, he died in a logging accident. I had suspected foul play and made a promise to myself that I would investigate it someday.

Mr. Fontaine closed my office door with a gentle thud. The sound brought me out of my shock.

"No sense getting everyone else in the office over here gawking at the mess," he exclaimed. His voice was calm and had no hint of stress, which was having its desired effect on me as well.

I handed him the note, looking out at what remained of the window, not saying a word.

"Well, what are you going to do, Mr. Hawes?" His calming tone left as he challenged me after reading the note. "Are you going to sit here all day like a statue, or are you going to earn your paycheck and investigate why someone feels threatened enough to throw a brick through your office window?"

*****

My mind came back to the present with the answer I had been searching for. I had heard it from my boss, whose murder I was going to be charged with if I stuck around. My ears now picked up other faint voices in the distance. I knew I had to hurry. I got up, forcing my legs to comply with my will. I quickened my pace as much as I could and scurried down the length of the shipping docks.

In the fog and darkness, I could make out the outline of several ships that were docked, but I needed to find one that was leaving tonight. Several yards in front of me was the CPR ticket office, and it still had a light on. I hurried over to the small office and quickly went up to the ticket counter. I must have startled the ticket agent because he looked at me with a harsh stare.

"Can I help you?"

"Yes, I need a ticket."

"Is everything all right?" the man asked. "You seem to be in an awful hurry, and there is blood on your pants leg!"

His face began to take on a slightly sinister smile. It must have been his old wrinkled face that made it look that way or the fact that I was suspicious of everyone that night. Yes, that was it. My imagination must be getting the best of me.

"There are no more passenger trains until tomorrow, but there is a ship leaving within the hour."

"What time did you say the next ship was leaving?" I asked, evading his question.

"There is a ship leaving within the hour. Where did you say you were heading?" A small glimmer in his eye now accompanied his sinister smile, which made him appear as if he knew something important that I didn't.

That look made me nervous.

"How much is the ticket?" I replied, trying to cautiously sidestep his question again.

He looked down at his price chart. Then sneaking a sly glance at me as if trying to determine the level of my desperation, he replied, "That will be ten dollars, one way, to the end of the line at Port Arthur."

In the distance, muffled footsteps began to get closer to the ticket office, but the combination of fog and darkness was too thick for the station light to cut through and let me see who was coming. I knew the ticket agent was taking advantage of my haste, but it didn't matter at this point.

"Okay I'll take it," I sputtered as I paid the man.

"Sailin' oan th' *Algoma*?" asked a surprisingly loud voice from behind me, which gave me a start.

Turning around, I saw a small man begin to appear out of the fog and darkness. He appeared to be Scottish, or perhaps he was Irish. I could never tell the difference.

"Aye, whit a grand ship she is too. Th' most powerful ship tae ever sail oan these waters."

Sizing up the man, suspiciously looking for any sign that he was one of my pursuers, I decided not to run and show my guilt.

Perhaps he doesn't know what I look like, I thought. Or perhaps my simple disguise would be enough to throw him off my trail long enough for me to get on the ship.

My disguise consisted only of the pair of reading glasses, which I wore on the end of my nose and the hat I had taken from my boss's office.

Trying to process what he had just said, I stammered, "Did you say the *Algoma*?"

The man continued to drone on. "Aye! She was built back in Scootlund, by master ship builders accustomed tae havin' their craft sail in th' north Atlantic. Sturdy she is. Th' first ay three new ships oan th' lake tae hae a steel hull."

Trying to take longer breaths and slow down my speech so I wouldn't give away my anxiety, I replied, "That's fascinating."

Still panicking, I realized it was too late to get a ticket on a different ship now as there was no time and it would bring even more attention to me if I tried. It was a cruel bit of irony that fate would have me escape town on the very ship that had caused me to flee it in the first place. The stranger started to rattle off more details of the ship, but I knew them very well.

The *Algoma* was the prize of the Canadian Pacific Railway. Well, her, and her two identical sister ships anyway, the *Athabasca* and *Alberta*. Put into service last year, they were the largest and most powerful ships to ever sail on the Great Lakes. Her steel construction made her considerably stronger than the wooden ships before her, and the seventeen hundred horsepower engines could move the two-hundred-and-sixty-five-foot ship at up to sixteen knots. She also had two masts rigged for sails that could further increase her capabilities. The trip from Owen Sound to Port Arthur could be made in just under thirty hours in relative comfort. Her cabins were well appointed, more like hotel suites than something you would expect to find on a ship. And they were also the first on the Great Lakes to use electric lights instead of oil lamps. She has one hundred and thirty first-class cabins and room for another six hundred in steerage, with the ability to haul two thousand tons of cargo besides. The ship was a monster.

I turned back to the ticket agent.

"How many passengers will be sailing on this voyage?" I asked, cutting off the stranger who hadn't stopped talking yet.

"So far, including yourself, there are only eleven passengers."

Hearing a commotion behind me, I fearfully turned, expecting to be grabbed by the short guy with the big voice. Instead, a woman was slowly appearing out of the dim and darkness, struggling with her luggage. Although she was walking toward me, the distance was too great and the light too faint to get a good look at her. There was however something that attracted me to her. I must have stared at her for a few seconds before I realized that the little guy was inching closer to me. We both looked at each other for a second, unsure what was going to happen. Suddenly, the woman, who was now only a dozen or so feet away, dropped her purse and began making a great deal of noise over it. The little man walked over to help her retrieve it. Seeing an opportunity, I turned and stepped through the gate on the far side of the ticket office.

Looking back, I saw the stranger looking right at me, but he made no attempt to follow as I started walking briskly toward the ship. The smoke stack was already blowing smoke as she was preparing for departure. I hurried aboard the monster more scared than I had ever been before in my life. I had no luggage, only the briefcase I was gripping tightly in my hand. In it contained something I had stolen from some very bad guys.

After boarding, I climbed the stairs to the main deck and headed to the back of the ship, hoping most of the passengers would stay in their cabins, leaving me to face my fears alone.

Leaning against the rail gave me a view of the entire dock, so I settled in and watched the activity or lack thereof. I wanted to see if I had been followed. I expected to see men or Mounties running around, trying to determine if I had gotten onboard or not, but there was no one. It was eerily silent. I looked back toward the ticket office and saw the woman boarding the ship, accompanied by the ship's porter, who had her luggage in tow. I watched as she strolled aboard. She walked with a graceful purpose, not looking to either side, as if not wanting to be distracted from whatever it was she was thinking about. A few minutes later, I made a mental note as I heard her in the center hallway leading to the rear cabins. With only eleven passengers on board, I was sure to run into her again before the voyage ended.

Staring back out at the dimly lit dock, my mind returned me back to the time the brick flew through my window a few years ago.

*****

"Are you going to sit here all day like a statue, or are you going to earn your paycheck and investigate why someone feels threatened enough to throw a brick through your office window?"

"What?" I replied as I looked up at him.

"They were probably right in thinking they could intimidate you so easy," he said in a mocking tone that I didn't appreciate. "They are probably laughing at you right now, thinking you messed your pants. Probably think you are halfway home to your mama's arms right now."

"Look here, Mr. Fontaine," I began to sputter as my blood began to boil.

"What, Mr. Hawes? What do you intend to do about it, stand up for yourself? I have news for you, Mr. Reporter. Your job is not about you! It is about those innocent people affected by the sinister events you are trying to get to the bottom of. It is about standing up for those who cannot stand up for themselves, protecting the people that are counting on you to do your job and uncover the unvarnished, unbiased, and honest-to-God truth. That's your job, Mr. Hawes, to expose those who prey on the innocent!"

"Stop," I shrieked. "Don't preach at me! You don't know me."

Cutting me off in midsentence, he continued, "Oh, I know you pretty well all right. Tell me about your parents again and how you feel about the circumstances surrounding their tragic deaths. Hmmm? Seems you jackrabbited out of there right quick after that."

Somewhere deep down inside, I snapped, and the anger and rage I had been trying to suppress for a very long time exploded into a loud groan, an unintelligible growl that reverberated off the office walls, until it was echoing back inside my head again.

Mr. Fontaine grabbed my arm and looked into my eyes from just inches away. So close, I could smell the sardines on his bad breath.

"Son, do you feel that anger right there in the pit of your belly, that fire?" he said as he poked his finger into my gut. "Don't ever forget that feeling. That feeling is called righteous indignation. It is what men are supposed to feel when someone we care about was wronged or harmed, when others try to make us feel inadequate or inferior and push us and bully us around. This is what drives men to seek justice on those who have broken the laws and done harm to their kin."

"I know," I snapped, my blood pressure still rising.

"Look, son. I do know you, and you are a good young man. But in these difficult times, good is not good enough. We need to strive to be great men. And the difference between good and being great is caring about others as much as we care about ourselves. Great men stand up for those who are being wronged and become personally involved in the outcome to make sure justice happens, by catching and exposing the treachery of those dastardly villains, so they can no longer prey on others. In doing so, they become the protectors of society and of the entire civilized world. Do not ever settle for being good, Mr. Hawes, when you have the ability to be great. And I believe, Mr. Hawes, that you have the rare ability to be great, if you so choose to."

I sat there in deep thought for a few minutes, running those words through my head over and over again.

He does know me, I said to myself, as guilt washed over me from running away from my problems again.

After a few moments of self-pity, my mind came to a new realization.

I do desire to be a great man. After all, what would I expect if someone had knowledge about my parents' death or could have even prevented it and did nothing, said nothing?

His speech had its intended effect on me. I took a deep breath as I crystallized my decision to keep investigating this story no matter what the cost. With this renewed vigor, I vowed to start digging deeper into my research, trying to find out who had threatened me and why.

Over the next few days, I went back and reread all of the articles I had written since I came to Owen Sound. The only thing that made sense was that these warnings were all related somehow to my articles on the railroad, but for the life of me, I could not find the connection. Deep down in my gut I knew that something didn't pass the sniff test. The railroad had a funny smell to it. I just couldn't figure out what they were trying to hide. Shoot, I still didn't know who it was that was trying to hide it in the first place. Even though I did not want to admit it, I had run out of ideas. So I decided to go back to the beginning and start over. I had too few clues to sink my teeth into, and the hunches I had all led me to a dead end. Yet I refused to give up. So I went down to the rail yard to talk to a few workers trying to dig up something under the guise that I was writing another promo piece for the paper. I wasn't sure what I was looking for specifically, but I was sure I would find it or it would find me.

When I arrived at the railyard, I headed down a track to where several men were gathered.

As I started to walk toward the crowd, a rough-looking man pointed his finger at me and yelled, "Get out of here. We don't need your kind of trouble." Then he walked over and grabbed me by the collar of my coat and escorted me on past the crowd. While the crowd was jeering and yelling, he whispered in my ear, "Tonight, eleven o'clock behind the Bucket of Blood, off the record."

With that, he reached the end of the railroad property and gave me a mighty push, so hard in fact that I almost fell over face first into the hard-packed earth. Luckily, I landed on my shoulder instead. This made the now distant crowd of railroad men roar with laughter in approval. It looks like it found me!

I got up and dusted myself off, excited that I finally had a potential lead. I quickly left and went back to the newspaper office to make some notes while my mind was churning with possibilities. After I wrote them all down, I burst into Mr. Fontaine's office to tell him of the new lead I had, but before I could say anything, I noticed he already had someone in his office. The man was huge, well over six feet tall, with an ugly look on his face. When he saw me, he stopped talking and left the room without saying another word. After he left, Mr. Fontaine got up and closed the door behind him.

"Who was that?" I asked. "And what did he want?"

"Never mind, nothing to concern yourself with," came the uneasy reply. "Now what was the reason you almost busted my door down to see me?"

I was so excited to tell my boss I finally had a lead that I spent the next fifteen minutes blathering on, too self-absorbed to notice that he didn't share my excitement. Then I left and started to make a list of questions I wanted to ask my informant.

*****

I arrived at the location a half hour early, and it seemed like forever waiting behind the saloon. I checked my pocket watch, and the time had already reached midnight. This was not a place you wanted to loiter after dark.

The Bucket of Blood was one of the four infamous bars on Damnation Corner. It had the reputation for drawing the roughest of men, but for some reason that night, all the action was over at the Pig's Ear tavern across the street. I was about ready to call it quits, when the rough railroad worker appeared from the shadows. He staggered over to where I was standing, pretending, I think, to be drunk in case anyone was watching and started peeing on the wall I was leaning against.

"Sorry, mate," he stammered loudly as his urine was now splashing dangerously close to my shoe.

Finished, he leaned over and told me to check out the three ships the Canadian Pacific Railway, or CPR, had purchased, but to do so cautiously as there were strange things happening with them and they were guarded at all times when in port by CPR constables.

He added, "Don't mess with them, they have more power here than the governor."

I asked the first of my prepared questions, but the man simply turned and walked away, back into one of the taverns.

*****

The next day I went to the CPR's administrative office and got stopped by a snooty-looking woman behind a large desk. I would say she looked like a librarian, with her prim outfit and harsh glare, as if I should be whispering and tiptoeing. The only problem with the librarian thing was that she did not look that intelligent or pretty.

Probably couldn't read at all. Perhaps a town like this is the place where librarian wannabes worked. Probably married to the mayor.

"Well, what do you want?" she rudely asked, as if she had just read my thoughts.

"I would like to see the CPR contracts and blueprints for the three new ships," I said. "I am a reporter and have been writing articles about the CPR."

I probably shouldn't have added that, as she acted real funny and said, "Ain't gonna talk to no reporter. Now git before I get in trouble."

With that, a couple of angry-looking men appeared near the desk. Realizing this could become an uglier situation any minute, I quickly turned and left, heading back toward town, puzzled by the weirdness of it all.

But I was desperate, so later that night, I did something completely out of character and broke into the records department room of the admin building and found the blueprints to the *Algoma*. The ship had been built too big to get through the Welland Canal, so it had to be cut in half and reassembled once transported past the canal, on the other side. That was public knowledge and had been reported in various newspapers at that time. What was not known, according to the blueprints, was that the ship was five feet longer after it was welded back together, and apparently, they had made a bulkhead wall two and a half feet away from either side of where it was cut in two. It also showed that there was a secret entrance into this dead space from the cabins directly above.

I put the blueprint back where I had taken it from and left quickly before I was discovered. On my way back to my office, I kept thinking about the ship being made five feet longer. *Why didn't they just have it made that way in the first place?* I decided that I should follow up on that and check it out for myself.

Halfway back to the office, I saw a pawnshop that had a sailor uniform hanging in the window, which gave me an idea. Since I had already broke my way into one building tonight, I decided that another was no big deal. So I broke in to the pawnshop and took the uniform and quickly changed clothes. Then I headed back to the docks dressed as a sailor and snuck aboard the *Algoma*. Luckily, it didn't take long for me to locate the secret entrance to the undocumented cargo hold in the middle of the ship. Once I climbed down the ladder, I discovered, or should I say uncovered, an international scandal with staggering implications. I grabbed some evidence and left the ship as fast as I could. Then I hurried back to my boarding room in town, trying to process what I had discovered.

My mind was overwhelmed, and I knew I was in over my head. After pacing for a while, I sat down on the edge of the bed. As the adrenaline wore off, I realized that I was exhausted mentally and physically, and I soon drifted off to sleep. I slept in late the next morning, then I spent hours pacing back and forth, trying to figure out what was going on.

Before I could get any of my thoughts written down in a logical manner, my editor, Mr. Fontaine, had a message delivered for me to meet him in his office right away. I finished getting dressed and headed to his office early that afternoon.

When I arrived, he closed his door behind me and ordered me to stop writing the articles. He sounded scared, and I think someone had threatened him to make me stop. We argued back and forth, out of earshot range, but in full view of the staff as well as the people out on the street through his windows. I had said some pretty strong things, calling him two-faced for telling me to ignore the threats but then changing his tune when apparently he had been threatened. I challenged his manhood and asked if he believed any of the stuff he had told me when the brick had smashed through my window. He looked at me as if he was working up another pretty speech. I wasn't in the mood, and I stormed out of his office, slamming the door behind me. I was too far along to stop now.

*****

After having several hours to let the anger and adrenaline wear off, I headed back to the office that evening to apologize and show him the evidence I had taken, knowing that he would be there late to get the final touches done for the morning paper. When I arrived, I found the building mostly empty, which was strange, as there should be people running all over the place, getting the final copies ready for print. Seeing that the light was still on in Mr. Fontaine's office, I walked back to apologize for my earlier outburst. When I opened the door, I found him slumped over his desk in a pool of blood. Rushing to his side, I was about to check his pulse when I saw him lift his head just a bit and look at me.

"Winston...," he said with the faintest of voices.

"Boss, what happened? Who did this to you?" I asked.

"Winston...I'm sorry."

"You're going to be just fine," I said, trying to reassure both of us. "I can get the doctor here in a few minutes."

"It's too late for me. Save yourself! Leave this town and never come back."

"Who did this to you?" I asked again as I saw the extent of the injuries to his face.

"Destroy whatever information you have uncovered. You do not know how powerful the men are that are behind this..."

"Boss?" I said.

"Cons," was the last thing he uttered. His head fell back to the desk, and he was no more.

Once I understood that he was indeed dead, the room started spinning on me. Everything began to turn dark, and I passed out.

*****

The trees were lazily dancing past my eyes, just as effortlessly as if some magician had made them detach their roots from the soil and float by on the evening wind. I watched giant pines and spruces, oaks and elms, and whole groves of birch trees that seem to go on forever. I spotted chestnuts and maples; redbuds, dogwoods, and willow trees. It seemed there was no end to the genus of trees that paraded past me, each of the non-evergreens exploding with brilliant gold, orange, and fiery red shades that made the city trees that were changing to their fall colors back home green with envy and pale by comparison.

Looking past the trees, I saw eagles and hawks and all kinds of winged creatures flying about, with gophers and chipmunks playing tag in the patches of tall grasses that waved hello in the wind. I felt like Aladdin riding a magic carpet to a different world, away from the stress and trouble of life in a bustling port city like Duluth, Minnesota. The contrast between the worlds I lived in and the one I now found myself traveling through was surreal. Pinching myself just to make sure I wasn't dreaming, I quickly determined that this was no illusion or trick played out on the simple minded. As impressive as that revelation was to my mind, I was spellbound and powerless to look away. My soul filled with much wonderment and amazement as I was awestruck at the sights my eyes beheld.

Unlike Aladdin, my magic carpet was a steam locomotive headed out into the wilderness of Canada, taking me to the cutting edge of North America's untamed frontier, where some of Canada's most rugged men had labored to build a city out of the frozen earth. Their efforts were fueled by the intersection of need, opportunity, and desire. Many were a lot like the famed mountain men of the Colorado Rockies, rustic individuals that could live off the land without the help of any modern conveniences, save a horse and a trusty rifle or some traps. Some were unskilled laborers, people down on their luck looking for work, only to find that their unlucky streak continued with the backbreaking work now required of them, while others were simply local folks who were motivated by the desire to survive another winter. As for myself, I had just accepted a job as a newspaper reporter for the *Owen Sound Times*. Owen Sound was a small port town in Ontario, Canada, with a population of approximately forty-five hundred people. Compared to the twenty-five thousand people that called Duluth, Minnesota, home, it was small. It was a long trip by train to Owen Sound from Duluth, with stops in Minneapolis, Chicago, Detroit, and Toronto on the way. My eyes were exhausted from taking in all the panoramic beauty that my window seat had provided. We were headed for Toronto, and darkness had begun to overtake the day, but yet I was reluctant to head to my sleeping berth and turn in for the night. So I moved to the club car to get a late snack and find another reason to evade sleep. Several minutes later, while eating a sandwich, I found that reason, or should I say, it found me.

"Hello, mind if I join ya?" asked the man who plopped down in the open seat across from me. Sticking his big hand out at me, he said, "My name is Dahlquist, but my friends call me JD."

"Hello, JD. My name is Hawes, Winston Hawes. Pleasure to meet your acquaintance," I said as I shook his hand. "Travel this way often?"

"No, this is my first time to visit Canada. How about you, Winston? May I call you Winston?" JD asked. Then without waiting for an answer, he continued by asking, "Are you going to Owen Sound?"

"Why, yes, I am," I replied, somewhat surprised by the question. As from what I was told, very few people get the chance to go there. "How about you?" I asked in return.

"Good golly, no!" JD said. Then he leaned over and whispered to me, making sure no one was observing him. "I heard stories."

"Really? I like a good story. What have you heard?" I asked in hushed tones that matched JD's sudden uneasiness. "Matter of fact, it is what I do, as I am a newspaper reporter."

"Sorry, old chap can't tell ya. You'll have to find that out for yourself." And with that, he got up, said "Good luck," and disappeared down the aisle and into the adjoining car.

*****

Slowly, I woke and started to come back to my senses after fainting. I had been dreaming about my first trip to Owen Sound a few years back. I looked around and realized I was in Mr. Fontaine's office and I was holding the hand of my dead boss. I guess I had fainted. Now he was lying on the floor next to me. I must have pulled him out of the chair when I fell. I had no idea how much time had passed; I just knew I had to get out of there. I stood up and looked around. Still there was no one to be seen. No one was looking in the window either. I glanced at my dead boss for the last time. Figuring I would need a disguise, I took his reading glasses off the desk and his hat off the coat rack, put them on, and ran out of the building. It was only a dozen or so blocks to the docks where I could catch a ship or train with any luck.

*****

The memories had stopped playing out inside my head. I was still standing at the rail of the ship, staring into the distance. Twenty boring minutes had passed, and the cold winter wind nipping at my cheeks was the only thing reminding me I was still alive. Perhaps I was going to get out of town unnoticed, I began to convince myself; after all, the ship was scheduled to leave at 9:00 p.m., which was rapidly approaching. The only activity so far had been a couple of crewmen preparing the ship for the voyage.

It wasn't long before I felt the ship rumble to life, and we began to pull away from the dock. The captain blew the ship's steam whistle, and our journey began. With my adrenaline rush coming to an end now that the ship was leaving the harbor, I decided I was going to find my cabin and collapse in a soft bed until breakfast. Pulling my ticket out of my pocket, I was shocked to discover that the old man at the ticket office had failed to include a cabin with the fare. I let a flurry of expletives fly into the evening air that would have made a sailor proud and my mother cry. This meant that I was sold a steerage ticket without a berth. I was beginning to feel like the old bugger did it on purpose. Maybe that was what the sly smile was all about. I was about to go into a full tantrum when reason temporarily grabbed control. Perhaps it was a misunderstanding. After all, I was in a hurry, and I did not tell him I wanted a cabin. I guess he assumed that since I had no luggage, I didn't need one. But then reason was overtaken by anger when I remembered that he charged me ten dollars for the ticket. Ten dollars for a first-class ticket with a cabin suite on a modern passenger ship like this was expensive, but not outrageously so. However, ten dollars for a steerage ticket was extortion. Still in shock and disbelief, I saw the words "second class" on my ticket, confirming the conclusion I had just came to. My blood began to boil. This means I won't be allowed above deck.

The only sheltered place for me on the ship now is below decks in the common area shared by all the poor passengers. With that realization, a cold chill ran down my spine. My paranoia kicked into high gear, replacing the anger that had suddenly appeared a moment ago. The ticket agent had set me up. He just confined me to the easiest place on the ship to be captured. I was probably going to be the only passenger of the eleven to be in the steerage common area. Anyone on the ship could be my pursuer. Maybe they all were. There was no room for error now. I had to think, come up with a plan. I had to find a place to hide.

*****

"Listen up ye bunch of lackeys! Mah nam is McDuff, an' Ah am haur tae retrieve some sensitife property swatched frae th' Canadian Pacific Railway. Th' bloke that has it is named Hawes, an' he is oan thes ship. Ah am offerin' ye fower limeys a chance tae make a lot ay money, two hunder dollars tae th' man who can deliver heem tae me haur in th' galley. We hae twintie-fower hoors tae fin' heem an' gie th' property back afore we reach Port Arthur. Onie questions?"

One of the four crewmen named Halverson took a step forward and asked, "What does he look like?"

McDuff eyed the man for a moment, then replied, "Ah laid eyes oan heem back at th' tickit office. He is taa, wi' dark hair stickin' oot frae under a hat an' is wearin' spectacles, an' haes blood oan his claes. He cam aboard wi' naethin' but a briefcase."

"So you want to talk to this man and retrieve what is in his briefcase?" asked another crewman named Duncan.

McDuff paused, walked over, and poked his finger into the man's chest for emphasis. With a snarl, he said, "Yeah, that's reit. An' en we're gonna kill heem deid. In case onie ay ye limeys has a problem wi' at, mah friend here is gonna help ye fin' heem."

Right on cue, another man entered the room. He was as big as a bear he was. Huge arms, barrel chest, face that looked like he had been in way too many fights. This guy seemed as if he could snap a man's neck as easy as if it were a twig.

"Weel, don't jist stain thaur gawkin', divide up in tae twos an' gie gonnae," McDuff barked, drawing their attention off the stranger and springing them into action.

*****

As my paranoia was still whirling away at full tilt, I noticed someone walking toward me. Seeing me look up, he hollered, "Excuse me, sir! I need to speak with you."

He was still half the ship's length away, but there was no one else on the starboard side deck. I wasn't going to wait and find out what he wanted to chat about. Whoever it was meant trouble for me. Either it was my pursuers wanting to do their worst or someone wanting to check my ticket, which, upon seeing it, would usher me below decks, which would bring me back to my pursuers who would do their worst. I took off walking in the opposite direction, toward the back of the ship. Turning to the aft, I quickly darted down the second hallway to my right. Looking for a place to hide, I started checking the doors to the first-class cabins, but they were all locked. I could tell the person behind me had quickened their pace by the sounds of their shoes slapping against the deck in the area I had just left. Coming to another hallway, I looked around both corners, but could see no one. Turning left, away from the sounds, brought me next to a staircase that led below decks. I needed to get out of the open, as I heard someone coming up the stairs, whistling. Discovering a door behind the staircase, I tried the doorknob. It turned, and I jumped inside without looking. Finding myself in a small life-jacket locker about the size of a large closet, it was all I could do to get the door closed quickly and quietly. Seconds later, I heard two sets of footsteps outside the locker. They paused and stopped a few feet from the door. Gently putting my ear up to the door, I could hear the sounds of two men talking. The only muffled words I could make out were "Hawes" and "Briefcase." With that, my fears had been confirmed, and my mania had reached a new pinnacle. Everything was starting to go black. I felt myself beginning to hyperventilate. The air became hot and stale. Claustrophobia was setting in. Perhaps if I closed my eyes tightly it would make the room stop spinning and keep it from closing in on me. But I knew it wouldn't work; I had already experienced this once today. It would only be a matter of time before I passed out. Pushing myself deeper into the locker, I tried to conceal myself. That was the last thing I remembered.

*****

I waited a few minutes to finish my sandwich. Then I followed after JD into the next car. He was sitting alone next to the window writing into a journal. When he looked up and saw me, he quickly put away the journal and stared at me.

"Mr. Dahlquist, do you mind if I join you for a while?" I asked. "I'm buying."

"I don't see why not. I have some spare time waiting for this train to get us to where we are going. But please call me JD."

"Thanks. Traveling by yourself can make even the stoutest heart anxious and homesick."

"Where's home?" asked JD.

"Well, it was Duluth, Minnesota. But there is not much left for me there but painful memories, so I am off to start my life somewhere fresh."

"I am sorry to hear that. Really, I am."

"Thank you. That is a very kind thing for you to say."

"So how did you choose the obscure little town of Owen Sound, Canada, to be the place you wanted to start over at?"

"Lucky, I guess!" I said with a chuckle. "I got offered a job, and it seemed foolish to turn it down."

"That is lucky. Good jobs are hard to come by, especially in a frontier town like Owen Sound."

"Where are you traveling to, JD?" I asked.

"Oh, I am headed to Toronto."

"So what do you do in Toronto?"

"I work for the railroad," he said somewhat anxiously.

"Oh, are you a conductor? I always thought that would be an interesting job."

"No," he replied uneasily. "I have a much different job for the railroad that I am not at liberty not talk about. Now if you will please excuse me, I think I am ready to turn in for the night."

With that, JD got up and went off to his sleeping car. I sat there thinking how strange this man was. Finally, my mind turned toward what I was going to find when I got to Owen Sound. Up ahead I could hear the engineer pull on the steam whistle.

*****

McDuff and the man who was as big as a bear, called Archer, were all that remained in the galley. The rumor is that Archer got his name in an act of piracy in the South Pacific when he was stabbed in the chest but still managed to pick up his assailant and throw him overboard with such a force that one of the witnesses said he looked like he was shot off the ship like an arrow. Maybe the four crewmen had also heard the rumor because they had scurried out rather quickly and started searching the ship for Hawes.

"What if we can't find the scallywag before we reach port?" Archer asked. As soon as the words left his mouth, he regretted it.

A slow evil grin crossed over his face. "That's somethin' ye don't need tae concern yerself wi', unless ye can't fin' heem," hissed McDuff. "So fur yer sake, ye better fin' heem."

Even though Archer towered over the small Scottish man, McDuff had always intimidated him. Of course, if you had seen the evil things Archer had seen McDuff do, you would be intimidated too. With that, Archer left the galley in search of some crewmen. Then it would be his turn to intimidate someone.

*****

"What have you gotten the two of us into? Making some quick cash rustling up a passenger is one thing, but killing a man is more than I bargained for."

"'Just help me find this passenger,' the man had said to us, 'and I will make it worth your while,'" replied the second sailor. "There aren't any laws about helping strangers and getting a little reward for doing so."

"Well, I want no part of it. I don't want that kind of trouble on my conscience."

"Conscience? Since when did you get one of those? Did you buy it back at port before we left?" mocked the second sailor. "If you paid money for it, you got ripped off!"

"Ha-ha. Like you don't have one. I have sailed with you on this ship since day one, almost two years ago. And for a couple more years on another ship before that. Don't go pulling the 'I'm a tough guy' act on me now. Besides, you only do that when you're scared."

"I'm not scared, I am worried! My gut says it will be us that winds up dead if we try to weasel out of this predicament. And what was with the little Irish guy sounding all tough and what not. He's lucky he has that big goon watching his back."

"Like you were going to put him in his place before he showed up."

"I might have," retorted the other. "And I would have won too, unless the wee squirt is a leprechaun."

Realizing they were in a predicament, the first sailor tried to lighten the mood by mocking McDuff.

"Aye! Me thinks th' wee squirt is a leprechaun, but it'd be heem that was hurtin' if we ever met in a dark alley. Ah hae th' secret o' how tae defeat leprechauns."

"Oh really, tell me what it is then."

"Cannae dae it. Then ye wid tell ev'body 'n' thare wid be na mair leprachauns or thair hidden gowld."

His humor finally met its mark, as the other sailor chuckled and played along.

"Did anyain teel ye, ye aren't reit in th' heed?"

"Aye! An' if ah were reit minded, ah would of dain something about 'at too."

Both sailors were laughing, with the tension having been temporarily broken up, and didn't notice the ship's captain walk up behind them.

"Crigger, Tibbs! Surely you don't mind sharing with your captain what is so funny about standing around and not doing your jobs," he blasted them.

"Our apologies, Captain," Tibbs said.

"See that it doesn't happen again!" Captain Ericson warned them. Then he turned and walked back toward the bridge.

With that, the two sailors abandoned the search and returned to their duties on the *Algoma*. Captain Ericson was a fair and decent man, and the crew mostly liked him, even though he commanded his ships with a firm grasp, not tolerating any tomfoolery when there was work to be done. And there was always work to be done.

*****

In the distance, I heard the ship's whistle sounding. My head hurt, the air was still, stale, and hard to breathe, and I was in total darkness. Where was I? Slowly I started to remember hiding in the life-jacket locker. How long had I been in here? Were my pursuers still outside the door? I had many questions but no answers. I tried to unbury myself from the life jackets in the darkness, but to no avail. I had to get out of here soon; I couldn't take being cooped up any longer. Frantically pushing against the life jackets, I started a chain reaction that caused the door to open and the jackets to spill out onto the deck. So much for being stealthy. I peered out of the locker. It was still night. The electric lights were on, lighting up the ship's corridors. To my amazement, the hallway was empty. Looking at my pocket watch, I realized I had been unconscious for over an hour. I untangled myself and started to climb out of the locker when I noticed I wasn't holding my briefcase. I dove back into the locker, throwing around life jackets like a madman searching for his sanity. It had to be in here somewhere. If my pursuers had found it, I would surely be dead by now. After throwing out a couple more life jackets, I spotted it lying against the back wall. What a relief. It hadn't been taken after all. However, I discovered that I had lost my hat and glasses in the fervor of the search. Oh well, no time to look for them now. I needed to find a place to hide, one that wouldn't make me pass out.

*****

"Pardon me, miss," the clumsy crewman apologized. He had almost run the beautiful woman over as he was hurriedly leaving a cabin. Not stopping to wait for an answer, the crewman continued down the hallway with great haste.

How rude, Catherine thought. As someone who had traveled upon ships a time or two in the past, she was more concerned with what he had been doing in the first-class section, particularly why he had been in a passenger's cabin than the crewman's lack of proper manners.

Ms. McGregor decided she would need to have a word or two with the captain about this. She would not however, let that keep her from enjoying an evening stroll first. The cold wind had subsided, being replaced by a light snow gently falling; and watching it from the ship's illuminated deck, swirling against the dark night sky filled with stars, made her feel like she was inside Van Gogh's *Starry Night* painting. The breeze was slight, and the lake had little ripples in it, instead of the waves one was accustomed to seeing this time of year. Looking out over the railing, she was absorbed deep in her own thoughts, thinking about how nice it would be to have found a special man to share the moment and her life with.

Catherine was a beautiful brunette with classic looks. Intelligent and charming, she had no trouble getting the attention of men. More than one had proposed to her over the years. But she was an idealist who could not bear the thought of sharing her life with someone who didn't reciprocate her zest for life. All the men she had met so far were pragmatic and boring, more concerned about acquiring stuff than they were about enjoying the spontaneous adventures of life. It wasn't that she despised having things.

Lord knows it is nice to lead a life of privilege, she thought. *But not at the expense of missing life all together. That's what was wrong with them!* Her inner monologue continued. *They were amassing wealth and privilege at the expense of enjoying life.*

Of course, she had always had suspicions that every suitor was only after a stake in her family fortune. She was wealthy beyond the common man's dreams. Having no brothers, the family fortune would be all hers one day. Her father was a shrewd businessman and controlled most of the natural resources along the North Shore of Lake Superior. A shipping magnate, he gradually leveraged his influence and began running his customers out of business by charging ever steeper prices to haul their precious cargoes to port. With little other transportation options, they saw no choice but to pay the price. Most realized too late how expensive that price really was. Getting to a point where they owed the shipping company more than they could pay, an agreement would be reached where they would sell their business to resolve the debt and thus avoid public disclosure and scorn. Having run this gambit for several years left him wealthy. It also left him with many enemies and few left to be conquered.

"I wish I could find a decent man to fall in love with me," she said to herself. "I doubt that I will ever be that lucky. The only men I have met are like my father. I need someone who is the opposite of him, someone who doesn't make acquiring things and money the entire goal of their existence."

*****

"Think, Hawes, think!" I silently shouted at myself. Where can you hide on the ship and not be found for the next twenty-four odd hours. Then suddenly, another thought popped into my brain. There were only eleven passengers onboard but room for over seven hundred. I needed to find an empty cabin to hide in. They couldn't possibly check them all, I reasoned. I will simply become a needle in the haystack. With that, I started checking doorknobs again, trying to find one that wasn't locked. This time, however, I promised myself, I would look before I leapt.

*****

"Come here ya filthy, good-for-nothing land lubbers," and with that, Archer began to unload his frustration on the suddenly timid sailors. "Ya best be explaining what happened with the life jackets!" Not waiting for either man to speak he continued, "Are ye two sorry excuses for sailors trying to attract the attention of the whole scurvy crew?"

The two crewmen looked at each other with a blank stare. They had no idea what he was talking about, but neither wanted to be the one to speak up and tell him so.

"What are ya staring at, ya lily livered barge rats? Clean up that there mess before I throw ya's both overboard!"

And with that, Crigger and Tibbs took off to find the mess, eager to be anywhere but there. Archer on the other hand felt much better after watching both men nearly trip over themselves to get out of there.

Once out of earshot range, Tibbs wisecracked, "For a big guy, you'd think he would be more popular."

Cracking up again, Crigger responded, "I think he must of seen your sailor skills because he called you a land lubber. I was ready to defend ya, but sadly tis true. Hence, from here on forward till eternity, I shall call ye L. L. Tibbs."

Not missing a beat, nor wanting to be out done, Tibbs responded, "And I think he saw your swabbing skills and was referring to ye when he be talking about a barge rat. Therefore, I shall call ye B. R. Crigger!"

With that, both men found themselves laughing again.

CHAPTER 2

The CPR

They were desperate, as the stakes were too high to fail. We knew there would never be another opportunity like this in our lifetime; therefore, we were aggressive and asked for the moon. To our surprise, they were happy to give it to us, and more.

—Octavius Prescott III, cofounder of
Canadian Pacific Railroad, 1880

Mr. Prescott paced the lobby. He was not used to being nervous, but today, he couldn't help it. He knew that in the course of the next hour, his career, future, and legacy would all be cemented in place. That is, if he could convince his audience to accept the business deal he was about to propose. He was as prepared as he could be, but you never know how things will work out with politicians. They were as slick as he was, but unlike him, their opinions changed like the wind. This made them difficult to deal with and dangerous. Get sideways with one of them, and they could literally ruin you in a matter of minutes. He continued to pace, as he was too full of energy to sit down and wait patiently to be ushered into the parliamentary meeting room. He kept running through all the possible objections and deal breakers in his head, knowing he had to answer each one as smoothly as possible.

Twenty-five minutes later, he stopped pacing as the doors opened and he was escorted into the room.

This was not his first time addressing a group of politicians; nonetheless, he caught his breath as he saw six of the nine lieutenant governors in the room. The only ones absent were the ones representing Prince Edward Island, Nova Scotia, and New Brunswick, which was okay, as his business wouldn't be in those areas anyway. He immediately knew that he had all of the right decision-makers present to move forward. Now it came down to luck and how good he was as a salesman. He worked the room by going to each lieutenant governor, introducing himself with a smile on his face and a firm handshake. He spent a few moments with each man, praising them over some of their past achievements and public successes. When he had finished making the rounds, everyone took to their seats and put their focus solely on him.

"Honorable and esteemed members of parliament, I find myself most privileged to have the honor of addressing you at such a time as this. I thank you for making time for me in your demanding schedules, and I promise not to squander it with something trivial and beneath your purview. Nor shall I waste it trying to impress you with verbosity and elocution. I do wish to commend this governing body, who, in 1871, had the wisdom and foresight to authorize the construction of the transcontinental railroad. In my humble opinion, this is the greatest need and most urgent priority of our young nation to accomplish. As with any competent leadership, a deadline must be set for achievement of this grand vision, which this group understood and set a very realistic deadline of ten years or less to complete the entire project."

Mr. Prescott paused to look around the room and noticed that everyone was sitting up straight and attentive in their chairs, eyes focused directly upon him. So far so good.

"Distinguished gentlemen, that was nine years ago, and where are we at? Are we close to meeting that goal? I suggest that it is self-evident. The answer is no! We are not 90 percent done, as the schedule dictates. Not due to any fault of your own, we have barely scratched the surface. Now I know that our exact progress has not been reported to the public for obvious reasons. However, that does not mean a determined person cannot find out the truth. According to my sources, I have discovered that we have less than 30 percent of the railway built. The most troubling part is that the 30 percent already done was the easiest part to accomplish. So what went wrong? Was it the vision, or was the timeline too aggressive? I say no. It was a combination of errors that led us here today. Instead of the progress that was promised, we have had scandals that have rocked our new nation, leading to the fall of several prominent politicians—you all know what and who I'm referring to! We've endured endless delays and cost overruns, which seem to have no end in sight. We have experienced ineptitude and gross inefficiencies and suffered from the feckless leadership in the very companies that have been laboring to bring this railway to completion.

"Gentlemen, the combination of all of these errors have become a source of national embarrassment! Frankly, in my opinion, we have become a laughingstock to the Americans who completed their transcontinental railroad two years before we even passed a resolution to build ours, and it only took them six years to complete it. That was eleven years ago! I ask each of you to think where we would be as a nation, if it had only taken us six years to complete our railroad."

He took another pause to let that sink in and make sure he still had everyone's attention. He knew this was a difficult part, as now he needed to ask for the moon. No one said a word. No one needed to. He had summed up the situation correctly, knowing the politicians needed to find a fast fix to the stagnating problem.

"Now please do not hear me wrong. My reason for being here is not to admire the problem nor to pour salt into a wound, but to offer a solution. I have assembled the finest business partners this country has ever seen, and we are asking for the opportunity—as patriots—to take over the entire project, and we will personally guarantee completion in no less than five years from today. These men I have chosen are already wealthy, successful businessmen who have shown the ability to get things done where others have failed. Gentlemen, just think what will happen to our economy once we get this railroad finished."

Mr. Prescott paused again to let them think on that point for a moment.

"We don't need to use our imaginations. It is self-evident, as plain as the noses on our very faces. This railroad will allow us to connect the rich raw materials and resources in the West to our manufacturing centers in the East. Just look at what happened to America's economy once they completed their transcontinental railroad. They exploded into a world economic superpower in just a few short years! That, distinguished gentlemen, is what is at stake today. The decision I am asking you to make is a simple one. Do nothing, and let Canada languish for another ten years and putter around with inept and incompetent people hoping they will finally get this project done, all the while driving up the cost and delaying our national rise to economic equality on the world stage with our neighbors to the South. Or change leadership on the project and let us help forge the nation we deserve to be. Urgency is tantamount to success, and our window for success is closing rapidly. Soon America will be too far ahead for us to catch up, and when that day comes, all of our dreams for a strong and vibrant Canada will have died a tragic and needless death."

Mr. Prescott stopped. This was the part where he waited for someone in the room to take charge of the discussion and answer his challenge. He didn't have to say it, but each man knew that his political career was on the line over this project.

Finally, after a lengthy pause the lieutenant governor of Ontario asked if he would step outside to the lobby while they discussed his proposal privately. He agreed and turned to leave the room but was stopped by the very question he was waiting for.

"Mr. Prescott, I have but just one question at this time. What do you require to make this happen, if we choose to do as you have proposed?"

Octavius paused and looked each man in the eye before answering. He did not want his response to appear hasty, but rather well thought out.

"That is a most excellent question. Much planning and thought has been given to that very question by my team. We are committing our best, and quite frankly, we are asking for yours in return. Specifically, we will need to take ownership over the existing rail lines so we will not have unnecessary conflict and delays dealing with people who have already proven they are not up to the challenge. We will of course require ownership of all the land that has already been granted to construct this rail line upon, and we will need a significant line of credit from the government to keep the supplies needed, arriving when necessary. Although my men are wealthy, no small group of men are wealthy enough to complete a project so grand as this on their own dime, nor should they be expected to. Lastly, we ask that our new company be exempt from taxes for a period of twenty years so we can recoup and profit from our endeavors on behalf of this great nation."

Once again, Octavius paused and waited for someone to break the silence. This time it didn't take very long.

"Thank you, Mr. Prescott. Please wait in the lobby as we discuss your proposal."

Octavius walked slowly and deliberately out to the lobby. Once there, he let out a slow breath and allowed himself a quick smile. He already knew that they were going to vote in his favor. No one had challenged anything he said or asked for proof on how his men could accomplish the task in five years. No one defended the lack of progress by the current companies. They were more desperate than he anticipated.

*****

The next day was a busy one. Mr. Prescott's new business partners had arrived one by one at the predetermined meeting place in a private room at the Russell House located just a few blocks from Parliament. They had all been there for at least twenty minutes and were still waiting for Octavius to arrive and tell them what news he had about yesterday's meeting with the government. Octavius however was in no hurry and preferred to let them wait. It was his way of reinforcing that he was in charge and they weren't. Meanwhile, he had went to the cigar store and purchased six of the most expensive cigars they had. He put them into his coat pocket and walked into the hotel an hour later. He went to the maître d'hôtel and told him to bring the best champagne he had into the room after his last guest arrived and he heard a commotion. Then he entered the private room.

"Gentlemen, please quiet down and take your seats. There is much to discuss."

The room settled down quickly as the men took a seat, waiting for him to speak.

"As you are all aware, I had a meeting with the government yesterday. Our expectations were that this would be the first of many meetings necessary to grease the wheels of progress."

The men chuckled at his little pun.

"We also fully expected to only have some lower-level officials at the meeting, and perhaps, if we were lucky, a lieutenant governor. But we were wrong, dead wrong."

He paused to let that sink in and let each man come up with their own conclusions before he would continue. He looked to see if their expressions changed, but he knew better. These men knew how to keep their thoughts from being displayed on their faces. That was one of the reasons he chose them.

"Go on," one of the men prodded him. "Can't stand suspense and drama. Spit it out, will ya."

Octavius smiled at the man. "What would you say if I told you that there were no less than six lieutenant governors present for the meeting?"

He heard a collective gasp from the men. Before they could speak, he continued, "And what would you say if I told you we do not need to grease the wheels to get a favorable outcome?"

"I'd say you were drunk," the man who hated suspense and drama replied.

"What favorable outcome are you referring to?" asked another.

"Yes, how favorable was it?" the fourth man in the room asked eagerly.

The room grew noisy with the sound of the men all talking and asking questions and speaking over each other like excited little kids on Christmas morning. He let it continue, waiting for it to die down on its own, which it did a few moments later when the door opened and a stranger walked into the room.

"Who are you and what right do you have to interrupt our meeting?" demanded the fourth man.

Octavius responded, "No need to worry, he is with me. I will introduce him to you in a moment. First, however, there is more that needs to be discussed about the meeting. Six lieutenant governors were at the meeting. All of them, out of their desperation to stay in power, were receptive to our business plan. In fact, they reached a unanimous decision within thirty minutes of the end of my presentation."

The room remained quiet. Every heartbeat had stopped. No one was breathing as they awaited the decision that was made. He had them right where he wanted them, and he enjoyed keeping them in suspense.

"Before I tell you the outcome, there is one little detail that remains undone. By the close of business today, we will need to officially establish and register our business with the government under the name of the Canadian Pacific Railway. Only then will the deal I negotiated be ready to be officially approved by the parliament. We will incorporate with me as the CEO and president. The four of you will become stakeholders, whose duties will be decided upon by me in due time. And this man who came in last, named McDuff, will become head of our security."

"Guid day tae ye gents," McDuff said as a way of introduction.

"Why do we need security?"

"Because the government just gave us twenty-five million acres of land, a six-hundred-and-twenty-five-thousand-dollar line of credit, ownership of all the railways already owned by the government, and a tax-exempt status for the next twenty years! They even threw in that we will be allowed to set the passenger and freight rates without interference for the next twenty years as well."

The room exploded with energy as everyone jumped up out of their chairs. Grown men hollered and cheered, not knowing what words to use to express what they were feeling at that particular moment. Christmas indeed had arrived for these fortunate men, one they would never forget.

As Octavius pulled out the six cigars from his pocket and passed them around, the maître d'hôtel entered the room with the champagne. He didn't know what to make of such a sight. It looked to him like pure chaos, so he hurried back out of the room hoping the ruckus would end quickly and not disturb the other guests. He would not be that fortunate.

One of the men in the room clinked his champagne glass to get everyone's attention.

"I propose a toast to Octavius. The man who is leading us to the promised land of wealth and unparalleled success."

Each man raised his glass and said, "Here, here!"

The celebration continued on for more than an hour, with the maître d'hôtel having to come back a few times with more champagne before Octavius called for everyone's attention.

"Gentlemen, we will have the rest of our lives to celebrate. Today, however, we need to get our business together—quite literally and figuratively!"

The men roared with laughter, obviously feeling the euphoric effects of too much champagne and good fortune.

"One month from today, we will all meet in a town called Owen Sound for our first business meeting. It is roughly three hundred and seventy-five miles west of here on the Georgian Bay. That is where our business will operate from, and that is where you will find out the roles I have chosen for you. Until that time, I charge that no man speaks to anyone outside of this room about our endeavor, as victory can be taken away as fast as it was given. Not until the decision is approved by the prime minister will it truly be a done deal."

After all the shareholders had left the room, Octavius closed the doors to have a private meeting with McDuff.

"Get yourself to Owen Sound quickly, and start recruiting a few useful men to be under your charge. I want men that will do what they are told with no questions asked, and can keep their mouths shut. The tougher the better. Take the five best men and give them the title of constable."

"Understuid."

"Once you get your men, I want you to go get the judges, Mounties, and influential officials on our side—anyone that can stand in our way. Do whatever it takes. Just be discreet. I will be there in a few days. We have much work to do. When we are done, we will own that town!"

"It will be dain as ye hae said."

With that, both men went their separate ways.

*****

Meanwhile, in Minnesota, Maxwell McGregor called the quarterly business meeting to order for McGregor Industries. The room was filled with men who cowered in his presence, not wanting to be the one to bring him news he didn't want to hear. One by one each man had to give a report on the state of the business that was under his responsibility. The only woman in the room was Catherine, Maxwell's only child. She was twenty years old and full of grace and beauty. She was also the only one who did not have to give a report.

"Let's start with new business development," Maxwell said with anticipation written across his face. It came as no surprise to anyone in the room as it was his favorite part of the meeting.

"Sir, I am pleased to announce that we are in negotiations with two different companies at this time. One is a lumber business, the other is a furniture manufacturer."

"Tell me about the lumber business."

"Yes, sir. By my estimation, we are on track to close on the lumber business within forty-five days. They have several lucrative land contracts, including one that is adjacent to the Superior National Forest. Plus, they have a profitable sawmill. Once we close the deal and merge it with our other lumber assets, we will be the third largest in the region."

"That is good news. Well done. Do you foresee any difficulty with the closing?"

"The negotiation has had its moments, but I am positive they see the value in our offer."

"Keep me up to date. I can add some additional leverage to the offer if it becomes necessary."

"Certainly, sir. Of course."

"Tell me more about the furniture business."

"Very well, sir, they are a second-generation family business that has been starting to expand their sales beyond our area. They began to use our shipping services last year to take their goods to Chicago and Detroit and have been fairly successful in gaining traction in those markets. They specialize in maple, instead of oak like the other furniture makers. Currently, we are at the tipping point with them on our freight rate, so they should be in default on their payments to us on the next shipping cycle."

"Very well. However, I have no interest in owning it long term. Once we get the furniture business, sell it for the best price in the Chicago market. Part of the purchase agreement will be a contract to purchase the raw maple lumber from our lumber mill for a period of five years at spot-market pricing plus 7 percent. Tell them the competitive advantage will be that it is cheaper to ship the raw materials versus the finished goods. But before we sell, we will have them produce all new furniture for our offices and my home. I also want my office walls and bookcases redone in maple, stained-reddish brown."

Maxwell turned his attention to the next man at the table.

"Let's go over the profit-and-loss statement. I want to see how our core business has been doing."

The next man stood up and began his presentation.

"Profits with our shipping business are up slightly over the previous quarter to the tune of a half a percentage point. Volume remained steady, but we were able to increase margins slightly—"

Maxwell interrupted the man. "That only averages out to 2 percentage points a year increase in our profits. That is not enough. That is not acceptable. Anything less than 12 percent annually, I will consider an outright failure. Have a thorough review done of all our clients and let me know where the drain on potential profits is coming from. We will not deleverage our business."

"Right away, sir," the man responded like a timid child.

Over the course of the next hour, every other man had given his presentation. However, Maxwell had hardly noticed, he kept thinking about that lumber business deal.

"Father, are you ready to adjourn the meeting, or is there something else on your mind for us to discuss?" Catherine said as all the men were sitting silently waiting to be dismissed while Maxwell was lost in his own thoughts.

Maxwell looked up and said, "Meeting adjourned."

Quickly, the men made their way out of the room and went their own separate ways. However, Catherine stayed behind.

"What's troubling, you dear?" Maxwell asked.

"Why is it that you push the men so hard when we are already among the wealthiest people in Minnesota?"

"That is how we stay rich. The moment we let up, someone else will take what we have from us. That is the very nature of business."

"What happens to those men who own the businesses you are buying?"

Maxwell smiled as he heard his daughter say the word "buying." She still had no clue he was ruthlessly running them out of business and taking their business from them to offset the debts they owed his shipping company.

"Who cares! If they were better business people, they would not be in the position that they find themselves in now. You need to understand that there are winners and losers in every contest and transaction in life, and I refuse to be a loser."

"When is enough too much? Can't we just maintain what we have and leave room for others to prosper as well? Is it necessary to conquer the whole world before your satisfied?"

Maxwell stopped to give his daughter his full attention. "I know business is difficult for you to grasp, but either you are growing or declining. There is no other option. You attack and defend. This is the very nature of life. If you don't believe me, look at the animals. They all attack that which is weaker than themselves and defend against the stronger. That is how they survive."

"So we are acting like animals then? What about when they hide in a hole in the ground?"

"What? My own daughter would have me disgrace our family name by hiding in a hole? I will not tuck my tail and run from any fight. It is not in my nature to do so! Now enough of this ridiculous conversation. I have more work to do."

Catherine left the room, once again disappointed with her father's avarice.

Meanwhile, Maxwell turned to the room on the right when he heard the door open and close. It was part of his three-room office, which led to the room he used to rest in after a long day.

"McDuff, what are you doing here? I did not expect to see you until the end of next week."

"Yer aff tae be glad ah arrived earlie, as ah hae intelligence that ye wull wantae hear."

"Interesting. What is it?"

"Ah wull ainlie share it wi' ye, if ye mak' me an equal cohort in yer business."

"What. That is outrageous! I doubt there is any news that you could share that would be worth even a tenth of my empire."

"Whin wis th' lest time mah wurds tae ye wur false?"

Maxwell chewed on that for a minute before speaking. "You know I trust you, but what you are asking is unprecedented."

"Yer choice. Bit ye shuid know that this is a wance in a lifetime type o' thing ah hae uncovered. Wull mak' yer wee empire mair lik' th' section o' toun whaur fowk beg fur breid."

Once again Maxwell stopped to digest the information. He took several puffs on his cigar before saying anything.

"McDuff, have a seat. It appears we have some things to iron out this morning between us."

McDuff grabbed a seat and proceeded to tell him about the CPR Railroad and everything he heard in the meeting. He even mentioned that he was hired as head of security for them.

Maxwell laughed at that. "Did they now? That is our good fortune. I will tell you what. If you use your skills and help me profit from this financially, I will make you a minor partner in the business. I will be back in touch with you in a few days to tell you what our next steps will be. In the meantime, here is a handful of gold coins to seal the deal in good faith."

*****

When McDuff finally arrived in Owen Sound a few days later, he understood why Mr. Prescott had chosen this town. It was small enough to become a company town and strategic enough to merge the shipping and rail business together. His first stop was the local bars, on damnation corner, to find men who would be loyal to him. He was looking for the best of the worst, and he had a plan how to find them. He went to the Blue Water saloon first and sat at a table to watch for an opportunity. He had been there no more than a half hour when a bunch of rough-looking men walked in and sat at the bar. He motioned to the bartender and told him to pour three of the five men a whiskey.

The bartender asked, "Which three?" to which he replied, "I don't care. You choose."

The bartender took his money for the drinks and walked back to the bar wondering what was going on. He poured the three drinks and gave one to the two guys on the end and one to the man in the middle. The three men drank their whiskey down in one shot, before the other two figured out they weren't getting any. When they questioned the bartender, he pointed over in McDuff's direction. The men turned and looked at McDuff who stared back. The two men who were left out got up and walked over to the table where McDuff was seated.

"What about us? You ain't gonna buy us a drink too?"

McDuff just stared at them, not saying a word.

"You deaf, mister?" they said to him.

McDuff finally spoke after a few more seconds of staring at the men.

"Ah tellt th' boozer keeper tae gie th' drinks tae th' three weakest men o' th' group."

"Why would you do that? Why would you not buy a drink for the strongest two?"

Unfortunately, he said it loud enough for the other three men to overhear. Now they had come over as well.

"Dae ye gree wi' wha th' boozer keeper chose as th' toughest amongt ye?"

The three who got the drinks all answered no, while the other two predictably answered yes, which caused the bickering in the group that McDuff wanted. He watched it get out of hand as the men started yelling and pushing at each other, trying to prove they were indeed the toughest of the group. McDuff amused himself and watched it go for a minute or two. Then he got their attention again.

"Gentlemen, na need tae let this git oot o' haun. Ah wis simply wanting tae knew wha wis th' toughest jimmy among ye. Fur am waantin' tae offer him a jab."

"What kind of job?"

"That is atween me 'n' th' toughest jimmy."

The men looked at McDuff and told him to find someone else. They changed their mind when McDuff pulled out a ten-dollar gold piece and put it on the table.

"Ye decide wha is th' toughest amongst ye. If he kin best me, ye kin haeth' gowd coin."

The men talked among each other. They decided that the little guy would not be much trouble for any of them, so it didn't matter who would fight him.

One of the two who didn't get a drink insisted on being the one to fight. He stepped forward and said, "I accept your challenge."

"Sae' ere urth' rules. Th' bloke that yields or is unable tae git up loses."

"Understood," replied the challenger.

"Boozer keeper, 'ere is a gowd coin fur ony damages that kin happen tae yer establishment," McDuff said as he flipped the barkeeper a different gold coin. "Ur ye ready tae commence?"

"Absolutely. Let's do this," said the man.

Before he could finish the sentence, McDuff picked up a chair and swung it into the side of the man's head and shoulder. It exploded into pieces, and the man hit the floor unconscious.

McDuff calmly turned his attention back to the remaining men. "He wis th' toughest amongst ye?" he asked in disbelief as the men kept glancing back and forth between McDuff and their friend lying in a lump on the floor. "A'body else waant a chance?"

This time the biggest of the four remaining men stepped forward.

"I'd like to see you hit me in the head with a chair. I'm twice your size," the man taunted McDuff.

"Ur ye ready tae commence?"

Instead of answering, the man took a swing at McDuff's head. He missed, as McDuff ducked under it with ease and countered with a left hook to the side of the man's ribs. The man grimaced in pain as he heard a rib snap, but managed to stay on his feet. The man stepped back gingerly to reassess his opponent. McDuff waited for him to make the next move. He didn't wait long as the man lunged forward and swung at his head again, this time lower than the last. Instead of ducking, McDuff pivoted to his left as the punch harmlessly went past. McDuff then countered with a roundhouse to the side of the man's head, connecting squarely with his ear. He went down and didn't get back up.

"Ah think tis best that ah fin' anither group o' men tae tak' up mah challenge."

Obviously, the remaining men agreed, as no one else stepped forward to challenge McDuff.

"Ah wull be back tomorrow nicht tae see if a'body else wants taetak' up mah challenge," he said so everyone in the bar could hear.

With that, he got up and left the Blue Water saloon and walked across the street to Coleman's and started his challenge all over.

By the time the night was over, he had been at four bars and no one had laid a blow on him. He knew word would quickly get around, and tomorrow he would find his men.

*****

The next day McDuff got up early and went to the telegraph office to send a message to his trusted associate Archer. Once he finished there, he went to the Royal Canadian Mounted Police (RCMP) office in town and asked for the officer in charge. A few moments later, a Mountie named Guy Bouchard introduced himself.

"What can I do for you?"

"Straight taeth' point. Ah lik' that. Is thare somewhere whaur we kin discuss hings in private?"

"Please, step into my office. Have a seat."

"You seem lik' a smart individual, sae ah wull git richt taeth' point. Owen sound is aboot tae become a major toon, as th' CPR Railroad is making tis country headquarters richt' ere. Ah hae bin sent tae git everything duin fur thair arrival."

"Very interesting. How can I help?"

"As heid o' security, a'm hoping fur some cooperation amongst ourselves."

"My duty is to uphold the law. If that is your goal as security, then I am sure we can get along splendidly."

"My goal is a mair than that, a'm feart. Thare is afftae be mair than a thousand warkers 'ere, 'n' some o' thaim kin git oot o' line. A'm needin' tae know that ye wull allow us tae handle th' discipline, sae that it doesn't interfere wi' oor business."

"You want us to abdicate our duties when it comes to your employees. Is that what you are asking?"

"Ah think yer drawing th' wrong conclusion. A'm ainlie offering tae hulp whin it comes tae oor warkers."

"Mounties are here to administer justice and uphold the laws for the safety of all people. To remain fair and impartial, we cannot allow others to be involved in that process. No matter how well their intentions are."

"A'm ainlie asking fur cooperation 'n' understanding that wull create a mutually benefitial kinship atween ye 'n' ah." With that, McDuff slid two five-dollar gold coins across the desk. "This is fur taking th' time tae hear mah offer."

Then he got up and left before Mountie Bouchard could say anything else. He then proceeded straight down his list of judges and other influential people and had the same conversation with them.

By the time he was done, it was time to go meet the evening train and welcome his associate Archer to town.

"Good tae see ye. We're gonnae hae a lot o' fun here. Let's heid ower tae th' saloon 'n' ah wull fill ye in."

"Aye, good to be back with you again. I've missed our adventures together."

"This wull be oor best adventure yit."

McDuff and Archer entered the Pig's Ear tavern and grabbed a table. As soon as they sat down, a crowd of rough men gathered around the table.

"Where here for the job," one of them said.

By the end of the night, they had found their five tough guys.

*****

Maxwell McGregor sat in his office looking at his vast holdings and trying to strategize how to add to it. This was nothing new for him, as he dedicated one full day per week to brainstorming on the topic. His thoughts were interrupted by one of his employees knocking on his office door.

"Come in," he replied.

"Sorry to bother you, sir, but I come about the lumber business we spoke of at the business meeting."

"Yes, how is that acquisition going?"

"Not very well, I am afraid. The man said he will never give into our demands and has threatened a lawsuit against us."

"A lawsuit, eh? On what grounds, that I am more successful than he is or that he owes me money for the last shipment of goods aboard my ships?"

"Extortion, sir."

"What? It can't be extortion if he agreed to the terms. He did sign the shipping agreement, did he not?"

"Yes, sir."

"Then I don't understand where he thinks he can refuse to pay me what he owes. What law gives him that right?"

"None, sir."

"So basically, he just realized that he is bankrupt and I hold all the collateral. He resents it and is blowing off some steam. He's got nothing, and he knows it," he said, pounding his fist on the desk. "Tell him he has one week to pay what he owes, or I will seize his business and everything else he owns."

"It will be done, sir. Thank you for your time." Then the diminutive employee scurried out the door and closed it quietly behind him.

Meanwhile, Maxwell went back to thoughts on how to grow his empire. Maybe he could own a bank. That brought a smile to his face. But his thoughts quickly returned to the CPR Railroad. He sent a message to McDuff via one of his ships going to Owen Sound to open up a brothel so that the women could get the railroad men to talk about things. Perhaps they would learn some more secrets.

*****

Three days later, the message was delivered by hand to McDuff. He let out a laugh when he read it. Then he found Archer and gave him orders to shake down every racket in town and recruit those men to work for McDuff. Anyone who refused could be dealt with anyway Archer saw fit. Archer relished these types of assignments. It is actually the thing that he does best.

By the end of the week, he had all the gambling in the town under their control and had brought in women from the big city to open the brothel. He also found a still operation that made moonshine and took that over too. Not long after, Guy Bouchard paid a visit to McDuff.

"It seems you have been very busy getting ready for your railroad business to come to town."

"How fur kind o' ye tae notice."

"It wasn't a compliment. I heard rumors that the town has a brothel now, thanks to you."

"A necessary evil tae keep th' men happy."

"So you admit it. I am placing you under arrest."

"Nae sae fest, laddie. We hae an agreement 'n' ye accepted mah gowd coins in exchange fur cooperation 'n' understanding. Sae noo yi'll need tae be understanding that ah expect yer cooperation."

"I agreed to you helping with the discipline of your employees."

"Aye 'n' this is an ounce o' prevention tae that effect. If they're happy, thay wull nae need discipline. Ah know this is nae easy fur ye, sae that is how come ah said it wull be mutually beneficial. Neist week ah wull stoap by wi' some o' th' profits fae oor business endeavor." McDuff then walked away, leaving the Mountie in the street by himself.

*****

Back in Minnesota, the diminutive man knocked on the door. "Come in."

"Mr. McGregor, the week is up, and we have yet to receive payment from the lumber company."

"What did he say when you demanded it."

"He said, um, that money didn't grow on trees, and he would pay us when he can."

"That's ironic coming from a man who makes his living off of trees. Get my coat. We're going to visit this man and see how smug he is to my face."

A short time later they arrived at the lumber mill. The diminutive man took him to the office of the foreman. Maxwell entered the room with an air of authority.

"Where is the owner?" he demanded.

"He left thirty minutes ago, to inspect to one of our properties, sir," answered the foreman.

"Then you will need to be the one to give me a tour of your operations."

"Not to be rude, sir, but who are you exactly?"

The diminutive man instinctively handled that question before Maxwell could say anything. It was better that way for all involved.

"This is Maxwell McGregor, founder and CEO of MMI Industries, and at present course, he will be the owner of this business by the end of the month. So for your sake, I would do as he asks."

The foreman wasn't sure about all that, so he stood his ground.

"Sorry, sir, but you will have to leave and come back to discuss this with the current owner."

Maxwell walked over to the man and stopped inside the man's personal space.

"I like an employee who will not be intimidated. I'll remember that when I take over."

Then he stepped back and looked over the operations he could see from there. He took a deep breath to enjoy the smell of the freshly sawn wood and then left.

Once outside, he spoke to the diminutive employee.

"Now let's go visit the furniture maker."

An hour later, Maxwell was at the small furniture workshop. He was impressed with the craftsmanship of the maple furniture he saw in the small showroom. He looked at a beautiful entryway door that was two inches thick and had ornate and intricate carvings and beautiful scroll work done on it.

"Go ahead and have this shipped to my office today," he said to the small diminutive man. "And have this bed frame shipped to my house. Catherine will love it."

As he had finished saying that, the shop owner had come up behind them.

"Excellent choice, sir. If you will follow me over to the cash register, we can finalize your payment on those."

"Payment will not be necessary, my good man. We will take this as interest on the amount of money you owe my shipping company. Hopefully, you will be able to resolve the debt quickly, or I may be required to take even more."

The man stood there with his mouth hanging open in a panic, not knowing what to say or do.

*****

Back in Owen Sound, Archer was in the brothel talking to the madam. He had previously given her instructions that the clients could either pay in cash or in valuable information. He was there to collect both. Most of the information so far was useless, but one thing she told him piqued his interest. He made a note to check it out that evening when it got dark out.

The next morning Archer immediately tracked down McDuff, who was in a newly rented building where he was making his office to his standards, to tell him what he discovered.

"Clear the room," Archer yelled as he entered to all the workers who were there fixing up the office.

Everyone stopped and looked at McDuff, not sure who to take orders from.

"Gang oan. Ye heard th' jimmy. A' body git oot 'n' gies a moment o' privacy."

Once the room was empty, Archer told McDuff the news.

"I found a counterfeiting operation here in town. It is a big one. Very sophisticated."

McDuff didn't say a word. He just stared off into the distance for a few moments.

"Boss, didn't you hear what I said?"

"Murdurr a' body wha knows aboot it. We wull replace thaim efter wi' oor loyal men. Fur noo, this is oor secret."

"As you say it will be done," replied Archer.

"Efter they're deid, shift th' equipment tae anither building fur safekeeping 'n' burn th' original building taeth' ground. Mak' it appear as thay died in a fire."

Archer left without saying another word.

McDuff left right after and headed to the telegraph office to send Octavius Prescott a message.

"Need tae catch up wi' immediately. (Stop) Git tae OS Wi' a' haste. (Stop)."

CHAPTER 3

The Times

I found out the hard way that being a newspaper man meant living a life of contradictions. For instance: I know many people but have no friends; I hear a lot of gossip and stories but have nothing of merit to write about; I am an optimist but must document every negative event that happens in society.

—Winston Hawes, reporter, *Owen Sound Times*, 1883

Even though I had only been on the job a few months, I had made the decision to turn in my resignation and return home with my tail between my legs. With an aura of failure hanging over my head, I walked into the editor's office to see my boss. Mr. Fontaine was seated behind his desk amidst a whirlwind of activity getting the final copy ready for print.

"What's up, kid?" he said as he looked up and saw the woeful expression on my face. "Looks like you spent the day picking splinters out of your britches."

"I made a mistake by taking this job. It isn't what I wanted or expected."

"Is that all that's got you down. Heck, that's easy. Just change your expectations."

"No, I'm serious."

"So am I. You were born for this job. I knew it from the minute I first saw you. You need to stop running from your problems and face them head on. Quitting would be a colossal mistake and a waste of talent. Now let's get down to the brass tacks and tell me what's bothering you."

I slumped down into the chair in front of his desk. "I don't want to bring more gloom and misery to people's lives. I want to write inspirational stories, uplifting stories that ease people burdens and lift their spirits."

"Why do people buy newspapers, Mr. Hawes?"

"I guess because they want to know what is going on in the world around them."

"That is exactly right. The news isn't about fairy tales, and we don't have the luxury of cherry-picking which stories we get to write about and which ones we ignore. It is our job to keep the public abreast of everything of importance that happens. This means we write both the good and the bad, about the villains and their victims, the tragedies and the triumphs, and even the minor scuffles and the kerfuffles that occur when it is noteworthy."

"Where's the honor in that? I don't want to be the town parrot. I want to make a difference."

"Do you want to know what the greatest ending ever written was?"

"Um, they lived happily ever after?"

"No! That is that fairy-tale logic again, and it's a lie. Those types of stories tell us that if we can get past this one big hurdle, life will be easy and nothing will ever challenge us or cause us pain and discomfort again."

"Sounds good to me."

"I've got news for you. Life is messy and hard and is meant to be a challenge. Mark my words, no life lived in relative ease, absent of challenges and obstacles ever made a good man better, nor did it allow him to accomplished anything decent and worthwhile with his life."

"So what's the answer then?"

"They got what they deserved."

"What? How is that the greatest ending ever written?"

"Hope and justice, my boy. That is what people want the most. They want people to get what they deserve, both good and bad. Justice for the wicked and hope for a better tomorrow. In my humble opinion, all of the things we want in life can be categorized by either hope or justice."

"That sounds too simplified to be true. Life is more complex than that. What about love and hate?"

"Love falls under hope. '*I want to find true love*' is another way of hoping for something good to happen, specifically that you find a beautiful woman to share your life with. Likewise, '*Someday that man is going to get his*' is a way of expressing that justice needs to be applied, as he has done something unfair and wrong."

"What about fear and happiness?"

"Think it through for yourself, it still fits. People want things to be fair, although life seldomly is. They want the sick to be well, the poor to get a job, the lonely to find a friend, the orphans to get adopted, the widows to get remarried, the wicked to be punished, and the evil to be eradicated from among them."

"What about mercy?"

"*Your Honor, my son was caught up with the wrong crowd. This isn't a representation of who he is or how he will behave in the future. I ask that you show my son leniency when you consider your judgment.*" Mr. Fontaine added, "Sounds like a mixture of hope and justice to me."

"And war?"

"You're an American, so let's take a look at two of America's wars. The Revolutionary War was about government oppressing man and denying them justice or a say in their future. That's why their new government was designed to be for the people, by the people, and of the people. Their civil war was about ensuring hope for future generations who had been denied it, by demanding freedom and equality for all."

"Okay. Let's just say you are right. How does that apply to my dissatisfaction with my job?"

"Everything. You said you want to make a difference and not add to people's misery. So do it. When you write about what is happening, don't just lazily report the facts like a parrot. A successful article will give the people what they are looking for the most. So make sure you give them a sense of hope or that justice was served. Of course, that means sometimes you will have to get involved and go find the answer for yourself. It won't always be obvious or easy to see."

My mind began to stir, thinking about what I had written versus how I had written my articles. Slowly, it began to click that this could work.

I left the room glad I had such a wise boss to learn from. I decided that I wasn't going to quit and that I never wanted to write a story again that didn't offer the reader hope or provide them with justice. I spent that night in my room rewriting the ending to all of my past articles, just to prove to myself that I could do it and it would work.

The next morning I awoke early with a fresh perspective and was eager to write something that would offer people hope. I had decided to find my own story instead of waiting for some unfortunate event to occur to some unsuspecting victim. I walked around town chatting with people and looking for some feel-good story to write about, but all I had uncovered was that a little boy's lost dog had returned home after being missing for three days. That qualified as a feel-good story, but did not offer an impact of the magnitude I desired. By lunchtime I was getting depressed with my lack of a breakthrough and went to the docks to watch the ships come and go. I began to wonder what stories they would tell if they could speak. That got me to thinking about far away distances and how they connected with Owen Sound, which eventually led me to think about the railroad and my own journey to Owen Sound.

That was it. The thought hit me like a slap in the back of the head. I will write a series of articles about the railroad that was endeavoring to span the country from ocean to ocean. It will fill the readers with awe and pride and give them hope for a more prosperous future.

The best part was that the company that was doing the construction, the Canadian Pacific Railway, was based right here in Owen Sound.

With this newfound inspiration, I decided to head over to the rail yard and start gathering background information. It took me about ten minutes to make my way there. The first person I saw was a train engineer who had just brought his train in to the station. He was walking around the engine inspecting the wheels and such. I watched him for about twenty minutes, taking notes on his activities. He was very thorough with his inspections. After he appeared to be satisfied with what he saw, he headed toward the station, which was in my general direction; so I walked over and asked if he could take a few minutes to discuss what it's like driving trains for a living. He told me he was still working and couldn't take the time right then to talk, but if I was willing to buy him some drinks at the bar that night, he would be happy to answer my questions. I agreed.

I headed back to my boarding room to get some questions ready for him. I had so many ideas floating through my mind that the time flew by. Before I knew it, I realized I was already late for the meeting I had set up. I hurried down to the Blue Water saloon and saw him sitting alone at a table in the back. He was still wearing his dirty overalls with a red kerchief around his neck and his striped hat with disheveled hair sticking out from underneath. His arms and, to a lesser extent, his face and white beard contained smudges of grease and soot.

"Hello, Mr. Gunderson," I said as I approached the table.

He looked at me as he pulled out his railroad pocket watch and glanced at it.

"You're late. Man could die of thirst waiting on you."

I quickly sat at the table and called the barkeeper over to get a couple of drinks ordered.

"What's it like driving one of those gigantic machines?"

"Not so fast, young man. First things first. First, we drink, then we talk." He paused to make sure I understood that this was nonnegotiable.

I nodded in agreement.

An hour later, after he had consumed every last dollar in my wallet, he signaled he was ready to answer my questions. So I re-asked my original question.

To my surprise, he responded, "Why don't you come and see for yourself? Tomorrow I make a short run to Toronto and back. You can ride in the engine with me and the fireman."

A huge smile appeared on my face as I immediately accepted his offer. He told me when and where to meet him and then left.

I sat there a few minutes after Otto Gunderson, the engineer, left the bar, not believing my luck. Before I got up, another man sat down at my table.

"Remember me? We met on the train a while back. Name is JD."

The memory slowly came back as I remembered my first train ride to Owen Sound.

"Yes, of course. Please have a seat. How have you been?"

"Doing well, thanks for asking."

"I thought you weren't coming to Owen Sound."

"I wasn't then, but times have changed, and my path has brought me here now."

"Do you still work for the railroad?"

"Yes. Can I buy you a drink? I owe you one from the last time we met."

"I'd settle for a bite to eat instead. I already have had more than my share of alcohol tonight, and I spent my last dollar talking to that engineer."

JD smiled and said that would be just fine. So we ordered food and waited for it to be delivered.

"So you've been a reporter here now for a few months, is that right?"

"Yes, that's right. Good memory."

"So how's it going? Written any good articles? Uncovered any nefarious plots?" JD said with a smirk on his face.

I chuckled. "No, nothing that unsavory, I'm afraid. Just the usual local stuff that happens between people in a town like this."

"Well, I'm sure things will pick up for you once you've been here a while."

"What do you mean by that?" I asked innocently.

"Corruption. Life is full of it. I'm sure you will run across it as a reporter."

"Oh," I replied. "Do you know of something that I need to be aware of?"

JD paused, as if he were struggling to decide to let me in on a secret or not. Before he said anything, our bowl of stew arrived, and it immediately distracted my mind from the conversation.

After taking a few bites, I regained my thoughts.

"You were about to say something, I think."

"If I was, I don't remember now," he offered as he stuffed a spoonful into his mouth.

"Corruption. I asked if you knew about any."

"No. Just talking in generalities. I haven't been in Owen Sound long enough to know anything like that."

"So how long are you planning on staying here?"

"As long as the job keeps me here."

"What is it you do for the railroad?"

"It's a trade secret, so I can only tell you off the record."

"Understood," I replied eagerly.

JD slowly looked around to make sure no one was eavesdropping on our conversation. Satisfied, he continued, "The CPR is looking at ways to keep their perishable food items fresh as they prepare to haul it across Canada. So that means we need to use special boxcars that use ice to keep things cold. These cars are special made by the CPR itself and have heavy insulation, floor drains, and roof hatches as well as ice bunkers on each end of the car."

"Why is that a trade secret?"

"Because secrecy helps guarantee success."

"So do you work on these cars as they travel from point to point?"

"No. We haven't begun to use any of them yet. They are all sitting in a rail yard in Toronto."

"I still don't understand then what you do."

"To make this endeavor a success, we have to have ice stations built up along the way to quickly load fresh ice onto the cars. My job is to figure out how many of these we will need and where to put them."

"Oh, that is a very interesting job for sure. So that is why you are in Owen Sound?"

"Yes. It is obvious that we will have to have one of these stations here. This will allow us to take fish off of the Great Lakes and transport it around Canada. It is also our main hub, so we will be switching a lot of trains here, which will need to be iced before they head out."

"So how many of these stations will be needed?"

"That, my friend, I cannot tell you."

Tired of getting nowhere, I decided to lay my cards on the table.

"Look, I want to write a story about the railroad that inspires people and gives them hope for a better future. Anything you can share with me that will help me accomplish that goal will be appreciated."

"Well, you will have a lot of content to choose from," JD said with a laugh. "Is that why you were spending all your money on the train engineer?"

"Yes. He is allowing me to ride in the engine on the trip to Toronto tomorrow."

"Is that so. Well, let me give you a warning. Be careful of the constables that patrol the rail yards. If they catch you doing that, they can throw you in jail without so much as even asking a question, or worse."

"Worse. What would be worse than that. Jail sounds pretty horrible to me," I exclaimed, slightly panicked at what I just got myself into.

"Worse is that they catch you during the journey, away from the station. You could disappear and never be found again."

"Now I know you are pulling my leg," I said somewhat hopefully.

JD just looked at me without saying a word. Then he got up and left. He seemed to do that a lot.

*****

The next morning I got up early and carefully made my way to the railroad to meet Otto. I was spooked by what JD had said, and I was looking over my shoulders constantly like a nervous hen, even though I noticed no one seemed to be paying any attention to my presence there. If they had, I was prepared to use my alibi as a reporter, which would work until I actually boarded the engine.

"Good morning. Glad to see you made it," said Otto. "Go ahead and climb aboard. I already told the fireman we were having a guest with us today. I will be aboard shortly, after I make sure everything is proper with the train."

Immediately, the alarm bells rang inside my head. He was going to get the constable and have me arrested.

Noticing my hesitation, he prodded me, "Go on. Hurry up and get aboard. We have a schedule to keep." And with that he pushed me toward the engine.

I was about to turn around and leave when the fireman reached his giant hand down to give me a hand getting up the ladder. I reluctantly grabbed it, knowing it was going to be my only chance to ride in the engine.

Once inside, I quickly looked around and got an adrenaline rush. Straight in front was a small door that opened to the steam boiler. It was open, and the fireman had resumed shoveling coal into it as fast as he could go. Above it were gauges and dials that looked menacing. Each with a line that showed a danger point, which seemed to be getting closer and closer to where the needle indicated. It was impossible to see outside the train from straight ahead as there were no windows, just the massive wall of steel that made up the end of the steam boiler. There was a small seat on each side of the engine that was basically a chair inside a window that stuck out from both sides of the train. I sat down and looked out the window. I saw the entire length of the engine stretched out in front of me. It looked like it didn't stop until it reached the horizon. I got back out of the seat, and looked around one more time and realized that there were only two seats: one for the engineer and one for the fireman. It looked like it was going to be a cramped ride after all. I turned my gaze back to the fireman, who had stopped shoveling coal for the moment. He glanced back at me, as if to say that one of the chairs belonged to him. I just stared back, not knowing what to say.

A few moments later, the engineer climbed aboard and said we were ready to begin our voyage. The fireman told him that the pressure in the boiler was sufficient to begin. So Otto reached up and pulled the chain to the steam whistle, which let everyone know to get out of the way before the train started to pull away from the rail yard. Then he began to move the levers and knobs that controlled the engine. Slowly, with a chug-chug, the engine crept forward and began to build speed. I looked out the side window from where I was standing and watched as the town of Owen Sound drifted past the window. Even though I had watched many trains come and go during my few months here, it was a completely different perspective to see the town move and the train stand still. I stayed quiet and watched until the town was behind us and we had entered into the Canadian wilderness. Before I opened my mouth to ask Otto any questions, he interrupted the silence.

"Well, what do you think? We are now traveling down the tracks at forty kilometers per hour, and we are pulling twenty-five fully loaded box cars behind us, each with forty-five metric tons of cargo."

"The amount of power needed to do that is extremely impressive. However, I did not anticipate that there would be so much smoke and coal dust flying around the inside of the engine," I said as I coughed, trying to clear my lungs of the smoke.

"Well, why on earth did you think we wore the red kerchiefs? It's not for fashion, you know."

I laughed. "I guess I just figured that out."

I proceeded to ask him a bunch of questions about the gauges and dials and everything that popped into my brain like an inquisitive schoolboy. Finally, after I had asked several questions rapid-fire, he gave me an order.

"Go ahead and sit over there in the fireman's chair. He won't be using it for a while. You will get more fresh air there."

I nodded and took a seat inside the window. The engineer was right; the smoke was not as thick. I looked forward and watched the giant pistons pumping back and forth on the wheels for a while until I got bored and leaned over to ask another question over the steady background noise that the engine made. Before I could say anything, Otto yelled over to me to keep an eye out for Indians.

"Indians? What for?" I yelled back.

"Just let me know if you see any. We need to be careful."

Over the next several hours, I didn't take my eye off the surroundings as we passed through. I had sighted deer, elk, and bear as well as badgers and other small animals, but no Indians. Finally, the scenery began to change, and I realized we were pulling into the outskirts of Toronto. I looked over at Otto, his kerchief was down, and he had a big grin on his face, which revealed to me that the thing about watching for Indians was just a ruse to keep me quiet.

As we began to slow to a stop at the Toronto rail yards, I became anxious again. I was worried about being seen by a constable while getting out of the engine. I leaned over and asked Otto how long before we made the return trip.

"It usually takes about two hours to get the train unhitched, turned around at the switching station, and reloaded for the return trip. Don't be late, or you will have to find your own way back. I will give two pulls on the steam whistle to warn you we are leaving instead of the customary one pull."

I nodded and hurriedly climbed out of the engine. Once my feet hit the ground, I looked around to see if anyone had observed me. It appears as if I got off unseen. I looked down at my pocket watch to make sure I knew when my two hours were up. When I looked back up, there was a large man standing in front of me. To my surprise, it was JD.

"Hurry up and follow me before you get seen. There are a lot of constables around here. More so than in Owen Sound."

With that, he hurriedly walked in a direction opposite of the station. I followed out of concern and curiosity, wondering where he was leading me. A few minutes later, we came up alongside a series of long buildings. He ducked in between the first two of them and walked halfway down their length before he stopped.

"Okay, we are safe here for the time being," he said. "If we get stopped, you are not a reporter but my assistant Gabriel Girard from Montreal. Understood?"

I agreed rather hesitantly, wondering what on earth was going on. Before I could ask any questions, he opened a small door to the building and disappeared through it. I followed. It was dimly lit inside by some windows high up near the roof. As my eyes adjusted, I saw it was filled with railroad boxcars. I followed JD as he approached one of them and climbed inside. He motioned for me to follow and then closed the sliding door to the boxcar behind us.

"This is one of the ice boxcars I was telling you about."

I looked around. It was definitely different than what I had imagined when he told me about them.

JD checked out the car to make sure we were alone. "I had to see you here in Toronto."

"Why? To show me these cars?"

"No, to tell you a secret that you must promise to never repeat, or else I will wind up dead."

I looked at him not knowing what to say. Why did he choose to trust me? What could this secret be? I had a thousand questions to ask.

"Can I trust you with my life?"

Again, I didn't know how to respond. No one has ever asked me that before.

"Um, yes. I promise that I will not reveal your secret. However, I must know why you are choosing me to tell it to. I barely know you."

"Because if I die, then I want you to publish everything I am about to tell you in your newspaper. But only if I am already dead. Do you understand?"

I took a deep breath and shook his hand. "Agreed."

"My name is not JD. That is my code name. They are initials that stand for Justice Department. I work for the United States government looking for the source of the largest US counterfeiting operation in the world. We have pinpointed its origin to the Owen Sound area. I took a job on the railroad as a cover so I can travel around and do my real job."

My knees buckled slightly as I digested this piece of information.

"Wow, I guess you do know about nefarious things going on," I said out loud without thinking about it.

"I could also use your help on this."

"How can I help you?"

"You're a reporter. You can go places and ask questions that I couldn't do without raising suspicions."

"I wouldn't have the first idea what to ask."

"I will let you know what I need. Then you can follow up and get back to me."

"How can we do this without being found out?"

"I will send my information to you in a code through paid personal advertisement in the Toronto newspaper, under the name of Jocko, and you can reply by using a coded sentence or two in your weekly article in the *Times*."

Just then the sound of footsteps could be heard against the gravel floor inside the building. JD quickly slipped a code book into my coat pocket before I knew what happened. The sound of the footsteps were getting louder and stopped just outside the car we were in. JD instantly changed the subject back to the inspection of the boxcar.

"So these are the drains in the floor to eliminate all the melting ice water during the journey."

As he finished his sentence, the door to the boxcar opened, and a man jumped inside.

"What have we here?" the man asked.

JD turned and addressed the man. "Hi, my name is JD Dahlquist, and this is my assistant Gabriel Girard. We are here inspecting the ice boxcars as part of our jobs with the railroad."

"And I am Remi Roy, a constable for the railroad. Mr. Dahlquist, I have heard of, but I have not heard of Gabriel Girard before."

"Like I said, he is my assistant out of Montreal. I hired him a few weeks ago and am getting him up to speed on our project."

"Go on then, don't let me stop you from your work."

"Thank you," said JD as he began to continue on with his fake educational talk. "See here the size of the ice bunker located on each end of the car. When we build an icing station, we will need to be able to have enough ice to be able to fill up to one hundred of these bunkers at a time. That breaks down to two bunkers per car times a maximum of fifty cars at a time."

I let out a loud whistle. "That will be a lot of ice indeed. But what will be the process of getting them loaded quickly enough? Fifty cars stretched out will mean the train will have to pull forward many different times to reach the loading platform."

I could tell that JD was proud that I could play along so seamlessly.

"We have done a lot of thinking about that very subject and have been testing out a few different designs for the construction of these ice stations. But alas, we do not have a great answer yet, except for more manpower on the ground."

The constable must have been satisfied with the conversation as he turned and left the boxcar without saying a word. JD then motioned for me to remain silent for a while as he continued talking about the ice stations just in case we were still being listened to.

After a what seemed like a long time, JD whispered to me that we needed to go to the train station together as that would be expected, and then I would have to leave separately without anyone noticing me, making my way back to the engine, to catch my ride back to Owen Sound.

After an indeterminate amount of time had passed, JD and I left the boxcar and made our way to the train station, acting as if everything were normal. Once there, we split up, and I made my way to the men's restroom. When I looked in the mirror, I noticed that my face was darkened by the smoke and coal dust from the ride in the engine. I wondered if the constable had noticed that as well in the dim lighting. I quickly washed my face to remove all of the offending stains I could, which didn't want to come off very easily. I stopped scrubbing when I heard the two whistles from the train. That was my signal that the train was about to leave. I looked at my pocket watch. It had only been an hour and a half. It was leaving thirty minutes faster than anticipated. I left the restroom and walked out of the station. In the distance, I saw the constable Remi Roy near the engine of the train. The engineer saw me and waved. I ducked back into the shadows of the building before the constable could spot me. When I looked back out, it appeared as if the constable was going to stand there until the train left. I quickly decided what needed to be done and circled my way around to the back of the train, trying to stay out of sight as much as possible. Luckily for me, there were two boxcars sitting on a side track next to the end of the train. I positioned myself behind them, so I was out of sight of the engine. I would wait for the train to start moving and then make a dash for the caboose and ride it back to Owen Sound. I heard the couplings holding the cars together pop with tension as the train tightened up and began to inch forward. Looking around one last time and seeing no one, I ran over to the caboose, climbed up the ladder, and opened the door to the inside. To my surprise, the car was occupied with a caboose man whose job was apparently to ride back there as well. I quickly introduced myself as Gabriel Girard, a CPR employee from Montreal. He looked surprised, but I explained that I needed to ask some questions to help us solve our ice-loading problem. He was eager to help. I remained unaware that Remi Roy had watched me board the train. The conversation on the return trip was pretty light, and I was glad for that. I forced myself to use the silence to come up with a plan for how to get off the train in Owen Sound without being observed. But every time I started to think about that pressing issue, my thoughts turned back to the conversation with JD. Who could be behind the world's largest counterfeiting operation? How have they gone undetected?

Where do they get rid of the money? Why Owen Sound? It was mind-boggling to think about, and I had no answers, except that I was afraid to get involved. What did I really know about JD? I have only spoken to him a couple of times. Perhaps he wasn't one of the good guys. Maybe he made all of this up for some reason. Before I knew it, we were pulling into Owen Sound, and I had failed to find a strategy for my exit. So when the train stopped, I winged it and extended an invitation to the caboose man to buy him a beer. We left the train together and walked to the edge of the rail yard. Once there, I told the guy that I forgot I had something important to do right then and would have to get him next time. Then I hightailed it down the street and out of sight.

CHAPTER 4

Empire Building

> Between a rock and a hard place, we were going to run out of cash, and it was unlikely we would get another grant from the government any time soon. We needed a new plan to keep it all going.
>
> —CPR executive, winter 1884

Octavius stood in the small meeting room in the new offices in Owen Sound with his business partners. He was the only one in the room who knew why he called the emergency meeting. The look on his face was grim, and his partners noticed it.

"Looks like you lost your last nickel," one of the partners exclaimed.

"We might have," Octavius replied, which made everyone in the room become quiet and serious. "I received word from McDuff last night that the pumps went out at the Silver Islet mining operation."

This made everyone gasp and start to ask questions all at once.

Octavius held up his hands to quiet the room. "I do not know the severity of the situation. McDuff is there now doing what can be done to get them running again. Until we hear further, we must begin to make preparations for the worst and hope it doesn't come to pass."

"What about our arrangement?"

"Our deal is still in place. We will be able to continue to skim off silver in exchange for information about which towns the railroad plans to run their lines through. Provided the mine can still produce silver."

"What do you mean by that?"

"The longer the mine goes without having the pumps running to keep the water from Lake Superior from flooding them, the more likely it becomes that the mine will cease to operate forever. The mine shaft runs out some two miles under Lake Superior and reaches almost two thousand feet deep."

One of the partners lamented, "Without the money we make from selling the silver, we will not be able to continue to fund the construction of the railroad, and we still have the mountains of British Columbia to pass through!"

"Now you get why I called the meeting! While we are waiting for more information from McDuff, we need to find another source of funding in case the mine is a bust. Does anyone have any suggestions?"

"What are the chances that the government will give us a bigger line of credit?

"Public opinion is the wind that fills the politician's sails, and unfortunately, the wind is currently against us. We will explore the possibility, but I would put our chances at less than 10 percent."

"Why can't we just run the same scheme of exchanging information for money with someone else. Should be easy enough to accomplish."

"It's a possibility, but we would need to find someone with enough money to be interested, but patient and dumb enough to keep being strung along while we continue to cash out on the deal. Those kinds of people don't grow on trees. I would put our odds of success at 5 percent or less—unless any of you know of such a person."

All of the men shook their heads, confirming what Octavius already knew with a high degree of confidence.

"What if we sell the grand lodges we have been building. The one at Lake Louise was very expensive and could fetch quite a penny."

FLEEING OWEN SOUND

"Gentlemen, we are expanding and growing, not diversifying and selling off. That would raise a public panic. No, what we need is a way to generate a lot of cash in a short amount of time, without anyone knowing what we are doing. The first inkling that gets out about our money troubles will open the door for someone else to swoop in and try to take it away from us, just like we had done several years ago."

"None of us has any more cash to pump into the business, so basically you want us to print money out of thin air," said one of the partners in frustration.

Everyone in the room was quiet, thinking about their predicament and what they could do to raise more capital. Octavius let this go on for a few moments before he broke the silence, because he already had the answer.

"That's exactly right. You, sir, are a genius."

"Thanks, but what did I say that was so genius?"

"Never mind for now. Meeting is dismissed. Everyone meet back here one week from today. By then we shall have our update from McDuff on how badly the mine was damaged."

*****

McDuff was already at the mine before the pumps had shut down. Maxwell McGregor had sent him there to diffuse the situation. He had been talking to the mine's owners about the shipment of coal they had been expecting to arrive. It had been overdue and was needed to keep the mine running all winter long. McDuff had assured them that it would get there before they had run out of coal. Now that they had missed that deadline, he had to convince them that it was still on its way and would get there before the ice got too thick and prevented it from getting there at all.

"MMI industries is daein' everything in tis power tae git that shipment 'ere in time," McDuff reassured the owners.

"Well, it sure doesn't seem like it. What is the holdup?"

"Ah heard we hud a mechanical issue wi' th' ship 'n' hud tae tow it back tae port. We hud hoped it wid be something we cuid quickly fix, bit it turned oot that that particular vessel wull need extensive repairs, 'n' wull nae be able tae mak' th' voyage."

"What!" screamed the owner. "If that coal doesn't show up, the mine will be lost forever. It will flood, and no pumps known to mankind will be able to remove that amount of water from those depths."

McDuff used a soft reassuring voice to calm the man down.

"We ur in th' process o' unloading th' coal faeth' disabled ship 'n' transferring it tae anither ship as we speak. A'm tellt that thay shuid be able tae mak' wey th'morr aefternoon. Wi' agreeable conditions, thay shuid be 'ere wi'yer coal in three days."

"Three days!" the man shrieked. "We ran out of coal last night! We had to evacuate all of the miners and close all of the shafts as a precaution. We have no way of knowing if they have started flooding yet or not."

"It's a predicament, that's fur sure."

"I will tell you something else. If the coal does not arrive in time and we lose the mine, I will personally sue MMI Industries for breach of contract and seek damages for the loss of the mine and its expected revenues for the foreseeable future."

McDuff looked into the man's eyes. "You kin huv a go, bit it's nae that fault o' MMI industries that we hud a mechanical issue wi 'th' ship. 'N' as ye kin see we, ur daein' everything in oor power tae git th' shipment oot 'ere as fest as we kin. Oan th' ither haun, it cuid be argued that yer responsible furth' incident by ordering th' shipment o' coal sae late intaeth' seezin. Hud ye ordered it, say twa weeks earlier, then ye wid nae be in sic a predicament, noo wid you."

"You don't have the right to try to turn this around on me. Your company accepted the contract. Perhaps if they had done better maintenance on their ships, this could have been avoided."

"Who knows. Mibbie it wull be fun oot that ye wur trying tae collect oanth' insurance policy, as th' mines hud run oot. Wance flooded thare wid be na wey tae gang doon 'n' confirm that, wid there?"

"Just tell your company they better make it here before disaster strikes," the owner said, trembling in anger, and then walked away before losing what was left of his mind.

"Very guid, sur. Ah shall relay yer concerns," McDuff said to the back of the owner.

Then he rode his horse back to Port Arthur and sent a telegram to Maxwell McGregor.

It read, "Everything gaun according tae plan. (Stop) Story bought. (Stop) Catch up wi' me in Port Arthur th' morra."

McDuff then found a room for the night.

The next day he boarded an MMI ship that had just arrived and went directly to Maxwell's private office onboard.

*****

"Come on in, McDuff," Maxwell said with a devious grin on his face. "Good work by the way. The mine is going to be a complete loss, which is going to drive Octavius Prescott back to needing me for a partner so I can infuse enough cash to keep his railroad solvent."

"A'm glad fur ye. However, ah wid lik' mah promised compensation."

"And just what was it we agreed to?" Maxwell said as a way of goading McDuff.

"Dinnae be playing games wi' me noo. Ye know exactly whit ye promised."

"Be a good sport and refresh my memory. I make so many promises to so many people."

"A'richt, wise guy. Ye promised me that ye wid pat me in yer wull tae inherit yer business empire whin ye died, as ye didnae wantae lea it tae yer daughter, seein she is clueless aboot business."

"Oh yes. I remember it, now that you mention it. I am in the process of having my new will revised as soon as possible and notarized. Then I will give you a copy of it for safekeeping. Of course, I will need to add language in it that nullifies it if I am murdered. Don't want to incentivize you to take over before it is my time to go."

"Ye hae na concern fae me oan that accoont."

"Good to know. Meet me back here in a month. Once the CPR comes begging to me to help them with their cash problem, we'll finalize it."

"That wasn't pairt o' oor wee agreement."

"It was implied. Why on earth would I make that kind of agreement if I get nothing in return. Yes, you made sure the mine was destroyed like I asked, and it will hurt their cash position. But the goal all along was to get my hooks sunk into their business. So once that happens, our deal will be finalized."

"'N' whit dae ah git if thay dinnae come tae ye?"

"You get nothing. The same as what I would get from it. So I guess you better be on your way to make sure that doesn't happen."

McDuff reluctantly agreed and then left the ship to board a different one to take him to Owen Sound. In two days' time, he will be back at his other job working for Octavius Prescott, trying to get him to add Mr. McGregor as a stakeholder.

*****

The following week Octavius and his partners had gathered for their follow-up meeting. Unlike the last meeting, his expression was not grim, and his partners noticed it immediately.

"Gentlemen, I have bad news. McDuff confirmed that the mine is a complete loss and is unlikely to ever reopen."

No one said a word. The men were thrown off by the contrast between the news they just heard and the upbeat expression on their CEO's face.

Octavius looked around the room at each man.

"So we will need to find another source of secret funding. Have any of you come up with anything since last week?"

"We could take on a silent partner, sell them a small piece of the action for the funding they could provide," answered one of the partners, just like McDuff had privately suggested to him earlier that day.

"Do you have someone in mind?"

"What about Maxwell McGregor? He has a lot of cash and influence."

"To me, that would be our last option. I do not wish to further dilute our profits at this stage of the game. Besides, I don't trust that he would play nicely with us," Octavius replied, shooting down the idea. "Unless you are willing to give up your seat to this newcomer."

"Absolutely not," replied the outraged man.

"I didn't think so. Anyone else have a bright idea?"

No one else dared to speak up, so Octavius continued.

"Fortunately, I have come up with an even better scheme than the one we had with the silver mine. The thought occurred to me last week when it was suggested we print money out of thin air," he lied. "The answer is counterfeit money."

The silence that followed deafened the room. No man dared to interrupt and ask a question, so they waited for him to continue, even though they had a million questions and just as many objections.

"We have the perfect opportunity to make as much money as we need. The trick will be to only make as much as necessary. If we get greedy, it will be easier for us to get caught. I know you all have a thousand questions, but just wait and here me out."

Octavius took the next two hours to explain his idea of using the *Algoma*, one of the three new and identical ships, as the place to hide the machine and print the counterfeit. He explained how they would only print American counterfeit so they would not get in trouble with the Canadian government and also how they would use the funny money to buy silver and other precious metals at Port Arthur, which they would then transport back and sell in the major cities of Ottawa, Toronto, and Montreal.

"Gentlemen, we have everything we need to pull this off, including the actual counterfeit plates, printing press, and supplies. But don't worry about the details, leave them to me. If you vote in favor, none of you will ever need to hear about this business again. All opposed say 'Nay.'"

No one opposed, so the meeting was adjourned, and Octavius send word to McDuff that he wanted to see him. It was time to put their plan into action.

McDuff met up with Octavius later that evening in a special pullman train car that doubled as a traveling office for Mr. Prescott III when he was about.

"Guid tae see ye again, sur. Whit dae ye wish tae discuss?"

"Brandy?"

"A'd prefer a guid whiskey if ye hae it."

"Certainly. How has the security been around our businesses?"

"Excellent, sur. We ur keeping oor eye oanth' local reporter, as he wis seen by constable Remi Roy in Toronto in one o' oor ice cars. He haes bin writing some harmless stories aboot th' railroad, and he wis usin' an alias by th' name o' Gabriel Girard. Bit ither than that, everything is richt as rain."

"Interesting. Keep him under your watch."

"As ye wish. Wis thare anythin' else?"

"Yes. I want to talk about that counterfeiting business you discovered in the outskirts of town here recently. Do we have everything we need to use it for our own purposes?"

"Everything haes bin shut doon, moved tae a secure site 'n' a' th' fowk that wis a pairt o' it hae bin eliminated."

"How much ink and paper do we have?"

"Archer 'n' ah counted twenty-five hundred unused sheets o' paper 'n' twa barrels o' ink," McDuff replied. However, he did not tell him about the two hundred sheets they found that had already been printed. He figured that was his finder's fee.

Octavius did the math in his head. With each sheet able to produce sixteen twenty-dollar bills, that means he can print an additional eight hundred thousand dollars of counterfeit money before they have to look for harder to get supplies. This is bigger than their six-hundred-and-twenty-five-thousand-dollar loan from the Canadian government. More than enough to make up for the silver-mine loss. This realization made Mr. Prescott's mood change from upbeat to giddiness in an instant.

"Outstanding! This is to remain our secret. Besides the stakeholders, whom I told during today's meeting, only you and Archer know about this. Next week we will be discretely moving the entire operation onboard the *Algoma* in the middle of the night. Get everything ready to move."

"It wull be dane as ye say, as lang as ah git mah promised compensation."

FLEEING OWEN SOUND

"Yes, of course. I will have the preferred railroad stocks delivered here to my private car by the end of the week. But this is to remain our little secret."

McDuff left the pullman car happy in his newfound fortune. He also realized that since the CPR no longer needed Maxwell's money, his deal with McGregor was never going to happen. He went to Damnation Corner to drink and think about how to turn this back around in his favor.

CHAPTER 5

Side Hustle

> After I heard their offer, it came out of the blue. The idea crossed my mind with such clarity it could not be ignored.
> I went over and over it, considering the possibilities.
> Then I quickly made up my mind. I can make this work.
> I'm going to go for it. I told them I would do it.
>
> —Thomas Ericson, *SS Algoma* captain, January 1885

It wasn't every day that the president of the CPR Railroad asked to meet with you. Mr. Octavius Prescott III was a busy man with no time to waste on things that were unimportant to the success of completing the transcontinental railroad through Canada. So naturally, Thomas was nervous and curious at the same time to find out what he wanted to meet with him about. As the captain of the *SS Algoma* steamship, Thomas was an employee of the CPR but was clueless as to why he wanted to talk to him. Fortunately, he was going to find out very soon, as he was to meet him at the Pig's Ear tavern on Damnation Corner at noon.

He arrived at the bar and stopped to look at his pocket watch one last time. He was ten minutes early. He decided to enter the bar and wait. It was surprisingly empty, even for that time of the day. He only saw two men: a short guy and a guy as big as a moose. They looked right at him when he entered and kept staring holes through him. He was about to say something when the small guy spoke from across the room.

"Captain Thomas, let me buy ye a whiskey afore yer meetin' begins."

It sounded like a good idea, so he accepted the offer and grabbed a seat at the bar. The small man sat next to him while the moose waited at the back of the saloon.

"They ca' me McDuff. A'm a constable fur th' CPR."

Seeing that the stranger already knew who he was, he nodded and sipped his whiskey. The man continued to speak.

"Mah jab is tae protect th' companies' best interests. If yer a guid employee 'n' dae whit yer tellt, ye wull hae naethin' tae fear fae me. Dae ah mak' masell clear?"

He nodded again, not sure how to respond to that.

"A nod's as guid as a wink tae a blind horse," he strangely replied as he got up and told Thomas to follow him to the back room.

Thomas finished his drink and followed him. The moose opened the door, and McDuff showed him in to the room. There was a table with a few chairs. McDuff announced the captain to the man sitting at the table, who was undoubtedly Mr. Prescott III. He looked like a fat cat railroad tycoon. As he entered the room, no one spoke but just stared at him, so he broke the awkward silence.

"Capt. Thomas Ericson at your service, sir."

Still, no one answered as the silence continued to hang in the room for what seemed like a full minute. Then Mr. Prescott III took a puff on his cigar and finally spoke.

"Thomas, before I tell you why I called you here I need to know what kind of man you are. Specifically, are you the kind of man that is willing to take some personal risk in order to achieve a great reward?"

"As a sailor and a captain, I risk my life every season sailing the dangerous waters of the Great Lakes, all for the reward of getting my agreed-upon salary. If that is what you are referring to, the answer is, yes, I am."

"A captain's courage is part of the risk I am talking about, but there is more than courage required. How much risk would you be willing to take to become one of the wealthiest men you know?"

He thought carefully for a moment before he answered. This is the type of question where a man's words might trap him in a situation he wished he wasn't in.

Now I understand the strange phrase the small guy had said to me, he thought. "I never heard of an offer to get rich that didn't require breaking the law. What exactly do you want me to do, because I won't kill somebody if that is what you are suggesting?"

"Oh goodness, no, my good man. That couldn't be farther from the truth. I have plenty of men that would be more qualified to do something like that than you. However, you are correct, what I am asking will require breaking a law. However, it's an American law, not one of ours."

"Okay, I am willing to listen to your offer."

Octavius smiled. "Great. But first I need you to understand the ground rules. Whether you accept or not, everything that is discussed in this saloon today is never to be discussed with another person as long as you live. If you do, I will need to put one of my more qualified men we previously spoke about in your path. Now the question is, are you going to walk out now, or do you still want to hear the offer?"

He knew walking out now was not an option, not if he wanted to remain a captain of his ship.

"I want to hear the offer," he replied. "But that doesn't mean I will automatically accept it once I discover what it is though."

"Courageous and cautious, those traits will indeed serve you well." Mr. Prescott leaned back in his chair and enjoyed his cigar for a few moments. Then he leaned forward and said, "I am a patriot, Captain Ericson. I am working night and day to get this transcontinental railway completed. Until we do, Canada will never become the nation it needs to be. America finished their transcontinental railroad in 1869. That was fifteen years ago!" He pounded his fist on the table in frustration. "Look what happened to their growth and prosperity once they got that done. That's what will happen to

Canada once we get ours completed." He paused to regain his composure. "Think about how exciting it would be to be a vital tool used to forge a nation, Thomas. Are you a patriot?"

"Of course, I am," he said half defensively and half out of pride."

"That's good. Because I need patriots who will do what it takes to lift this nation off of its knees and into greatness."

"So how can I help?"

"I am glad you asked. The CPR is in trouble. The cost of building this railroad is greater than anyone could have anticipated, and we are going to soon become bankrupt, unless we find a creative way to raise some new money. The problem is that our politicians will not give us any more loans. They told us they have given us everything they are going to at this point. Stupid, bickering, self-serving politicians—"

"How quickly?" Thomas interrupted, unaware that this was such a dire situation.

"Soon," came the reply. "Months, if not sooner. We are living on borrowed time."

"I do not have any money to invest."

Octavius laughed. "No, my dear captain, I don't need the money you have. I need the money you can provide." Before Thomas could say anything else, he continued, "I met a man who provided a way for me to create as much American money as I want. The problem is that I need a place to make it, that will never be discovered by the US Secret Service."

"Counterfeit money!" He whistled, thinking about the possibilities and the danger. "So again, why mc?"

"Because I want to run my counterfeit operation out of the five-foot secret cargo hold in the bottom of my ship. Even though I have three identical ships. The *Algoma* goes from Owen Sound, Canada, to Sault Ste. Marie, Canada, to Port Arthur, Canada, and back. It is the only one of the three ships that never sails in US waters, so it can never be searched by the Americans even if they discovered what we are doing. They would have to get the Canadian government to agree, which they won't, once they understand we are using the counterfeit American money to finish building our nation." He paused to let that sink in. It took a few minutes as his head was still spinning with possibilities.

"No risk should be undertaken without a reward, and great risk deserves a great reward, sir. What is my great reward for allowing this counterfeit operation to be run aboard my ship?"

"Land, Thomas, thousands of acres of land. The government gave the CPR twenty-five-million acres of land to build this railway on. Some of the land will become insanely valuable, some worthless. Do you know what the difference will be? I will tell you. The land near the towns where the railway is going to go through will increase in value a hundredfold or more. I will sell you some of this prime land at a price of only one dollar an acre. Once the railroad goes through, you can sell it back for a hundred dollars an acre or more to someone else."

Then his eyes lit up like Christmas when he was a boy, all full of magical wonderment and excitement.

"Can I sleep on it and get back to you in the morning?" Thomas asked.

Octavius made a show of pulling out his pocket watch and looking at the time.

"I can give you an hour. Time is of the essence. If not, I have other captains I can make this offer to," he said, insinuating that he would no longer be the captain of the *Algoma*.

"I understand how the cash will help the railroad, but I did not hear the details on how you were going to get the money off the ship and distributed without being discovered," Thomas continued. "I am only asking because if the details aren't right, this venture will be discovered. Just think what would happen if the ship was hijacked by pirates or there was a mutiny because our little operation was discovered."

Mr. Prescott III looked at him carefully. "You have a good head on your shoulders. Those are excellent questions, which further proves you are the right man for the job. As such, I will leave those details up to the captain of the ship."

"I will be back in one hour," he said as he stood and headed for the door.

The moose opened it for him; and he walked out of the bar, into the bright daylight, and straight across the street to the Bucket of Blood tavern where he sat at the bar and had another whiskey poured. His mind started hatching a plan to get his own piece of the action on top of what was offered by the railroad. By the time his hour was up, he was back at the Pig's Ear telling Mr. Prescott III that he was his man.

"As long as I am in charge of what happens on the ship, I am willing to play my part in this venture. To seal the deal, I am going to give you one hundred dollars for the deed to one hundred acres of prime railroad land in Calgary or Edmonton, whichever one the railroad will end up running through. And I want the tracks to cut right through the middle of my acreage."

Octavius smiled. "But of course. I see you are a shrewd businessman as well. I shall have the deed for you tomorrow, but remember this is privileged information. You must not tell others where we plan to lay the track." With that, he got up and walked out of the room, ending the meeting.

*****

Five days later, the equipment had been brought aboard the ship in unmarked crates during the middle of the night and stored on the main deck. After the men who brought the crates aboard left the ship, McDuff ordered two of his constables to move the crates down to the second deck and into room number 70. Then he and Archer brought it down into the secret hold and reassembled the machine, using the instructions they had made when they took it apart. After that was completed, the supplies of ink and paper were stockpiled in the hold next to the machine. McDuff then locked the entrance to the secret hold and told Captain Thomas, who was standing guard in the corridor next to room number 70, that everything was ready to go. Once McDuff left, Thomas made his way to his office and called his trusted porter Bryson to join him.

"Come on in and close the door," he said as he heard him knock on the door.

"Yes, Captain. You wished to see me?"

"Mr. Bryson, you have been under my command for quite some time now, is that correct?"

"Yes, Captain. You hired me to join you on the *Algoma* as soon as she came into service."

"I have kept my eye on you, and I think you are wasting your time as a porter."

Bryson blinked a few times, thinking he was getting sacked. "Captain, I have always done everything you asked to the best of my abilities."

Captain Ericson smiled as he realized what the porter was thinking. "Relax, Mr. Bryson. I am not going to fire you. Instead, I am going to offer you an opportunity to go into business with me."

A wave of relief and surprise washed over his face. "Thank you, Captain, but I don't understand. I have no money to invest nor any business acumen required to become a business partner."

"This is a unique offer. All I need from you is for your continued loyalty to me, some difficult work, and the ability to keep your mouth shut. If you can do those three things, I will give you 25 percent of the profits of this business adventure. By my estimation, you could retire in five years if all goes according to plan."

"Captain, I am honored by your confidence in me. I will do whatever you say. Just please tell me what kind of business we are going to be in."

"We are going to become entrepreneurs," exclaimed the captain. "I know you don't understand just yet, but let's shake on it to seal the deal, and then I will show you what I have in mind."

After shaking hands, the captain led him over to second-class cabin number 70 in the middle of the ship. He looked to make sure they were not being seen by anyone, then unlocked the door, ushered him inside, and closed the door quickly. Then he locked the door again.

"What are we doing in this cabin, Captain? Is this where you are going to run the business from?"

Captain Ericson didn't say a word. Instead, he went over to the closet and pulled up a trapdoor in the floor.

The captain then found the light switch in the closet and turned on the lights in the cargo hold below.

"Follow me," he said as he climbed down the twenty-foot ladder through the trapdoor in the floor.

A few moments later, both men reached the bottom. They were standing in a room five feet wide and eighteen feet across in the bottom of the ship. In it was an odd machine that looked like a printing press, and there were a bunch of supply crates stacked neatly against the wall.

"What is this place, Captain?" Bryson said out of curiosity.

"This is a secret cargo hold in the middle of the ship. No one knows it is here. This is where the ship was cut in half to get through the locks at the Welland Canal, and then spliced back together on the other side. When it was put back together, they made a watertight bulkhead wall two and a half feet on either side of the cut line to seal off any potential damage in case the ship's welds sprung a leak. This room is on the port side of the ship. There is an identical one on the starboard side of the ship, separated by this five-foot-long wall in between them. After it left the shipyard when the ships were reassembled, the CPR privately cut secret entrances into the closet floors of cabin 70 and cabin 71, which are directly above them."

"So then what does this machine do?"

"It prints counterfeit American money. Twenty-dollar bills to be exact."

"I do not know how to run this machine, and I don't want to be stuck in this tiny hold all day even if I did know how to run it."

"Not to worry. That is not your part in all this. The CPR Railroad owns this machine, and they will choose a noncrew member to run it as needed. But enough of that. Let's get back to my office so I can tell you how we make our money on this deal."

Ten minutes later, they were both back in the captain's office. Bryson had a thousand questions, but he knew enough to wait and let the captain explain his plan first.

"You were born in Halifax, weren't you?"

"That is correct, sir."

"Good, that's very good. I am a patriot, Mr. Bryson. Are you?"

"Of course, sir. Why do you ask?"

"The CPR needs to raise some extra funds to complete the railroad. That is why there is a machine on this ship that can counterfeit American twenty-dollar bills. I am the only crew member to their knowledge that knows it exists, and I am trusting you with that knowledge. If you tell anyone, we will both wind up dead. Do you understand?"

"Yes, Captain," he said as he sat down in the chair next to him. It was necessary as his knees felt like they were going to give out.

"Our opportunity lies in the fact that the CPR is not keeping track of how much counterfeit is printed off of the machine. So we are going to print off some extra money for ourselves. In fact, I need to get our hands on ten thousand dollars to get our business off the ground."

"I don't understand, Captain. Can't we just print whatever we need?"

"No, we need to get a legitimate business started so that we can explain our sudden wealth. Otherwise, people will ask where we got all of our money, and we will not be able to answer them."

"You are very smart, Captain. What kind of business are we going to start?"

"I heard rumor about a mine on Isle Royale that found silver as well as copper. It has not been reported yet because they do not want to worry about poachers and claim jumpers rushing to the island. So they are stockpiling their treasure until such time as they can make the most profit. For ten thousand dollars, I am going to become a 10 percent owner of the mine."

"What about me, sir? I thought I was going to be a partner?"

"Yes, you are. Not as an owner of the mine, but as my personal business assistant. It would look suspicious if a porter with no resources was able to become an owner of a mine. Again, we must make everything look proper and above suspicion."

"I see, sir. So how then do I become wealthy?"

"So here is my plan. They are only going to make the counterfeit while we are docked at Owen Sound. So they are not bouncing around in the rough water when they do it. So after they finish, we make some extra counterfeit before each voyage. On our way to Port Arthur, when we stop at Sault Ste. Marie to pick up passengers, we will exchange this counterfeit American money with real Canadian money two for one. We will then stockpile this Canadian money in the purser's safe, which only you and I have access to. We keep repeating this process until we build up enough Canadian money for the next step, which is to stop about a mile off of Isle Royale in the middle of the night and have silver from my mine secretly brought aboard the ship, which we will pay for with the Canadian money. We will then take the silver to Port Arthur, where we will sell it on the docks for a profit. Whatever we make on the selling of the silver, I will give you 25 percent of the profit, right off the top."

"Who are we going to sell it to?"

"The CPR itself, my son. That is the beauty of it all. Their plan is to make the counterfeit money to purchase the silver at Port Arthur that was mined at the Silver Islet Mine before its demise. But we are going to sell them our silver as well for their counterfeit money. We will use some of it for our exchange program in Sault Ste. Marie, and the rest we can spend in Owen Sound on whatever we want. Then we keep repeating the process until we are rich."

"I am afraid you lost me, sir. It was too much to take in all at once. Can you say it one more time?"

"We buy silver from my mine on Isle Royale, who gets paid for the silver they produce tax free because they never reported digging up the silver nor selling it. I get the silver at a 100 percent profit since we paid for it with the Canadian money we bought with the counterfeit American bills. Then we sell the silver to the CPR in Port Arthur, who will pay a premium price to buy it, since they will be paying for it in counterfeit money. We then take the counterfeit money from the sale of our silver and give you 25 percent, which you can keep and spend or trade two for one for real Canadian cash when we stop at Sault Ste. Marie."

Bryson was still chewing on the information, so Captain Ericson made it as simple as possible.

"Here is an example. Over time, we have exchanged ten thousand counterfeit dollars for five thousand dollars of Canadian currency. We then take it and purchase five thousand dollars of silver from my mine and sell it in Port Arthur for six thousand to the CPR, which will be using more counterfeit money. I then give you 25 percent of the six thousand in counterfeit, which equals fifteen hundred dollars that you can do with what you please. Since your yearly salary as a porter is only eight hundred and twenty-three dollars, that represents a very nice increase in lifestyle. In fact, each time we sell the silver, you will make the equivalent of two years' worth of income. We do this two or three times a season, and you can retire in five years."

The wheels finally clicked in Bryson's head. He smiled and said, "Thank you, Captain, for this amazing opportunity. I am your man."

After Bryson left the office, the captain went back over his numbers again. Using the same example that he gave Bryson, his mining operation would make five thousand of profit on the sale of the silver to him. As 10-percent owner, that equals five hundred dollars of income. When he sells the silver to the CPR for six thousand, he keeps 75 percent, which is forty-five hundred dollars of profit. Added together and he makes five thousand per cycle. By his estimations, they can safely do three cycles per year, which means he would get fifteen thousand per year in income plus the increased value of his mining operation, plus the land investment opportunity that he is getting from the CPR to run this operation for them. He closed his eyes and started dreaming of all the things he wanted to buy with his newfound wealth.

*****

One week later, Captain Thomas made his way to the nondescript building on the street he was told about. It was on a back street, not a main thoroughfare. He got out and paid the horse and buggy driver, and then he watched the buggy leave. Except for him, the street was otherwise deserted. He used the door knocker to announce his presence. A few moments later, he was ushered inside.

"Good day to you, sir. Can I help you?" the unkept young man asked.

"Yes. I was told I could find a particular person here who recently discovered something of value on Isle Royale."

"I'm afraid you've been given some bum information, sir."

"Perhaps there is someone else here I can speak to? I have a business proposition I would like to discuss."

"Please wait here for a moment."

Five minutes later, the unkept young man appeared with an older man who looked like his relative.

"What is this all about? We have no time to waste with people trying to sell us stuff we don't need. Now go away."

Captain Thomas didn't move. "I am here to buy, not sell, my good sir."

"What is it that you think we have for sale here?"

"This is a business, isn't it? The very nature of business is to buy and sell. Let's sit down and have a private conversation. I know about what you found on the Isle."

"Is that so? And who gave you this preposterous information?"

"An Indian acquaintance of mine named Gitchie Manito."

The man blinked. "Never heard of him."

Thomas pulled out his wallet and showed the ten grand to the man. "I bet this jogs your memory."

"We don't need a partner."

"My good fellow, I can help you with the thing you need the most. I can get you paid for the silver you dig up and get it off of the Isle with no one the wiser."

"And just how can you do that?"

An hour later, Thomas left the nondescript office on the deserted back street as a partner in the mining operation.

CHAPTER 6

A Dangerous Game

> Isolated and outnumbered, I found myself
> engaged in a deadly game of hide-and-seek. The
> penalty for losing would be catastrophic.
>
> —Winston Hawes, 1885

It was almost midnight, and I had been frantically looking for a cabin to hide in for quite some time now. I had started at the back of the ship and was working my way toward the front. Seeing a restroom, I cautiously opened the door and went in. I went into a stall and pulled my pants down to look at my leg more closely. It was just a scratch. It hadn't bled at all. It must have been Mr. Fontaine's blood that got on my pants leg. I got dressed again and left the stall. I had turned the sink on and was splashing cold water on my face when I heard voices outside the door. Quickly turning off the water, I ran back inside the stall and closed the door just as two men walked in.

"Wa haven't we foond thes man yit?" the frustrated McDuff barked at Archer while he glanced around the room.

"We've checked the second deck, and he isn't there, which means he must be hidin' in one of the cabins on the main deck," Archer replied, trying to impress his boss.

"Onie signs ay heem at aw?"

"The men have started at the back of the ship checking cabins, workin' their way to the front. We thinks he hid in a life-jacket locker at one point, but no one has seen the lad yet."

"You stupid oaf. Thes means he knows we ur oan th' ship searchin' fur heem. 'At will make heem harder tae fin'. Dae ye know how many places thaur ur fur a man tae squirrel awa' oan a ship loch thes?"

"We'll find him," answered Archer, trying his best to sound confident.

"Ye better dae it fest," warned McDuff. "Ah am gonnae th' cargo hold tae gie plan B pit intae place."

"Plan B? What's plan B?"

"Don't ye be worryin' yer wee heed aboot' at. It's jist some insurance in case ye fail me."

As they were talking, the door opened again, and a passenger walked in.

McDuff and Archer immediately stopped their conversation.

"Good evenin', sir. I am CPR constable McDuff. May I be seein' yer ticket?"

"I don't have it with me, it's in my cabin. I don't understand why you would need to see it again. The purser checked it when we boarded as he showed me to my room."

"I be sorry ferth' trouble, sir, but I will need tae' go wi' ye tae yer room tae be seein' yer ticket. We be havin' a stowaway onboard," he lied.

I stayed hidden for a while after I heard the men leave the restroom. My mind was turning over everything I had just heard. I now knew that the Scottish-Irish guy from the ticket office was the man in charge of finding me, and that he had a plan B in case he couldn't, and that he was one of the constables I had been warned about. I also knew that there were at least three other men helping him search for me. They were searching the main deck currently, and they had already searched steerage and second class on the between deck. I couldn't stop my mind from pondering what plan B was and why the Scottish-Irish constable didn't nab me at the ticket office. While I was thinking on these things, my body began to tell me that

I was too tired to continue running. It was past midnight. I decided to try to get some sleep in the only place I knew was safe. I made my way back to the life-jacket locker and promptly went to sleep.

At seven-thirty in the morning, my body awoke out of pain. My body had knotted up from the awkward, cramped quarters I had fallen asleep in. Slowly, I stood up in the locker and stretched to get the kinks out of my muscles. I could hear nothing outside of the door. The question now became, how was I going to survive another day at sea before we docked at Port Arthur?

*****

"Captain, there is a woman here who requests a word with you," first mate Ethan Ralston said.

"Very well, show her to the bridge, Mr. Ralston." *I wonder what this is about*, the captain thought.

A few moments later, Mr. Ralston returned to the bridge with Catherine.

"Captain, thank you for seeing me. I know you are a busy man," the woman exclaimed.

"It's not a problem at all. What can your captain do for you?"

"If it's not too much trouble, I would like to speak privately with you. It is important."

"Very well. Mr. Ralston, you have the bridge until I return."

"Aye, sir!" Mr. Ralston replied as he moved beside the captain to take over control of the ship.

"Shall we step into my quarters? It is probably the only place on the ship where I can guarantee our conversation will remain private. Of course, we could also take a stroll on the deck, if you would prefer, Miss…" The captain paused as he realized Ralston had not properly introduced them. He made a mental note to talk to him about that later. "I'm terribly sorry, I'm afraid we haven't been properly introduced."

"McGregor," Catherine replied. "And your quarters will do just fine."

They walked to the stairs and proceeded to go down one level below to the main deck. The captain reluctantly unlocked his door and swung it open.

Catherine stepped inside and was amazed at the decor of the room. It had been made to look as if you just stepped back two hundred years in time. There was an old-world globe, probably three feet in diameter, between two stuffed leather chairs, which were beside the desk. The desk was large and made out of beautiful teakwood. It was full of ornate scrollwork and carvings. A map table was in the middle of the room and had several old charts and maps rolled out over it. Near the porthole was a sextant and a spyglass. Off to the other side of the room was a leather sofa, and on the wall hung a portrait of Ponce De Leon.

"Captain, this is completely unexpected. Surely this isn't typical among modern ships."

"No, it isn't. In fact, it is one of a kind, to the best of my knowledge. I spent a good portion of my life savings to make this happen. I have always admired the great explorers of the past, so I tried to recreate what I thought an ancient explorer's quarters would look like. Besides, this room helps me relax and keep everything in perspective."

Catherine continued to stare at the furnishings. She really felt like she was in a ship from ages past. "Why the picture of Ponce De Leon?"

"Because of the fountain of youth, of course."

"You don't actually believe in that, do you, Captain?"

"No, I do not believe that it is an actual destination or place. However, I do believe in the noble quest it represents."

"Which is what exactly?"

"The search for the one thing in the world that makes you feel young and full of life. The very thing that gives you energy and purpose to keep going on. For most, it is love or power."

"I am most curious, Captain, what is that one thing for you?"

"Early on in my life, I discovered mine was sailing on the open sea, being tested by the wind and waves and proving mastery over them by bringing my ship safely into port. That is when I feel life is full of vigor and purpose and accomplishment. What about you?"

"I have never thought of it that way before. I guess, I am unsure of what it would be."

"Your still young, you'll have time to figure it out. Now, what did you need to talk to me about?" the captain said as he politely changed the subject.

"Captain, I think you have a thief in your crew. Last night I happened to see a sailor on this ship leaving a passenger's room in such haste that he actually ran into me in the corridor. He didn't stop to see if I was all right, but he did yell 'excuse me' as he continued running away."

"I see. I am very glad you brought this to my attention discreetly. First of all, are you all right?"

"Yes, he just startled me more than anything."

"Can you describe him? Did he have anything in his hands? And do you remember what cabin it was?"

"It was a first-class cabin, but other than that, no. I'm sorry I can't remember any of the details. I was pretty startled by the whole thing."

"Don't worry, Ms. McGregor, we will find this man and determine what no good he's been up to. I have zero tolerance for these types of matters and will not hesitate to lock him in the brig in the bottom of the ship if I find any wrongdoing."

Satisfied with his response to her concerns over the crewman's strange behavior, Catherine thanked him and headed back to her cabin to order room service for breakfast.

Meanwhile, Thomas returned to the bridge in a huff.

"Mr. Ralston!" the captain yelled. "Do you know who that was?"

"No, sir."

"Well, neither did I. Never, ever bring a passenger to see me without introducing them to me first, or I will be finding me a new first mate. Is that clear?"

"Yes, sir. My apologies, sir. She was just so pretty I must have forgotten my manners, sir."

The captain stared a hole through the poor first mate for what seemed like eternity. Then he pointed his finger at the man, as if he was going to yell some more; but instead, he turned and left the bridge, going back to his quarters.

"Wow, I'm glad that was you and not me," said Bryson, the purser, with a mocking grin on his face. "I would stay clear of the captain as much as possible for the rest of the trip if I were you."

"Why did the captain get so upset over something so simple?"

"I reckon it had something to do with the fact that he did not want to get questioned by the daughter of his biggest competitor in the shipping business."

"What?"

"Catherine McGregor is the heiress of Maxwell McGregor Industries. You know, MMI Shipping, which controls almost all the vessels on the Great Lakes. It is the CPR's main competition."

With that, Ralston's stomach turned sour as the gravity of his blunder began to sink in.

"Bryson," the captain yelled from the hallway.

*****

I had left the life-jacket locker and resumed my search for a better hiding spot. I also realized that I had to find a separate hiding place for the briefcase. If captured, it would be my only chip left in the poker game of life. I had just got to the bottom of the stairwell when I was seen.

"Hey, you!"

My head spun around, and I saw someone running down the hall at me. I took off running as fast as I could. Stealth was no longer an option. I needed to create some separation between my pursuer and myself so I could lose him in the maze of passageways and stairwells. I turned and ran toward the front of the ship.

"Stop and I'll go easy on ya," my pursuer yelled.

I could tell from the sound of his voice that I had put some distance between us already. I just needed to find a place to duck into so he can run past me. I turned down another hallway to the right and then made another quick right around the dining room. Now I was headed aft. When I got to the back of the ship, I saw another staircase and quickly climbed up to the main deck. I turned right and was still running at full speed. I tried to stop quickly, but I tripped and fell awkwardly in the process, narrowly avoiding a woman who was unlocking her cabin door. Sprawled out on the floor, I got up quickly and saw the woman I had watched boarding the ship last night.

"Miss, I don't have time to explain," I said, looking over my shoulder to see if my pursuer was catching up. "But please take my briefcase and hide it in your cabin. I will come back for it later."

She had a bewildered look in her eyes and didn't respond at all. It was as if she hadn't heard me.

"Miss, please help me. It is a matter of life and death." Handing her the briefcase, I gently shoved her into her room and closed the door. Then I took off running again. I could hear my pursuer breathing hard as he was running up the stairs and almost at the corner where he would be able to see me again. Ahead, I saw some lifeboats suspended above the cabins on their davits. I ran to it, jumped, and pulled myself in, concentrating on trying to keep my breathing quiet.

*****

After a few seconds had passed, Catherine started to open the door again. She saw another man running past her door. He glanced at her as he ran past, but didn't stop. Quickly, she closed the door and locked it. She sat on the edge of her bed trying to figure out what was going on, wondering how many times she was going to get run into in the corridors when she realized that she was holding the first man's briefcase.

A few minutes later a knock on the door startled her. Still in a daze, she said, "Who is it?"

"It is the ship's purser, Mr. Bryson," the man said.

"What can I do for you?"

"I am sorry to bother you at this early hour, but I believe I left another passenger's piece of luggage in your room last night."

Immediately, she realized she needed to hide the briefcase.

"Oh really, I haven't seen anything," she lied as she started to look for a place to hide it.

"I still need to come in and check for myself. This is very embarrassing for me to have lost it, and I am afraid the captain will hear of it if I do not find it quickly. It will only take a moment."

"Just a minute," she said, realizing he was not going to go away. "I need to put a robe on."

She quickly took the briefcase, threw it in her empty suitcase, and closed the latch. Putting a robe on over her dress, she wrapped a towel around her head as if she had just washed her hair and opened the door.

"What did you say you were looking for?" she demanded.

"Sorry to bother you, miss. But I think I mixed up a man's briefcase in with your luggage. May I come in and take a quick look?"

"If it can't wait until after breakfast," she said, playing the ruse out.

With that, the man entered the room and began looking around. It appeared as if he was looking for the man who left the briefcase and not the briefcase itself as he glanced everywhere.

"My luggage is over there," she pointed.

The man looked at the suitcases and was about to open one when she protested.

"What kind of man are you, trying to rummage through a lady's personal effects? The captain shall hear about this!"

The man stopped. He knew full well what would happen if she went to the captain again.

"My apologies, miss. Sometimes I get a little too zealous in doing my job. A word to the captain will not be necessary."

"Well, it seems that you have a couple of things you are trying to keep from the captain, don't you?" she said as she realized he was the man who almost knocked her over earlier.

Under his forced smile, she could see the anger in his eyes as he apologized again. He excused himself and left her cabin.

*****

I waited for an hour in the lifeboat before I felt it was safe to get out. As soon as I did, I headed for the cabin where I had left my briefcase. After nervously knocking on the door, the beautiful woman answered it. When the door opened, I was speechless. A wonderful perfumed smell hit my nostrils, and I was instantly under its spell. I took a good look at her face, and her eyes drew me in. They were the most beautiful eyes I had ever seen. I forgot why I was there. Time stood still—that is, until she said, "You must be here for your briefcase. Why don't you come in, and I will get it for you?"

Still in a trance, I followed her into her room as she closed the door behind me.

"I am glad we finally got to meet. My name is Ms. McGregor, but you can call me Catherine. And your name is Mr. Hawes."

"Why, yes, it is," I said. "Have we met before? Surely, I would have remembered that."

She laughed and said, "Yes and no. We have not met before, but I have followed your newspaper articles, so I feel like I know you already. Somehow, I find your articles are different from the other ones I read. I am not angry when I am done reading them."

"Oh, how kind of you," I offered.

"I have some breakfast remaining from where I had ordered room service. Why don't you finish it up? You must be hungry."

I realized I was hungry after not eating since breakfast yesterday, so I accepted her offer. Not knowing what else to say, I picked up a piece of toast and oafishly shoved it into my mouth.

"Well, I do have something else to tell you," she said very softly as she handed my briefcase back to me.

"Yes?" I said, trying not to spit crumbs out as I spoke. I wondered where this was going to go, thinking I was still in the lifeboat dreaming.

"I did something bad. However, it was for good reasons. I hope you will not think too badly of me after I tell you."

"That would be impossible, Ms. McGregor, I mean, Catherine," I said as I used her first name for the first time.

"I threw a brick through your newspaper window," she said tentatively, waiting to see my reaction.

Stunned, I said, "You…why on earth would you do that?"

"I'm not sure I should say just yet. But I did it to help you, not to harm you."

"I don't understand. How could that help me?"

"What's in the briefcase, Mr. Hawes?"

"Please call me Winston," I quickly replied. "And I'm not sure I follow."

"Why were those men chasing you? Surely it had to do something with your briefcase, or else you would not have given it to me to keep it safe."

"You are right on your assumptions. Those men do want what is in my briefcase."

"Why?"

"I will tell you if you do not think too badly of me," I said back in kind. Having finished the toast, I picked up the remaining bacon off her plate.

"Impossible."

I pinched myself just to make sure I wasn't dreaming this whole conversation in my head. Nope. I was awake all right.

I swallowed the bacon and said, "It is because I stole it from them, and they desperately want it back."

I watched her expression to see if she was going to throw me out of her room. She didn't.

"I know," she replied, smiling at me.

Instantly, alarm bells went off in my head. She is one of them. How stupid could I be? Why would a beautiful woman such as her be interested in a guy like me? Stupid, stupid, stupid. I looked at the food as if it had been poisoned and turned to go to the door, but she grabbed my hand. It felt wonderful. I stopped instantly, hoping she would never let go.

She looked at me and said, "I knew I could trust you to tell the truth, Winston."

"What?" I said, dumbfounded.

"I have been following you for a long time, since just before I threw that brick through your window."

"Why?" was all I could get out.

"Because you are different than all the other men I know. You see, my father is a ruthless businessman. He owns MMI Shipping. I know what ruthless men are like, and I know you are not that type of man."

I just looked at her. Nothing came to mind to say.

"You are trying to do the opposite of my father, and I respect that. You are trying to stop the evil deeds of men like him and set things right by exposing the truth in your articles."

I still had nothing to say. My mind was like a lump of oatmeal, too thick to process anything.

"I read all your newspaper articles. I even did some digging myself, as I suspected that my father's business might somehow be involved. He controls the shipping on the Great Lakes. There was no way he was going to let the CPR just launch three new megaships unchallenged in his backyard."

"So is he involved?" I asked.

"Not directly, at least not that I have discovered. But I do know some things that I am not sure you do."

"What would that be?"

"That the CPR cares more about their railroad than they do about their shipping business."

"Why do you say that?"

"Because my father tried to blackmail them into being a partner in the shipping business, and they didn't flinch."

"Wouldn't that mean the opposite? That they do care about the shipping business?"

"No, because my father gave them an all-or-none proposition. Either they would share their shipping revenues and let him continue to set the pricing for cargo on the Great Lakes, or he would drive them out of business."

"Maybe they didn't believe he was capable of doing that?"

"Trust me. Everyone in the industry knows my father is capable of doing that. In fact, he has done it many times before."

"How do you know that?"

"Because my father has no sons, just me. And he thinks that women are not smart enough to understand the complexity of business dealings, so he has let me sit in on some meetings he shouldn't have."

"Why would he do that?"

"He told me my beauty would present a distraction and give him the upper hand in negotiations."

"Well, he was right about that!" I said before I thought about what I was saying.

Catherine blushed slightly. Then she changed the subject.

"What's in the briefcase, Winston?"

I wanted to tell her, but didn't want to drag her into the trouble I was already in.

"I can't tell you. It's not safe for you to know."

"Okay," she said. "I trust you."

"Thank you," I sighed, relieved I did not have to lie to her about it. "Tell me more about this meeting you attended with your father, purely as a distraction."

Catherine blushed again. "It was a meeting with Octavius Prescott III. He is the CEO of the CPR company. A very powerful man who is building the transcontinental railroad in Canada. He also owns the three newest ships on the Great Lakes."

Winston interrupted, "I know. This ship we are on is one of them. I was doing stories about the railroad when apparently you threw a brick through my window to stop me."

"Not to stop you but to warn you about the danger. I was hoping to meet up with you to discuss what I knew, but that became too difficult for me."

"So what was the conversation in the meeting about?"

"My father said he knew what was going on and that he wanted a piece of the action. In fact, he said he was going to be their partner. The railroad man was furious. He demanded to know what my father knew about his company. My father said he knew everything, including the fact that the company was running out of money to finish the railroad and that they were stealing silver from the mine at silver islet to keep things going."

"Wow. That connects a few dots for me. So did he say anything else?"

"My father just said that it would be really unfortunate if the silver mine went dry, then they would be in a real pickle and that if they waited until they were that desperate before coming to accept his generous offer, the price would be triple."

"The man knows how to negotiate." I whistled as my mind was whirling away. "Wait, didn't that mine flood recently?"

"Yes, and it was no accident either. Mr. Prescott III stormed out of the office and slammed the door behind him. You could hear him yelling in the hallway that no one was going to railroad him. Which in a way was kind of funny that the railroad man would use that phrase. As soon as he left our house, another man entered the room. I do not know where he came from. It was a man I had never met before—that is, until I boarded this ship. I was so startled to see him at the ticket office, I actually dropped my purse."

"The small Scottish-Irish guy?" I said, slightly panicked.

"Yes. That's the same guy. Anyway, my father told him that he would underbid everyone to get the contract to ship the coal that was needed to keep the pumps running at the mine during the winter. He told this man once that happens to make sure that the coal never gets there."

"That way the pumps would stop and the mine would flood. Brilliant…and ruthless," I interjected. "So your father followed through with his threat to cripple the illegal cash flow that was keeping the CPR running."

"Yes. My father was extremely happy to hear the news when it happened. He expected Mr. Prescott III to grovel back to his office within days. But he never did. He wondered where they found a new source of money."

I glanced down at my briefcase. "I know the answer to that. I also know something you don't."

"What is that, Winston?"

"That the Scottish-Irish Guy is named McDuff, and he works for the CPR Railroad as a constable. I can only surmise that since he came into the meeting after Mr. Prescott III left, that his loyalties lie with your father and not with the CPR."

*****

Crigger went to find Tibbs. When he found him, he pulled him aside where no one else could hear him.

"What is it?"

"I was swabbing the decks by the captain's office, trying to stay busy and out of the path of the leprechaun."

"And?"

Well, that's when I saw the first mate go into his office."

"So?"

"They were talking loudly, and I heard the captain say that we were going to make an unscheduled stop tonight, as an emergency training drill. Said we were going to lower the lifeboats and everything."

"Really, that is odd."

"There's more. The first mate left the captain's quarters in a hurry. Luckily, I heard the door begin to open, so I looked down and pretended to be swabbing the deck real good. A few moments later, I heard the captain talking to someone else in his office. He said that they were going to meet up with someone named Itchy Mosquito and bring something back aboard the ship."

"What? I don't believe you. I guarantee you there is no one on the planet named Itchy Mosquito. You must have gotten into the rum again?"

"What rum?"

"Never mind that nonsense," said Crigger. "I wonder what they could be bringing aboard."

"I don't know, and I don't wanna know."

"You haven't told anyone else about this, have you?"

"No, who would I tell?"

"Make sure you don't. We've got enough trouble with the leprechaun and his goon. Don't be needing anymore. You better get back to swabbing before anyone misses you."

"Right, good thinking."

"And don't bother me again unless you hear a story about a mermaid."

"You didn't hear…" He paused to make the other man listen more closely. "Nah, never mind. I heard that was just a big fish tale anyways," cracked Tibbs.

Crigger shook his head chuckling and then left Tibbs to his chores.

*****

McDuff was in a foul mood, even worse than usual. He couldn't understand what was so difficult in finding one man on this ship.

"He's git tae be hid awa' real guid by noo. Tis bin ten hours," he said. "Whit areas hae we nae searched yit?"

Archer thought for a moment and then said, "We have not searched the cargo holds, nor the crew's berths."

"Git thaim searched reit awa' 'n' *then* report back 'ere tae me. A'm starting tae doubt yer abilities tae fin' him."

Archer left to go search them himself.

Meanwhile, McDuff made his way down to the second deck and into the food storage room, where found his special marked box behind the huge mound of potatoes. He opened it carefully and put the contents inside his jacket to conceal them. Then making sure he hadn't been noticed, he left the food storage room and proceeded down the hall and stopped at the second-class cabin number 71. Looking around to make sure no one was watching, he opened the door to the cabin, entered, and quickly closed it again. Then he went to the closet and lifted the trap door in the floor and climbed down the ladder to the secret cargo hold in the bottom of the ship. It was only five feet wide and went eighteen feet across to the middle of the ship. There, a wall separated an identical space on the other side of the ship. MacDuff was on the space on the starboard side of the ship. That was where the bags of money and supplies were stored. He moved some of the bags until he had cleared a small area against the bulkhead wall and the middle wall that separated the two rooms in half. This was almost the exact middle of the ship. He took the contents out of his jacket and carefully placed the TNT against the two walls. He then trailed the fuse out to the edge of the money bags and buried the TNT under the money bags, leaving only an inch of the fuse wire exposed.

"Nobody wull fin' that 'til tis tae late. Plan B is noo operational." He grinned and climbed back up the ladder into the closet. He then put the trap door back in place and then waited at the door, listening to make sure he would be able to leave unseen. Once he was out of the room, he made his way to the captain's quarters, where he unlocked the door and went in unannounced.

*****

An hour later, the captain entered his room, only to find McDuff sitting in his chair behind his desk with his feet propped up on it, smoking one of his cigars.

"How did you get into my office? I shall have you arrested and put into the brig for this," the captain exclaimed.

"Relax, Thomas. Ye know ye hae na authority tae dae ony sic thing. Ah tak' mah orders faeth' CPR, wha by th' wey owns this ship. Noo be a guid laddie 'n' hae a seat. We hae a few hings tae discuss."

Captain Ericson sat down as he was told, wary of whatever this little guy was going to discuss with him. He may work for the CPR as a constable, but that didn't mean he had to like him.

"A'm waantin' tae know whaur yer loyalties lie."

"I don't understand."

"Let me spell it oot fur ye then. Yer nae helping this reporter, Hawes, hide, urr ye?"

"No, why would I do that?"

"Sin ye asked, ah wull tell ye how come. Yi'll want th' briefcase fur yersel', sae ye kin sell it taeth' hi'est bidder."

"You've lost your mind. I have no interest with whatever is in this man's briefcase. And I have not seen this man nor helped him evade capture by you or your men either."

"Whatever's in th' briefcase?" McDuff mocked the captain's words. "Dinnae be expecting me tae think that ye dinnae know that he haes th' missing counterfeit plates. Especially sin ye know aboot th' counterfeiting machine in th' secret cargo haud."

Even though the captain's face went a little paler than normal, he sat up a little straighter in his chair. He wanted the man to have to look up at him.

"You know very well that I know about the counterfeit operation being run aboard this ship. If you remember our original conversation at the Pig's Ear, I am a patriot, and I am doing my job. Nothing more, nothing less. I have no interest in the counterfeiting business. My reward is land, remember? If the plates are missing, it is you that let them get taken, not me. It was your job as constable to run the protection for the operation."

McDuff stood up and locked eyes with that captain. "We'll juist see aboot that, Thomas. A'm sure afore this trip is ower, we wull talk again aboot this." He turned to leave the room but stopped a few feet from the door. "Ye better hawp ah fin' this guy quickly."

The door slammed shut, and the captain got up from the chair.

I wonder how much that guy knows? he thought. Then he set off to find Bryson, the purser.

*****

"So why is that guy from my father's office on this ship?" asked Catherine.

"He's the guy who is chasing me to get my briefcase. I overheard him tell some goon in the bathroom that he was looking for me. I guess this means that your father figured out where the CPR got their money after he flooded their mine shaft."

"I don't understand. What does your briefcase have to do with that?"

"I stole what is in the briefcase from the CPR, from off this very ship. If your father is after it, then he knows what's in it and why this ship is special."

"So what do we do next?"

"First off, I need to keep away from you so I don't drag you into my troubles. Then I need to find a place to hide the briefcase until we get to Port Arthur. After that, I need to find a way to get off the ship and give the briefcase to the American authorities."

"No!" said Catherine resolutely. "He saw me at the ticket office. He knows who I am and that I got on the ship. He works for my father, so you will be safer with me as he would not be allowed to harm me."

I was about to protest when she grabbed my hand to stop me from leaving. Then she put her finger over my lips and said, "Hush."

My mind immediately turned to mush. My brain was a bowl of oatmeal all over again.

"Okay," was all I could mumble.

"Now that that's settled," Catherine said. "You were right about finding a place to hide the briefcase. Let's think for a moment about a place they would never look."

It took me a few minutes to begin to think at all.

"I've got an idea," I finally said. "How about you hide it and not tell me where. That way if I am captured, I will not be able to tell them where it is."

"We are not splitting up. I made that abundantly clear."

"Fine, but if we are captured, they are not going to beat the information out of a woman, especially as one as beautiful as you. And if they tried, I would tear them to pieces."

Catherine looked Winston in the eye. "Do you really believe that?"

"Of course, I do. They would never hurt you, you said so yourself," Winston exclaimed, missing her point entirely.

*****

The captain finally caught up with Bryson, the purser, and ushered him to a place they could talk privately.

"Things are going to get out of hand. Do you know where the briefcase man is hiding?"

"Not for sure, but I do have my suspicions that he could be with or have stashed the briefcase with Ms. McGregor."

"Why do you think that?"

"I am pretty sure I saw her standing in the doorway holding the briefcase at one point, and then when I went back to check her room, she acted very defiantly. She had even wrapped a towel around her head like she had just washed her hair."

"Very well, do what you can to retrieve that briefcase before the others do. Then bring it to my office, and wait for me there."

"Yes, Captain."

"There's another matter we need to attend to."

"What would that be, sir?"

"As you know, we are scheduled to stop a mile off Isle Royale tonight to meet the Indian Gitchie Manito. He is going to row out to us with another shipment."

"Good old Gitchie Manito, how much is he bringing?"

"This is the last drop of the season, so I told him to bring double the normal amount."

"Luckily, sir, I already have enough in the safe to cover that. It would have been difficult to run it off and get it swapped out at Sault Ste. Marie with the constable aboard."

And with the counterfeit plates missing, thought the captain. "Good thinking, Bryson. We will need to make sure that McDuff and Archer do not catch wind of what we are doing."

"We will also need to find a new place to hide it until we reach Port Arthur. Where do you suggest, Captain?"

"No, put it in the food pantry like we always do. No one will look for it while it is there. Then we will transfer it to the starboard side secret hold."

"Yes, Captain. I understand. What would you have me do to make sure McDuff is out of the way?"

"Find the briefcase, remove the contents, and lock them in your safe, then rehide the briefcase with some counterfeit money in it and keep them occupied looking for it. When the time comes, you can help them discover it by leading them on a wild-goose chase while the shipment is being received."

"You are a shrewd one, Captain. I shall make it happen. However, I do have a suggestion to make."

"Go ahead, spit it out. We don't have all day."

"Let's have Duncan and Halverson load the shipment into the pantry while I handle McDuff. I won't be able to be in two places at the same time."

"Okay. But it's your head if they screw it up," said the captain.

With that, both men left and went their separate ways.

*****

Catherine looked at Winston. She marveled at how he had not picked up on her feelings for him. Why is it that the men she didn't want to give her attention always did, and now the man she does want to give her attention is clueless of her feelings? As she was pondering this, she began to realize that this meant that she is the one pursuing and not the one being pursued. Deep down she liked that, the feeling of being in control and not waiting for life to just happen by chance, and it made her fall for Winston even more.

Perhaps the pursuit of love was her fountain of youth, she thought.

"Before I can help make any decisions on what to do, I need to understand exactly what the situation is," Catherine said to Winston, answering his question.

Winston was out of options, so he said, "Let's find a different place to have this conversation, and I will tell you everything. But I do not feel that we are safe here."

"Fine, let's go to the cabin across the hall. That way we can hear if anyone breaks into my cabin to try to get us or the briefcase."

Without waiting for an answer, Catherine went to the door and listened for any sounds in the hallway. Hearing none, she cracked the door open and looked down the hall. Seeing no one, she walked across the hall and tried the door. It was locked. She pulled out her room key and put it in the door lock. It turned only slightly. Taking a hairpin, she put it in the lock and fiddled with it for a few seconds until the door opened. Then she motioned for Winston to come across to the other room and lock her cabin door behind him.

"Wow. Where did you learn to do that?" Winston asked once they had settled into the new room.

"I learned it from a man who proposed marriage to me once," she said, hoping to get a jealous reaction from him, which didn't appear to work. So she continued on, "Okay, now we are safe. Please tell me what is going on."

"Once I arrived at Owen Sound, I wanted to write a feel-good story. But instead of making people swell with pride, they became nervous. The more I reported on it, the more nervous people seemed to get. One day I got a tip from a man named JD who I had originally met on the train ride that brought me to Owen Sound in the first place. At first, I thought this was just a random meeting, but then I remembered seeing him again at the rail yard in Owen Sound, even though he said he was only going to Toronto. I later discovered who he really was. He is with the American Secret Service. He told me that Owen Sound was the counterfeiting capital of the world in US currency and he was there undercover to figure out who was doing it. He asked me to help by inserting code words into my newspaper articles so he could communicate with his superiors back in Washington. I agreed to help him investigate as well as send the coded messages in my articles. It took almost a year before we had stumbled across the link between my articles on the railroad and the counterfeit. In fact, it was JD who had pointed me in the right direction one night in the alley behind the Bucket of Blood tavern. That's when he told me to check out the three ships that the CPR had just purchased. I had decided no time better than the present to check them out, so I headed toward the docks. On my way there, I saw a pawnshop that had a sailor uniform hanging in the window. It gave me an idea, so I broke in and took it. Then I ran back to the newspaper office a few blocks away and changed clothes. Then I headed back to the docks dressed as a sailor and snuck aboard the only ship at the docks that night. It was the *SS Algoma*. While I was aboard the ship, I heard people talking through the open stairwell down below me. So I snuck down the stairs far enough to catch what they were saying. They said that they needed to print an extra thousand, as their guy in Sault Ste. Marie had a place to get rid of the extra money. They then went their separate ways on the deck below me. So I followed one of the men who was walking toward the middle of the ship and watched him enter room number 70. A few minutes later, he came back out and continued walking away from me, so I made my way down the hallway and entered that very same room. I was surprised that the door was unlocked, but even more surprised when I saw the open trap door in the closet floor. So I looked down the hole and saw the printing press down there. I knew this was a once-in-a lifetime opportunity, so I quickly climbed down and took the engraving plates off the machine and then got off that ship as fast as I could without being seen. That is what I stole, and that is what is in the briefcase."

Catherine didn't know what to say. This was not what she had expected to hear. *I expected it contained incriminating information that my father was using as leverage over the railroad*, she thought.

"Later that night, I wrote my last article on the railway project. I included the words *Golden Spike*. That was the code words which indicated the engraving plates from the counterfeit machine had been found and recovered. To everyone else, it was just a reference to the not-too-distant completion of the railway when they would drive the last symbolic spike to signal the project was completed. It went out in the morning edition of the paper yesterday."

"So how did the bad guys figure out you had it?" asked Catherine.

"That part is still a mystery to me, unless they had suspected JD all along and forced him to talk."

"Or unless someone figured out your code in the newspaper," she replied. "What else was in cabin 70?"

Winston thought for a moment. "It was a standard second-class cabin. It had a dresser and two bunk beds, besides the closet with the trap door, of course. Why?"

"Where is the last place they are going to search for the missing plates?" she replied. "We could hide them in the dresser."

"That is true, but we would have to break in to put them there, and then break in to remove them again, before we get off the ship. That is asking too much."

"Well then, what about the captain's quarters? That is about as private as you can get on a ship."

"Again, too hard to get in and out when we need to."

"Well, where do you think we should hide them?"

Winston thought for a moment and said, "I will be back in a half hour. Wait here, no matter what happens. If I don't return by then, go back to your cabin and pretend you know nothing."

She went to say something in protest, but Winston winked at her and said it would be all right. Then he got up and walked out of the room without the briefcase. Catherine didn't notice this, as her mind started down the possibilities of what that wink really meant.

*****

A half hour had come and gone and Catherine was beginning to worry about him even more since he was late. She started pacing back and forth in the room, when she heard a commotion across the hall. She went up and put her ear to the door. She recognized the man's voice. It was the purser who was giving orders to a sailor by the sounds of it. He told him to wait in the hallway beside the door so that when it was opened, he would not be visible to whoever had opened the door. If he clenched his fist, it was the signal that they would both force their way into the room. Catherine started to panic, wondering what they would do once they discovered the room was empty. Then she noticed the briefcase up against the side of the chair where Winston had been sitting. She put her ear back to the door as she heard knocking.

"Ms. McGregor, I apologize, but I need to speak to you about something urgent."

A few seconds later, there was a second attempt to knock on the door. Perhaps they thought she was asleep by now. There was a moment of silence before the porter whispered a little too loudly to the sailor and told him to get ready, as he has the master key from the chief steward that unlocks all the rooms on the ship. She heard the key unlock the door and then she heard the sound of someone falling to the floor with a thud. Then the door closed, and nothing else could be heard. She was still wondering what happened when there was a soft knock on the door she was now leaning against.

"Catherine, it's me. Hurry up and open the door," she heard Winston say.

She immediately opened the door and saw Winston standing there in a sailor uniform. He quickly entered the room and closed the door. Catherine was so relieved to see him back safely, she instinctively wrapped her arms around him and gave him the tightest hug, like a mother protecting her child.

"Hi, beautiful. Glad to see you too," he said as she let go, realizing what she had done.

Then it registered what he had said, and she gave him a second hug, this time not as a mother protecting a child.

"I was so worried about you. Where did you go? Why were you late? How did you get back to this room without being seen? The bad guys are searching my room right now!" she fearfully said. "And what are you doing in the sailor suit?"

Winston calmed her down and said, "There's more things we need to discuss. First of all, the porter is in your room taking a nap. Unfortunately, I think I broke a knuckle hitting him in the back of the head."

She looked at his hand, which was already swollen and bruised.

"Let me fix that up for you," she replied.

"No time. The second thing is, I took the master key ring from him that unlocks all the rooms on the ship. We can enter any room we want at any time. That is what I went to look for when I left."

Before she could say anything, he continued. "The third thing is that we now know you're not safe. It won't take Bryson long to regain consciousness and figure out what happened."

"So what is our next move?"

"Well, there is one more thing I need to tell you."

Catherine smiled as she looked into his eyes and said, "Tell me anything you want."

"I think you were right. We should hide the counterfeit plates in the captain's office now that we have the master key ring. Getting in and out won't be much of a problem for us anymore."

Catherine's smile slowly faded off her face. "Sure, that makes sense," was all she could force herself to say.

"I also think that we should stay in this room as much as possible to keep an eye on your room. They will probably suspect that you will be coming back to it at some point. Now you wait here while I go hide these plates. I will be back as soon as possible."

This time when he winked at her, she got mad.

Just what kind of moron is this man? she thought.

Winston started to walk to the door, but stopped short and turned back around to face Catherine.

"There really is something else I want to say that is important."

Catherine assumed it was more briefcase talk, so she coldly said, "Can't it wait until you come back?"

"No, and If I don't get it out now, I never will," Winston stammered as he took a deep breath and slowly let it out. "When I came to Owen Sound, it was because they were the only newspaper that would hire me. I felt this was the lucky break I needed, as it offered me an honorable way to escape my past and to get the new start I desperately needed—"

"What was so bad that you needed to escape your past?" interrupted Catherine, confused as to where this conversation was headed.

Winston took another deep breath before continuing, as this was the first time he had talked about this to anyone other than his dead boss.

"Back in Duluth, my dad owned a successful logging business, but he was murdered while I was away for my senior year at college. As soon as I received the news, I quit college and came home. It took me two days to get back. But there was nothing to come home to, as I discovered my mom dead in the kitchen when I got there. Apparently, she committed suicide over her broken heart. I tried to get the police to give me answers to who had done this, but the case was never solved, and I was never told anything. Even so, I have my suspicions as to who was responsible."

"That is the most horrible thing I have ever heard. I am so sorry for your loss."

Winston paused to keep his composure, then he continued, "I wouldn't have told you any of this if I didn't need to. Look, the truth is that I am falling for you, and I think the feeling is mutual. But before I can go down that path with you and see where it goes, I need to lay all my cards on the table up front. I do not want to start out by holding back on something like this."

Catherine blushed and smiled. "I am falling for you as well. You are unlike any other man I have met so far in my life. Whatever it is, I am sure we can get past it."

Not knowing how else to say it, Winston just said it as a plain fact.

"I am confident it was your father who killed my dad to gain control of the family logging business. He was the one who purchased it after my dad's death for pennies on the dollar. He was the only one who had motive and opportunity. You said yourself that your father was a ruthless businessman, capable of doing anything to advance his business interests. I can't forgive him for what he has done. I'm sorry, I just can't. If I can prove it, I will get him arrested and put on trial for my dad's murder and causing my mom's suicide. And I know that this is going to be something that will keep us from moving forward."

Catherine stepped back a step or two and felt like she was just punched in the gut. Then as tears streamed down her face, she said very softly, "Winston, thank you for telling me this. I know that was difficult to do." She sniffed and then wiped her eyes. "I know my father is ruthless and has been out of control for a long time. Even so, I never really thought he was capable of murder—"

Winston started to interrupt, but Catherine gestured with her hands that he should stop.

"Please listen to my heart. I chose you over my family long ago when I threw that brick through your window. And everything I have learned about you since that day has made me fall in love with you even more. I realize that nothing said or done could bring back the love of your parents, and if it is true what you say about my father, then he deserves everything he has coming to him, and I give you my promise that I will personally help you get justice for your parents. But you are mistaken, this will not keep us apart, because I have already started down that path with you to see where our relationship goes."

Winston blinked, the room started spinning, and he felt like he was going to pass out, until Catherine reached up and put her hands on his face and kissed him for the first time.

CHAPTER 7

A Painful Message

A message had been delivered. Patience had run its course, and it was time to make a choice. Keep playing the game or give them what they want. The decision would affect more lives than just mine.

—Winston Hawes, reporter, *Owen Sound Times*, 1885

"Whit's yer excuse this time, fur nae finding him yit?" McDuff asked Archer. "Ne'er mynd, ah don't wantae hear it. Ah reckon a'm needin' tae send a message that we ur serious. Go fin' me a sailor laddie, 'n' bring him tae me."

Archer nodded and left immediately.

The game just turned deadly, he realized.

Archer made his way back to the crews' quarters on the aft end of the ship on deck two. There he found the second engineer who had just finished his twelve-hour, midnight-to-noon shift and was getting ready to hit the bunk for some well-deserved shut-eye. Archer shoved his constable badge in his face and asked what his name was.

"Second Engineer Niklas. Is there a problem with the boilers?"

"No, something else is the problem. Follow me."

And with that Archer made his way back to McDuff with Niklas following behind. Once they reached the brig, Archer grabbed

Niklas by the shirt collar and threw him violently down to the floor at McDuff's feet.

"Don't you get up, until I get back," he sneered. Then he left the man with McDuff while he went to get some witnesses.

Fifteen minutes later, he had found two sailors, Crigger and Tibbs, and brought them back to the room as well.

"Dae ye know how come ah brought ye wee sailor ladies 'ere?"

No one said a word.

"Sae ye kin see fur yourselves that a'm nae fooling aroond!"

Archer snatched the mop that was still in Tibb's hand and broke off the handle over his knee.

"Archer is go'in tae gie this bloke a beating evry hauf oor until ye bring me Hawes or his briefcase."

Archer then proceeded to give the first beating while both sailors were in the room to helplessly watch. After he was finished, Niklas was unconscious and bleeding from his head and probably had his arm broken, trying to shield the blows from raining down on him. Crigger and Tibbs got out of that room as soon as they were allowed to leave.

Once they were a safe distance away, they stopped to catch their breath and tried to keep from losing it.

"I told you those guys were nothing but trouble," said Crigger.

"What are we going to do, tell the captain?" asked Tibbs.

"No. We are going to do exactly what they asked us to do. We are going to find this Hawes before anyone else does."

"I can't do it. I can't turn him over to the bear and the leprechaun. They will kill him for sure."

"Yes, and they are going to kill Niklas if we don't."

"What if we find Hawes, take his briefcase, and warn him to hide. Then we bring the briefcase back and get the reward, save Niklas's life, and spare the live of Hawes?" asked Tibbs. "Everybody wins!"

"If we can make it work, that will be plan A. If not, we have to trade Hawes for Niklas."

Just then they saw Bryson wobbling slowly their way. He looked like he dried out a saloon. They ran to where he was, and each man put an arm under one of his shoulders to help him stand.

"What happened to you?"

Bryson wasn't willing to admit to these men what happened, as what he was doing for the captain was a secret.

"Take me to my cabin. I need to lie down. I must have eaten something that disagreed with me," he lied. "And tell the captain to come see me when he has a chance."

By the time they had gotten Bryson to his room and went and relayed the message to the captain, they had wasted twenty minutes. There were only a few minutes left before the next beating of Niklas.

*****

Winston did not pass out. Instead, he had never felt more alive. He felt like a circus performer who could tame lions while doing backflips on a unicycle. After the kiss, they held hands and shared their hearts for what felt like eternity. Then Winston let go of Catherine as he felt the ship slowing down. They must be getting ready to dock at Sault Ste. Marie to take on more passengers. He knew this meant that the captain would have to be on the bridge to dock the ship, so he decided this was the perfect opportunity to hide the plates in his office.

"I will be back, but I have to go hide these plates while we still can," he said while he took the plates out of the briefcase and tucked them under his shirt. "Wait here and do not open the door for anyone. Remember I have the key, so even if it sounds like me, do not open the door." Then he winked at her and left the room.

The hallway was still empty, but the door to Catherine's room was open, which meant that Bryson was awake and had left. Winston closed the door and quickly made his way toward the captain's quarters. Luck was on his side as he only encountered two passengers on his way there. He quickly let himself in the room and closed the door. Slowly he looked around the room to identify the perfect hiding spot. His eyes stopped on the large old-world globe that was standing in the center of the room, against the wall between the stuffed leather chairs. He went over and examined the base of it. Lifting the globe up ever so slightly, he saw that the base had a hollow area underneath it; so he quickly took the two counterfeit plates, the front and back side of a twenty-dollar bill, and put them underneath, and then set it back down on top of them. As he was doing so, he heard the sound of someone putting a key in the door lock. He quickly ran over to the closet and got inside, just getting the door closed as he heard the captain and Bryson enter the room. Bryson was filling him in on what had happened to him and that he suspected that it was Winston dressed as a sailor that attacked him. The captain sat down at his desk just to the left of the globe and had his back to the closet. Winston could see Bryson through the slats in the closet door. Both men were between his hiding spot and the exit door.

"I'm sure your head hurts, but you only have yourself to blame. In fact, from my point of view, you got what you deserved for being stupid! How could you mistake the man you are trying to capture as one of our crew and then try to use him to capture himself?"

"Captain, I can understand your disappointment in my misfortune—"

"Save it," the captain said, cutting him off. "I don't give two hoots about this man. I only care about our side business going off as planned tonight. The rest of this is just a distraction we can use to keep McDuff and Archer off our tails."

"Yes, Captain. I understand."

"It will be disaster for both of us if they ever discover what we are doing right under their noses. In fact, those two would not even be on this ship today if it weren't for that reporter trying to escape with their counterfeit plates."

"Yes, Captain."

"Now you remember what your job is for the rest of the day, don't you?"

"Find the counterfeit plates before McDuff does. Hide them in the purser's safe. Then hide the briefcase somewhere else to keep McDuff hunting for it and out of our way while we meet Gitchie Manito's rowboat tonight and load the silver from your mine on Isle

Royale onto the ship in exchange for the Canadian cash we got from the excess counterfeit money. Hide the silver in the galley until we reach Port Arthur, where we will sell it to the CPR for a huge profit. Then we retrieve the plates and give them to McDuff, so business can go back to normal."

"Good. Now get out of my office and make it happen just like that!" ordered Captain Ericson.

With that, Bryson left immediately, not wasting any time to get back to his mission. The captain also got up and made his way over to his private restroom and closed the door. Winston waited about fifteen seconds to make sure he was staying in there and then made his way out of the closet and over to the cabin door. Then he quickly left the room and locked the door back behind him.

Moments later, he unlocked the door to the cabin across from Catherine's room and told her what he just overheard.

*****

Crigger and Tibbs knew that a half hour had passed and the Niklas was probably getting beaten again. They had failed so far to find this man or his briefcase and knew that they only had so much time left before it was one of them getting beaten up while others were made to search.

"We need to get a plan together on how to find this guy."

"No kidding. What do you have in mind?"

"Think like him. I mean what would we do if we were in his shoes? Where would we hide?"

"Some place warm and out of sight. Somewhere where there was more than one way in and out so we couldn't be cornered. Someplace smart, where people would not think to look."

"Sounds good. And how many places are there like that on this ship?"

"I don't know. But I do know he will not be in a cabin. That is where everyone else is expecting him to be. That would be a stupid hiding place. Only one way in and out. You would be trapped like a rat, and it would only be a matter of time before they found you."

"I agree completely, that would also rule out hiding in one of the lifeboats. Too cold. Man could freeze to death in one of those."

"Okay. I like where this is going," replied Crigger. "So if we eliminate the cabins and the lifeboats, what does that leave us?"

"Below decks. My guess is that he is possibly hiding as one of the crew in plain sight, probably in the engine room as no one really knows what those guys look like anyway. There are multiple ways in and out, and it is warm."

"Let's go check there next! I bet you are right."

With that, both men made their way down to the engine room. They walked from one end to the other and made sure they recognized each of the sailors they came across. Then they did it again. Still they came up empty.

"Now what?" said Crigger, disappointedly.

"We check out the other areas where passengers wouldn't be expected to be."

"Like where?"

"How about the cargo holds?"

"Brilliant!" said Crigger, suddenly enthusiastic again.

*****

Catherine looked at Winston. Worry was etched across her face.

"It appears as if every single person on this ship is looking for you," she said.

Winston felt the ship's engines come to life. He realized this meant that they were leaving Sault Ste. Marie.

"It is going to be a very trying eighteen hours until we get to Port Arthur," Winston said.

Suddenly, there was voices in the hallway.

"Ms. McGregor, this is Bryson, the porter. Please open the door for me."

Winston and Catherine stopped talking, waiting to hear what was going to happen in the room across the hall. To their surprise, the door to their room opened, and Bryson walked in and closed the door behind him.

"Hello," he said with a forced smile. "I hope I didn't disturb anything."

Both Winston and Catherine remained frozen, unable to breathe or move.

"It appears that you forgot what room was yours. But that's okay. Once I awoke from the nasty little bump on the back of my head, I started to think about how Winston could have gotten a sailor uniform on and happened by chance to be the one that I had follow me to your room. Then I figured out that he was already headed to your room when I ran across him. But then I thought, if he was, why weren't you there when we opened the door before he so rudely knocked me unconscious. Then it came to me. Because you were in the room across the hall, so you could keep an eye on things. Pretty clever, but I guess I am smarter for having figured it out so quickly," Bryson gloated.

"What are you going to do with us?" asked Winston.

"Right to the point. I like that, so I will get right to the point myself. I am going to take your briefcase and its contents and then I am going to turn you over to McDuff. He has been wanting to have a discussion with you for quite a while now."

Winston was silent as he kept his eyes on Bryson and started inching his way between Catherine, the briefcase, and Bryson. He knew this man wanted revenge for knocking him out earlier, so he was preparing for the worst. Bryson noticed him positioning himself, so he quickly grabbed Catherine's arm and pulled her over to him.

"Stop," she said. "You're hurting my arm."

"Do you hear her? Pick up the briefcase and hand it over to me, or she will get hurt more than she already has."

Winston reluctantly took the extra two steps needed and reached down and picked the briefcase off the floor, then handed it toward Bryson.

"Take it, just let her go. You can have the briefcase, and you have me. You don't need her for anything."

A wicked smile came across Bryson's face as he shoved Catherine toward Winston as hard as he could. As Winston reached out to catch her, Bryson quickly took a step forward and punched Winston in the side of the head, who went down like a sack of potatoes. Bryson then helped Catherine up who had also fallen to the floor.

"If you want to see him alive again, you better come with me quietly and not draw any attention to yourself."

Catherine looked at Winston lying unconscious on the floor. She knew she had no alternative than to go along with what she was told to do at this time. She nodded in agreement, not saying a word. The silent treatment was her way of being defiant without making things worse. It also made her feel like she had some measure of control.

Bryson took her to the bridge and told the captain that she requested to speak to him again on some urgent matter. The captain looked at Bryson and realized he was holding the briefcase.

"Very well," he said. "Mr. Ralston, you have the bridge."

"Aye, sir," came the reply.

Then the captain left with Bryson and Ms. McGregor. Once they had arrived in his cabin, Bryson filled him in on the current situation.

"Good job! Now leave the briefcase here with the woman and me. Go find McDuff and take him to where you left Winston. That will fit in nicely with our plans of keeping McDuff distracted. Then get back here as quickly as you can without being observed."

"Right away, Captain," replied Bryson as he made haste to go find McDuff.

"Why don't you grab a seat and make yourself comfortable. You are going to be here for a while," Captain Ericson told Catherine. "And you can call me Thomas when it is just the two of us in the room."

Catherine looked at Thomas but said nothing. She was still in the mood to dish out the silent treatment.

"As long as you are quiet and behave, you will not have any trouble from me. Do you understand?"

She stared at him, refusing to even blink. Underneath her calm demeanor, her brain was frantically trying to figure out how to help Winston out of his situation.

For all I know, the first man I truly loved could be dead, she thought. *No, I cannot afford to think that way, I must be strong.*

*****

Crigger and Tibbs had just finished searching the cargo hold. He was not there either.

"Poor old Niklas. He must have gotten two more beatings since we left."

"That's why we can't give up. We now know that he isn't in the bottom of the ship, so let's work our way back up to the top."

Both men continued talking among themselves as they made their way up to the second deck. That is where they ran into Bryson again.

"What are you two doing down in the cargo holds…never mind," he continued. "Do you know where I can find the constable McDuff?"

"Aye, we saw him down by the brig a while ago," Tibbs answered.

Bryson didn't waste any time as he made a beeline to the brig at the bottom of the ship.

Tibbs let out a chuckle. "I guess mama was right, you need to be careful what you ask for."

"Hope he gets beaten instead of Niklas. I never did like that man," added Crigger.

"I wonder why he wanted to find the constable?"

"Not our concern."

"It kind of is, as we now have a difficult decision to make."

"Which is?"

"If we find Hawes or the briefcase and bring it to McDuff, maybe it will be Bryson we save from getting a beating and not Niklas."

"That would be tragic. But we have no way of knowing if that will even happen. No, we must continue under the assumption that it will be Niklas that we save from a beating. Now stop talking so we can get back to searching the top deck."

"I thought we were working our way up to the top," Tibbs wisecracked. "I always felt I was captain material."

Crigger wasn't amused. "Look, if Bryson was looking on the second deck for McDuff, then he would have stumbled across our guy if he had been hiding there. And we just searched the bottom deck, and he wasn't there. So we need to resume our search on the top deck because that is where he is. It is simple logic."

"You said it."

*****

The captain put the briefcase on his desk and opened it up. His face turned beet red, and he pounded his fist on the desk.

"Where are they?" he said forcefully to Catherine.

Catherine continued her silent treatment. She just stared right back at the captain, wishing he would just fall over dead.

Thomas got up from behind the desk holding the briefcase in this right hand, shaking it as he spoke.

"I am not the bad guy here. I am the one trying to save your life and Winston's by trading the contents of this briefcase for your safety."

Catherine saw right through this lie.

Sure, she thought, *that's why your crew knocked Winston unconscious and is now turning him over to McDuff on your orders.* She said nothing.

The captain read the contempt on her face, so he tried a different tact.

"If you don't tell me where it is, you will suffer the same fate as Winston! Don't force me to turn you over to McDuff as well. He is a constable for the CPR Railroad and is under orders to recover the materials stolen from the railroad at all costs. You are on the wrong side of the law here, Ms. McGregor, and the law always wins in the end."

Catherine let a small smile play out across her face as she knew that McDuff was also in cahoots with her father, which meant that she knew more about this than the captain did. She also knew the contents of the briefcase were illegal; therefore, they were also on the wrong side of the law. She decided it was time to press the captain for some answers.

"What was supposed to be in the briefcase that belongs to the CPR?" she asked innocently, breaking her silence.

The captain was unsure how to answer her. If he refused to answer, then he would lose an opportunity to further a dialogue that could lead to learning its whereabouts. However, if he admitted what was in there, he would be admitting that he knows about the counterfeiting going on. Silence hung in the air as he thought about it.

"I don't know," he finally said.

"So you are telling me that anything could have been in that briefcase when you looked in it, and you would not have known if it was the right stuff?"

Thomas was beginning to hate this woman more than he already had. He was now wondering if he should continue playing out this lie or try another answer.

He responded, "I'll be the one asking the questions from now on. And yes, I do know what was supposed to be in the briefcase. For your information, it is money, Ms. McGregor. I just said I didn't know as a polite way of saying it was none of your business."

"Your momma must be proud to know that her son thinks lying to women is considered polite."

That was the last straw. There would be no more talking to this woman. He would wait for McDuff to beat the information out of Winston instead. He went over and tied Ms. McGregor to the chair and put a gag in her mouth to shut her up. He wondered what was taking Bryson so long to get back.

*****

Bryson had finally reached the brig. He saw McDuff and Archer standing over the top of Niklas, the second engineer, who was sitting in a chair and looked like he had been in a pub brawl. Once Archer saw Bryson, he moved in his direction in a very threatening manner.

Bryson held his hands up for him to stop and said, "I found Winston. I knocked him unconscious in a cabin, and I came to take you to him."

McDuff said, "Guid wirk 'n' none tae soon. Ah dinnae think yer poor sailor matey cuid hae taken ony mair interrogation. Tak' Archer 'ere wi' ye tae whaur ye say he is, then bring him back 'ere tae me."

"What about the reward? I heard that you offered two hundred dollars to the person who found him or his briefcase?"

"Aye, wance he is 'ere in th' brig wi' me, ye shall git yer reward. Dinnae ye worry yer wee heid aboot that."

McDuff smiled a sinister smile as Archer motioned for Bryson to leave and show him where Winston was.

*****

Crigger and Tibbs had started to search the top deck at the aft end of the ship. They had only been at it a few minutes when they heard a groaning sound come from inside one of the cabins. They stopped and put their ears to the door to listen.

"Sounds like you waking up in the morning, except not as loud," said Crigger to Tibbs. "Disturbs the whole crew."

"You're right. It definitely is the sound of someone coming back from the dead," replied Tibbs. "You know how hard I sleep after working my fingers to the bone all day long on this here ship."

"I bet it is the guy we are looking for. We should go in and check it out."

Tibbs checked the door. It was unlocked, so he opened it and they both went inside. There they discovered Winston sitting on the floor holding his head, looking dazed and confused.

"They must have knocked him out!" said Tibbs.

"I bet they are coming back for him. We should get him out of here so we can exchange him for Niklas."

"Where are we going to hide him?"

"Well, he is wearing a sailor uniform. Let's move him down to the crew's quarters and put him in your bunk. If someone sees him, they will just think it is you goofing off again.

"Very funny! That only happened once, and I was sick. I think the cook tried to poison me with his awful food."

"Do you have a better plan?"

"No."

"Then let's get a move on while we still can," ordered Crigger.

The two men each grabbed one of Winston's arms and lifted him to his feet. Then they quickly left the room and went down to the second deck to the aft crew's quarters. Winston was walking in step, with assistance, but appeared to not be fully aware of what was going on.

*****

Bryson and Archer reached the cabin where Winston had been unconscious. The door was slightly open and was the first clue that something was wrong. Bryson quickly pushed the door open and stepped into the room. Archer followed. The room was empty.

"Uh, I know this looks bad, but he was here ten minutes ago. I swear it. I knocked him out myself."

Archer looked at Bryson. "Well, then he couldn't have gotten very far. Let's find him before he gets a chance to hide again! Believe me, neither of us wants to go back and tell McDuff that he got away."

"Let's split up. You go one way and I will go the other to double our chances of finding him. We will meet back here at this room in fifteen minutes," suggested Bryson.

Archer poked his finger deep into Bryson's chest. "You better be back here and not make me come look for you as well."

Bryson got the point, literally. "Absolutely," he said.

With that, both men split up, and Bryson made haste to get to the captain's office and update him. When he got there, he saw that Catherine was tied and gagged and the captain's face was red.

"What happened, Captain?"

"I'll tell you what!" Thomas thundered. "The briefcase is empty! And now McDuff has Winston, and we have no hope of recovering the plates."

"That's not true Captain, McDuff does not have Winston. He wasn't in the room when I got back there to hand him over."

Catherine overheard the conversation and hope filled her heart as Winston was still alive, and there was still a chance they might escape. She wondered how Winston managed to get away in time.

"How in the Sam Hill did you screw that up?" yelled the captain.

"We could still find him or the plates first. I am sure that your guest here can help us with that," Bryson suggested as he dodged the question.

"No! Under no circumstances is that gag to be removed. Every time she opens her mouth to speak, my headache gets worse."

Bryson wondered what had happened between them while he was gone. Instead of pushing the conversation, he told the captain that he had to hurry to get back to meet Archer and pretend to help him find Winston. Then he left to go back to the room.

*****

Down in the crew's quarters, Crigger and Tibbs had put Winston in Tibbs's bunk and made him comfortable.

"Why are you helping me? Do I know you?"

"I guess we kind of know you. You must have taken a nasty fall, because we found you lying on the floor. You asked us to help you find your briefcase," Crigger lied as he winked at Tibbs. "If you tell us where it is, we will go get it and bring it back to you."

"I don't remember. My head hurts."

"Well, you just lie here and get some rest while I look after you," Crigger replied. "I will send my mate here to go find your briefcase for you. Pretty soon you will be as right as rain."

Crigger stepped away from the bunk, so Winston could not hear him talking to Tibbs.

"I will stay here with this Winston fella while you go and negotiate the release of Niklas in exchange for this guy."

Tibbs objected, "I thought plan A was to trade the briefcase so no one else would get hurt."

"Time is running out on plan A. I am not sure how much longer Niklas can hold out."

"At least, let me go see if they are going to beat up Bryson instead on Niklas. If so, we have all the time we need."

Crigger reluctantly agreed. "But hurry back and let me know what is going on before you go off doing something else!"

*****

Several minutes later, Tibbs had snuck his way down to the brig area where Niklas was being held and beaten. From his vantage point, he could see the cell without being observed very easily. McDuff was next to Niklas, who was sitting in a chair with his back to him. Archer was not there, and neither was Bryson. This was bad news. He was pondering what to do when he saw Archer return and speak with McDuff. Although he could not hear what was being said, he was glad to see that both men quickly left and Niklas was now alone. Tibbs waited to make sure they were gone and this wasn't some sort of trap. Then he crept out from his vantage point and made his way to Niklas.

"Don't worry, mate. I am going to get you to safety," he said as he approached the chair.

Niklas didn't respond as he was slumped over unconscious. Only the ropes were keeping him in the chair. Tibbs untied Niklas and put him over his shoulder like a fireman and began the trek back to the crew's quarters where Crigger and Winston were. His muscles were strained to their limits by the time he got back, but he managed to get there unseen. Crigger helped him gently set Niklas down in an open bunk.

"How did you get him freed?" Crigger asked incredulously.

"I was watching when all of a sudden the leprechaun left with the bear and Niklas was all alone, so I took advantage of the opportunity and hightailed it back here with him."

"Thank God Almighty, he is finally safe."

"Yes, but now we have another problem. How can we hide two men in the bunks? We can't pretend it is both of us."

"We will have to let Winston go. Niklas is our concern at this point."

Both men agreed that this was the best course of action. They gently shook Winston until he was fully awake. Then they explained to him that he wasn't safe there and needed to go find a place to hide from McDuff until they reached port. Winston, who had regained most of his senses by this time, looked over at Niklas lying in the next bunk. It sent a shudder through out his body as he saw the extend of the injuries this man had acquired. He thanked the two men for their kindness and quickly left to find Catherine.

*****

Instead of heading off into a different direction as suggested, Archer followed Bryson to the captain's office when they split up, and then he hurried back to tell McDuff about it. When McDuff heard the news, he smelled a double cross with the captain and headed there as soon as Archer was finished speaking. It didn't take long for him to reach the captain's quarters and barge into the office unannounced.

"How did you get in here!" shouted the captain.

"Ye mist hae forgot that a'm a constable. As sic, ah hae th' ability tae go wherever ah please."

McDuff looked over and saw Catherine tied and gagged, sitting on the captain's expensive leather couch.

"Did ah interrupt something private? Ms. McGregor is sure a sight tae behold. Ah wull gie ye that. Ah didnae tak' ye fur th' kind o' jimmy that liked tae tie up yer girlfriends though."

The captain replied with a gauged amount of anger in his voice. "She is not my girlfriend. She is being interrogated as to the whereabouts of Mr. Hawes, who you so kindly asked me to help you find."

"'N' ye fin' th' gag helps her tae spill th' beans? Is that it?"

Thinking quickly, he replied, "It is a precaution to make sure she doesn't scream and draw unwanted attention. I was just telling her that I was about to remove the gag, if she behaves."

"That wilnae be necessary, Thomas. Yer correct that she kin hulp us fin' whit we ur lookin' fur. Ah wull tak' her wi' me 'n' finish asking th' questions mah wey. Ah appreciate ye finding her fur me."

He knew better than to protest. In fact, he was happy it was working out this way. This would keep McDuff distracted while they got ready for the meeting with Gitchie Manito.

"Not a problem," Thomas replied. "Happy to help."

*****

Niklas was still unconscious after they moved him into Tibbs's bunk. His arm was broken, and his leg appeared to be as well. His head was bruised and bloodied, and his face was swollen and disfigured. He looked like he had been trampled by a stampede of wild horses. He definitely needed to be in a doctor's care. But that wasn't an option right now as they were unsure which of the crew could be trusted.

"Tibbs, you need to go steal some laudanum from the medical supplies to help Niklas deal with the pain. If he wakes up without it, everyone on this ship will know where he is from the screaming."

"How much is needed? I don't know anything about medicines."

"Take everything you can find. No one will miss it until we get ready to set sail on the next voyage, and by then you and I will be long gone. I don't plan on sailing on this ship anymore. Not when the constable is allowed to beat the crew. No, sir! This is my last time sailing for the CPR."

"Rightly said, I'm with you," replied Tibbs, who then left on his urgent humanitarian mission.

*****

"Captain, to the bridge," came the announcement over the ship's speakers.

The captain looked at McDuff after hearing the announcement.

"I need to excuse myself from this meeting and head to the bridge," he stated with a tone of authority.

McDuff looked at him for a moment before saying anything. "It seems lik' yer wantid elsewhere, Thomas. Dinnae let me keep ye fae daein' yer jab."

Thomas started to walk past McDuff to the door, when McDuff grabbed hold of his arm.

"Whilest yer aff daein' yer sailor duties, a'm needin' fur ye tae deliver a message fur me. Ye dinnae hae ony issue wi' that, doo ye?"

Before the captain spoke, McDuff answered for him. "O' coorse nae, a'm sure ye'll be happy tae hulp." Then McDuff told him the message and sent him on his way.

*****

"Captain, sir. We are approaching White Fish point. It is custom for the captain to be on the bridge for this part of the voyage," First Mate Ralston said as the captain entered the bridge.

"Very well, I have command of the ship. Mr. Ralston is temporarily relieved."

Now White Fish Point is the most treacherous part of the journey, known to sailors as the graveyard of the Great Lakes. All ships entering or leaving Lake Superior must pass through this area, and all captains had standing orders for their crews to be on full alert until they had safely made it past this dangerous zone, and they never left the passage to be navigated by anyone other than themselves. Captain Thomas ran the calculations through his head. If things went according to plan, they would safely pass this point at 4:00 p.m., and then it would be smooth sailing until their secret unscheduled stop.

"Mr. Ralston, please update me on the current conditions of the weather and this ship," ordered the captain to the first mate.

"Winds are fresh, east by southeast," came the reply. "We are running full sail and steam power at standby. Seas are relatively calm with three footers. Barometric pressure has been falling slightly. Looks like we could be in for some bad weather in the next few hours, if it keeps falling much farther."

"Did you get an updated weather report when we stopped at Sault Ste. Marie?"

"No, sir, I was on the bridge the whole time."

"Very well," replied the captain, remembering why his first mate was on the bridge when they stopped to make the counterfeit transfer.

*****

Archer was not at the room when Bryson got there. Instead, he had went back to the brig to watch Niklas and wait for McDuff to return. Perhaps he would get some answers out of him before McDuff got there.

That would be good, he thought as an evil grin crept out across his face.

Once he arrived at the brig, the grin had disappeared.

"Where is he?" Archer yelled loud enough to rival the ship's steam whistle. He was sure that McDuff was going to lose it when he found out. Intuition told him that there was not enough time to go find Niklas before McDuff came back. Not knowing what else to do, he sat in the chair and waited for McDuff to return, preparing himself to weather the storm. His thoughts were interrupted by an announcement over the loudspeakers that was repeated twice.

"Mr. Hawes, we congratulate you on your excellent game of hide-and-seek. To recover something delicate that you misplaced during the game, we ask that you report to the lost-and-found office located next to the brig as soon as possible."

Archer was trying to understand the meaning of the message when McDuff appeared with Catherine beside him. She looked angry, defiant, and terrified at the same time.

"Whit dae ye think o' mah wee message?" McDuff asked triumphantly. "Tis time we stopped chasing efter him 'n' mak' him come tae us."

Archer stood up, relieved that his boss was happy, even though Niklas was gone, and even happier that he would no longer need to keep tearing the ship apart looking for Winston.

"Perfect! I wonder how long it will take for him to show up?"

"If he is smart, it wilnae tak' ony time at a' fur him tae mak' his move. Noo dae as ah say sae we kin welcom him properly."

*****

Winston stopped dead in his tracks as soon as he heard the announcement. This meant that they had Catherine. He knew that if he showed up with the plates, they would never get out of the bottom of the ship alive, so he needed to figure out how to rescue Catherine without getting captured himself. Then his thoughts went to the poor sailor Niklas he had seen and the beating he had taken, undoubtedly by the same men who now held Catherine. The image in his brain was too powerful for him, and it took everything he had to keep from passing out right then and there. It also caused something deep and primal to course through his body for the first time in his life, as he sprang him into motion and headed back to the crew's quarters to find the two sailors who helped him. When he entered the room, both sailors looked at him as if they knew he was coming back.

"We heard the announcement. We figured you would be coming back here," Crigger said. "What is it that they have of yours? Surely, it's not the briefcase, or they would have no need for you."

"They have taken the woman I have fallen in love with, Ms. McGregor, captive."

"That's a tough blow, mate. Wouldn't want to be in your shoes," Crigger responded.

"Her shoes either," added Tibbs.

"What may I ask happened to your crewmate?" Winston asked, looking over at the beat-up sailor in the bunk.

"I'll tell ya for sure. He had the life beaten out of him because no one could find you or your briefcase. He was made an example to what will happen to the rest of us."

"They took a mop handle and beat him about the head while we were forced to watch. They broke his arm as he tried to shield his head from the blows," added Tibbs.

"They told us he would get a beating every thirty minutes until they got what they wanted."

"He was with them for almost three hours before we could rescue him."

Winston's blood began to boil. "Guys, I promise I had no idea. I would have turned myself in had I known this was going to happen."

Crigger and Tibbs glanced at each other for a moment, then at Niklas, then back to Winston.

"What are you going to do about it, now that you do know?" Crigger asked.

"I am going to rescue Catherine and get her to a safe place, then I am going to the authorities with enough information to put them away for a long time."

Neither man said a word. They just looked silently at Winston and then went back to taking care of Niklas. Winston, realizing that he was on his own, took the master keys from his pocket and stuffed them under the mattress next to him when no one was looking. Then he left to go rescue Catherine.

A hundred thoughts went through his mind, from creating a diversion to stealing a weapon. But his mind kept returning to the image of Niklas. No, he needed to go straight there and give himself up, hoping he can convince them to release Catherine in the process. He couldn't waste time trying to come up with another plan.

*****

"Weel noo, lookie whit we hae' ere. If it is nae Mr. Hawes," McDuff said to Archer as he saw Winston walking toward the brig.

"He came quickly, just like you said he would," replied Archer.

"We hae bin expecting ye," McDuff said to Winston as he drew near. "Thare be na need fur ony further misfortune. We jist need ye tae return whit ye teuk."

Winston entered the brig where McDuff was standing. Archer was off to the side of the room next to an empty chair. There was no sign of Catherine anywhere.

"Come hae a sit 'n' lets hae a discussion lik' civilized men," McDuff said as he pointed to the chair.

Winston stopped where he was at. "Before I agree to anything, I need to make sure that Catherine goes free, unharmed."

"Aye, sae yi'll want tae negotiate then, is that th' plan?"

"It's not a negotiation. It's a demand!" Winston said defiantly. "I don't talk unless she is let go, right now."

"Yer nae in ony position tae be making demands. We wull fin' th' plates noo that ye 'n' Catherine ur in oor possession. We kin murdurr ye baith 'n' tear th' ship apairt at port if we hae tae."

"That is where you are wrong. You need both of us alive because I know more about what's going on than either of you do."

"What's he talking about?" Archer asked McDuff.

"He's bluffing. He's git naethin. This is jist a pathetic attempt tae save his life 'n' his girlfriend's."

"On the contrary, I am a reporter, and it is my job to learn secrets. For example, I know that you are employed as a constable for the CPR and that you also are on the payroll of McGregor Industries as a spy."

McDuff stepped closer to Winston and said in almost a whisper, "Ye better be havin that seat noo. It appears we dae hae mair tae discuss."

Winston sat down. "First, I need to see that Catherine is released."

"She's in a safe place fur noo. Naethin tae worry aboot. Wance wur dane 'ere, ah wull tell ye whaur ye kin fin' 'ere safe 'n' sound. Ah promise. As fur yer secret, mah loyalties ur wi' th' hi'est bidder."

"Where is she being kept?"

"Tell me whaur th' plate be 'n' ah wull tell ye. 'N' while yer thinking aboot it, ah wull tell ye a secret. Archer murdered Mr. Fontaine tae keep him fae printing yer lest message in yer article."

Winston looked at McDuff in surprise.

"Ye thought ye wur bein' sae clever, workin' wi' that undercover secret service agent. He hud some misfortune yesterday as weel. Whit exactly happened?" McDuff asked Archer.

"Apparently, he had too much to drink and fell asleep right there on the railroad tracks, made quite a mess when the morning train arrived."

"How did you know about JD?"

"Did ye think yer wee trip tae Toronto wis a secret? Otto Gunderson, th' train worker, tellt us a' aboot th' trip th' nicht afore ye left. We hud eyes oan ye th' hail time. We even heard th' chat in th' train carriage atween ye, or shuid ah say Gabriel Girard 'n' JD, or shuid ah say Jocko. Or wis it Justice Department, th' secret service agent? That wis mah favorite yin by th' wey."

Winston looked sick to his stomach.

McDuff looked at Winston, waiting for his answer on where the plates were hidden.

"A dinnae hae a' day laddie. This is th' lest time a'm asking nicely, afore ah let Archer fin' awa' tae dispose o' ye."

"I always wanted to see how fast a man could swim. Maybe he can keep pace with the ship all the way to Port Arthur!" Archer said with a cruel laugh. "Better yet, I can take bets on how long he will keep up before he drowns."

"Ah say he lasts na mair than twa minutes wi' thae winter conditions."

Winston knew he had to come up with something quickly. Before he knew what he said, he blurted out, "The captain has them."

CHAPTER 8

The Rise of Crigger and Tibbs

Evil ran unchecked aboard the ship and violently murdered one of our own. We were angry and decided no more. It was time to take a stand; revenge was ours to have, and we were out for blood.

—Crew, *SS Algoma*

McDuff looked at Winston, trying to gauge whether his answer was the truth or a bluff.

"Does he noo. 'N' how come wouldn't he hae brought thaim tae me if he did hae thaim?"

Winston looked back at McDuff. "I answered your question as to where the plates are. If you want more questions answered, you need to give me something in return."

"Ga git th' wifie 'n' bring her 'ere," McDuff ordered Archer. "Fur yer sake, ah hawp whit ye hae tae say is true 'n' worth mah time," he said to Winston.

"It will," promised Winston. "I just don't think you're going to believe it at first."

*****

A few minutes later, Archer returned with Catherine. She had her hands tied behind her back and there was a gag in her mouth.

Archer pushed her down until she was sitting on the floor against a wall.

"Untie her!" Winston demanded. "I promise on my life, that she will not attempt to leave or to scream."

McDuff stared at Winston for a moment, then turned and walked over and removed her gag. He left her hands tied behind her however.

"Na tell me whit ye know."

Winston looked at Catherine. She mouthed the words, "Thank you," but her voice had no volume behind it. Winston then turned to look at McDuff again.

"You said that your loyalties were with the highest bidder. Is that true?"

"Aye, whit o' it?"

"I am willing to pay you for our freedom."

"Wi' whit, th' counterfeit plates? They wur mines tae begin wi'. Sae ah think nae."

"No. I already told you about those. I have other information that will make you wealthy beyond your dreams."

"Ga oan. Tell me whit it's then."

"Not until I have your word that we have reached a business deal. The information for the release of both Catherine and myself, unharmed."

"Ainlie if ah kin verify it's true, 'n' ah wull indeed be able tae be made wealthy fae it."

"You've got yourself a deal," said Winston. Then he proceeded to tell them everything he knew about the captain's side hustle, including the secret rendezvous with Gitchie Manito later that night off Isle Royale.

Winston was right. He didn't believe it. McDuff told Archer to guard the prisoners while he went to have words with the captain. Deep down McDuff had known there was something off about the captain. But this couldn't be true. No matter, in a few minutes he would know if Winston was telling the truth. He made his way to the bridge.

"Thomas. A'm needin' tae hae a word wi' ye in private."

Captain Ericson didn't look back at the man who spoke to him. Instead, he ordered a crew member to go get First Mate Ralston out of his bunk and to the bridge.

"My time is yours as soon as my first mate arrives. In the meantime, you can wait for me in my quarters. I'm sure you'll know where to find it."

McDuff leaned against the wall and said, "Na need. Ah wull wait reit 'ere. A lot kin be learned by observing someone daein' his jab."

"Weather report!" growled the captain for the second time in the last half hour.

"Barometric pressure is at 1005.2 and falling, Captain. Waves are at 7 to 10 feet with winds gusting to 10 mph."

"Very well. Come find me if the pressure drops below one thousand. Mr. Ralston, you have the bridge," the captain said as the first mate entered the bridge. Then he left the bridge with McDuff following behind.

"This better be important," the captain said once they reached his office. "There is a major storm system forming out there, and we still don't know how bad it's going to get."

"Aye, indeed. An' a' heard some troubling tings that a'm waantin' tae discuss wi' ye, Thomas."

The captain sat down behind his desk while McDuff remained standing.

At least, they were now at eye level with each other, he thought. "And what would that be?" he questioned.

"That yer in possession o' th' plates 'n' hae nae brought thaim tae me."

"That's rubbish. Who told you such nonsense, and what need would I have with the plates?"

"Aye, that wid be Mr. Hawes hisself. We hae captured baith he 'n' his wifie. 'N' that is th' quaistion ah wis hawping ye wid answer fur me, Thomas."

The captain banged his fist on his desk as he stood up.

"I don't have time for this. Like I told you a few moments ago, there is a dangerous storm brewing out there. In case you didn't know,

November is when the deadliest storms hit the Great Lakes! The most shipwrecks and loss of life occur on them in November. Now, as a constable of the CPR, you are entitled to search my quarters if you like, but you will not keep me from returning to the bridge, to do my *jab* as you call it, and ensure the safety of this ship."

"Okay, Thomas, go 'n' sail yer ship. But we wull be huvin wurds aboot this again real soon. Ye better hawp ah dae nae fin' oot yer trying tae double cross me by playing baith ends against th' middle. Fur ah wull be keeping mah eye oan ye."

McDuff left and went back to the brig. Once there, he told Archer to take Winston and Catherine and put them in the secret hold below room number 71 and tie them up so they can't escape.

Back on the bridge, Captain Thomas felt the eyes of his crew looking at him.

"You all have jobs to do, so get to it!" he groused.

*****

Niklas was now gasping for his last breaths of air. The laudanum seemed to be keeping the pain from being unbearable, but he must have suffered organ damage in the beatings. Crigger and Tibbs were doing everything they could to help their beaten crewmate from dying, but soon realized they were unsuccessful in doing so.

"He's gone," whispered Tibbs a few moments later as he noticed the man had stopped breathing. He reached up and gently closed the man's terror-stricken eyes.

Crigger stopped what he was doing as he felt hot tears running down his cheeks.

"We can't let them get away with this! I don't care what it takes."

Tibbs nodded in agreement. "What are we going to do?"

"We're going to kill the leprechaun and his goon. That's what we're going to do. Then we are going to throw their bodies overboard so they are never found and leave this ship at Port Arthur and find a land job. I'm done being a sailor."

"I'm with you one hundred percent. But we need to make them suffer more than Niklas did, and there is something else we need to do as well. We need to rescue Winston and his girlfriend. They are just as innocent as Niklas was."

"Right you are. I couldn't have said it better."

"What are we going to do with Niklas's body?"

After a lengthy discussion, the men decided to leave Niklas where he was for the time being and to focus first on revenge.

Over the next hour, they spent their time switching between grieving for a lost friend and plotting to avenge his death. Finally, Crigger decided enough was enough.

"Niklas is dead. We need to start looking for Winston and his girlfriend before they are as well. Pretty soon it will be almost impossible to move around on the main deck because of this storm."

"Where are we going to start looking. We weren't that successful in our search for Hawes were we. We didn't find him in time to save Niklas's life."

"This time is different. We know who has them, so we know they aren't hiding in the open like last time."

"So where do you suggest we start."

"We found Niklas in the brig, which is in the bottom of the ship. So my guess is that we start searching all the nooks and crannies in the bottom of the ship."

"That makes sense. Let's go."

"Wait, I remember that Winston slid his hand under the mattress before leaving to get his girlfriend. Maybe he left something behind that will help us."

Crigger reached under the mattress and found the master key ring. "Well, would you look at that. We can unlock any door on the ship with these."

"What if we come upon the leprechaun and the bear first?"

"We kidnap them and torture them like they did Niklas. Then we put them in the lifeboat to be used in the fake drill. When they reach the water, we cut the lines and they will drown out in the middle of the lake or be smashed to pieces against the rocks."

"I like it, but there is one problem. I don't think we can knock them out by ourselves."

"Good point."

"What is?"

"We will need help, so let's look through all the medical supplies you stole. I am sure there is something there that we can use to our advantage."

"Whatever you do, let's not use the laudanum on them. I want them to feel everything."

Crigger looked through the medicines.

"This will do nicely," he said as he pulled a bottle of chloroform out of the pile. "We will sneak up from behind and use this to knock them out like the dentists do."

"Hold on a minute. You're telling me that you had a dentist sneak up behind you and knock you out with chloroform before?" Tibbs asked innocently.

Playing along, Crigger said, "Sure did, happened while I was in Chicago several years back. The worst of it was when I came too, I was missing two teeth and had a tattoo on my tongue." Then he quickly stuck his tongue out at Tibbs for emphasis.

"That explains it then."

"Explains what?"

"All those nasty-looking white bumps on your tongue."

*****

"The storm is getting stronger. Give me a weather report." Before he got a reply, the captain yelled out again, "Weather report!"

"Barometric pressure is at 998.1 and still falling, Captain. Waves are 10 to 12 feet with winds gusting to 20 mph."

"Mr. Ralston, what does the barometer reading say to you?"

"It means that there is the possibility of a major storm ahead, sir."

"Wrong. It means there is definitely a major storm ahead as we crossed under 1000.0 mb in pressure. You need to know what these markers are if you want to make a good captain someday."

"Yes, sir."

"The question now is how low is the pressure going to go."

"That is a good question, sir."

"So far we have dropped 15 millibars in the past six hours. If it keeps dropping at that rate, it will be near 980 mb when we reach Port Arthur, which would make it a storm as strong as a hurricane."

"Sir, correct me if I am wrong, but I have never heard of that happening on the Great Lakes before."

"That's because it hasn't. That's why I anticipate it is going to let up soon. But for the sake of safety, give me full steam power in addition to running the sails. Perhaps we can outrun it and get to Port Arthur before it gets too bad to sail in. At least, we are past White Fish Point, so we have nothing but open water in front of us."

"Aye, Captain."

"And I want another pressure reading at the top of the hour. I will be in my quarters. Ralston has the bridge," the captain said for everyone to hear. "Bryson follow me. We need to discuss the safety of the passengers in case this does get worse."

Bryson immediately followed him to his quarters. "Sir, we do not have a protocol in place for something like this."

"I am well aware of that. I called you here to talk about our meeting with Gitchie Manito tonight. He is going to have a devil of a time rowing out to meet us if that storm gets much worse."

"Oh, good point, Captain. Should we find a way to call it off."

"No. We have no way of communicating with him at this point. And I know him, he will die trying to get to us. Instead, we will need to make sure that we have everything ready to go. Speed will be tantamount to success. The longer he stays alongside the ship, the better chance he has of a wave crashing his rowboat into the side of us and sinking him."

"Understood, sir. I will have the cash preloaded into a lifeboat an hour before we get to our spot, and it will be ready to be lowered once we see him."

"Very good. Make sure the money is in waterproof bags. It's going to be miserable out there when we make the transaction. We also need to make sure no one interferes with us. I don't trust those constables aboard my ship."

"Maybe we can use the storm to our advantage."

"Yes, excellent idea. We can make a ship wide announcement that everyone needs to stay off the decks because of the wind and the waves. We can even blow the foghorns to make people afraid of the storm."

"Good thinking, sir. I do have a concern though. What happens if someone sees us lower a lifeboat?"

"We can tell them it was a rescue operation for some fool who didn't heed the warnings to stay off the decks and was washed overboard."

*****

McDuff told Archer to go keep tabs on the captain. Then turned his stare at his two captives with evil intent written across his face.

Catherine spoke first. "I think the motion is going to make me sick. It is a really rough ride down here."

"That wull be th' least o` yer troubles, dearie. Ye better git used tae bein' ere 'til ah git whit a'm waantin'."

"We had a deal!" Winston yelled at him.

"Tis true, bit it's nae finished yit as we hae nae fun th' counterfeit plates."

"The deal was that I told you about the captain's get-rich-quick scheme that you can take over, in exchange for both of our lives."

"True, we did gree tae that. Bit a'm feart ah aye need th' plates."

"Why, isn't that enough money?"

"Sin ye asked sae nicely, ah wull spill th' beans. Th' CPR haes na mair need fur th' counterfeit business, as th' railway wull be completed th'morra. Sae thay instructed me tae sell th' machine taeth' hi'est bidder. Which happens tae be Catherine's da."

"How would he even know about it?" asked Catherine.

"Fur ah tellt him. Mind ye, ah tellt ye mah services gaed tae th' hi'est bidder? Weel ah hud a deal wi' yer da tae be written intae his wull as th' sole inheritor o' his empire. Maxwell McGregor 'n' McDuff industries soonds lik' a proper business name tae me. It lik' th' ring tae it."

"I don't believe it for a second," she retorted.

"Tis true, dearie. He knew ye wern't smart enough or tough enough tae run it wance he wis deid. A' ah hud tae dae wis tae git him oan as a stakeholder in th' railroad. Wance we fun oot thay wur desperate 'n' wur taking silver faeth' silver mines in exchange fur secrets, we foud oor opportunity 'n' destroyed th' mine."

"So if that is true, it still doesn't explain why you need the counterfeit plates."

"Wance ah hud discovered th' counterfeit business 'n' teuk it ower, ah sold it taeth' CPR fur a tidy piece o' preferred stock. Therefore, thay declined tae add yer faither oan, sin thair financial problems hud bin solved."

Winston interrupted, "So you screwed yourself out of the inheritance. Ha-ha. You got what you deserved."

"Nae sae fest. Ah renegotiated wi' Mr. McGregor wance ah tellt him o'th' counterfeit machine. Seems he hud fancied owning his ain bank. Sae by mah count. Ah git stock in th' railroad, git tae be th' sole heir o' MMI Industries, 'n' hae th' captains land scheme in mah back pocket. Nae tae mention that ah wull ain that mines o' his afore tis dane."

"I hope it's worth it. Because just as quick as you got it, it will be taken away from you. You will never get away with this," Catherine scolded him.

"Och, did ah forgoat tae mention that th' CPR wants me tae sink th' ship tae cover thair tracks. 'N' Catherine's da wants me tae sink th' ship as revenge fur nae letting him oan as a stakeholder in th' railroad 'n' tae send a powerful message tae his competitors."

Winston and Catherine just stared at each other without saying a word.

"Noo wi' that said, if ye tell me whaur th' plates ur, ah wull release ye afore ah sink th' ship. Ye hae mah promise."

Catherine decided to give him the silent treatment, and Winston followed her lead.

"If ye dinnae wantae tell me richt noo, that's okay. A'm willing tae let ye sit doon 'ere fur th' rest o' th' voyage. Bit, ah wid be worried if ah wur ye aboot staying tae lang...boom!" McDuff let out an evil laugh and then went up the ladder and sealed the trap door behind him, making it pitch black in the cargo hold.

Catherine leaned over into the side of Winston. "I'm scared! I don't think that evil man plans to let us go, no matter what."

"Don't you worry. I promise we will get out of this alive and well," he said, trying his best to give her hope.

"Even if we do, what would happen to me? My dad disinherited me from his will. I have no money, no place to go."

"I'm sure that McDuff was just saying things to scare us into telling him where the plates are hidden."

"No, I am sure that my father is capable of doing that. I know how he talks down to me when he discusses business."

"Things always look the darkest before something amazing happens."

"Look, I'm not naïve. I know you are just trying to encourage me in this hopeless situation. And I really think it's sweet. But these men are not like you, they are ruthless killers. After all, you are the one that told me my Father murdered your parents."

Winston let that sink in before answering. "Do you think I am a great man?"

"What? I don't think now is the proper time to discuss such things. We can do that when and if we get out of here alive," she said in a slightly rebuking way.

Winston continued, "My boss, who I found out was murdered by Archer yesterday, once told me the difference between a good man and a great man. He said that great men care as much about others as they do about themselves. They protect the victims by standing up to the villains to make sure they get served justice for their evil deeds and by doing so, become protectors of everything good and noble and wonderful about society."

Catherine let those words sink in, allowing it to change her attitude.

Softly, she answered, "Yes. That is exactly why I fell in love with you. You are different than the other men, who only care about themselves and their empires."

"Then trust me when I tell you that we will get out of this somehow, and I will finish what I started and bring these men to justice."

Catherine nudged in tighter against Winston in the darkness. "I believe in you. I just hope it happens before I get sick from the waves tossing this ship up and down."

*****

"Captain, the barometer is now down to 995.6 mb," Mr. Ralston reported at the appointed time at the top of the hour.

"My gut tells me we are going to be in for one of those big November storms we all fear."

"I think you may be right, sir. Should we turn around?"

"What, and head back to White Fish Point? Are you crazy? That is the worst place to get caught in a storm. We will be blown into the rocks and scuttled before we know what happens."

"Sorry, sir, this is my first major storm."

"Then pay attention, and be quiet unless I ask you for something."

"Aye, sir."

The captain made a ship wide announcement.

"Attention! We are sailing into some bad weather, and I expect the voyage might get a little rough. Since we have passed White Fish Point, we will continue on to Port Arthur as scheduled. I advise all passengers to stay in their cabins. That will be all for now."

*****

McDuff and Archer met up in the brig.

"Did ye hear that announcement? Th' captain is trying tae gang as planned wi' th' special stoap, even wi' th' storm bearing doon oan us."

Archer nodded that he had heard the announcement.

"Whit a piece o' guid fortuin. We wull tak' th' machine apairt noo 'n' pat it in yin o' th' lifeboats. Whin thay stoap tae catch up wi' th' Indian, we wull git aff 'n' blaw up th' ship. It wull be blamed oan th' waither."

Archer laughed. "Sounds good. But how are we going to blow up the ship?"

"Ye lea that tae me."

"What about the plates? Don't we still need them?"

"Aye, we wull git thaim whin th' time is richt."

"What is your plan?"

"We let thaim git scared bein' alone in th' darkness, rocking back 'n' forth by th' tough seas fur a few hours. Whin we come back, thay wull be happy tae tell us, juist tae git oot o' thare."

"And what if that isn't enough to get them to tell us?"

"Lea that tae me. Then it's juist a maiter o' threatening tae git frisky wi' his wifie. If he's smart, he wil nae let me git tae far, as ah micht hae tae much fun tae halt."

"When do I get to have some of the fun?"

McDuff thought for a moment. "Ah will flip ye fur it whin th' time comes…heids ah win, tails ye lose."

Unfortunately for Archer, he stopped listening after the first sentence and didn't pick up on the no-win scenario.

"Noo lets git tae tearing th' machine apairt. Time's a wasting."

That was the end of the conversation as both men made their way to cargo hold through room number 70 and began to disassemble the machine.

*****

"Shh. Be quiet for a minute. I think I hear someone talking in the next room," cautioned Winston.

"Do you think it is one of the crew? Perhaps we can yell to get their attention."

"No, let's wait to see what happens first. I do not want them to come back and rough us up or put a gag in our mouth if it's McDuff."

"What is that sound? Are you sure it is coming from the other cargo hold? It sounds like metal clinking against metal. You don't think we are sinking, do you?" Catherine whispered in the darkness.

"No. I think it is coming from the identical cargo hold to our right. It sounds like someone working on a machine."

"Do you think it is engine trouble?"

"No. We wouldn't hear that from here. We are in the middle of the ship, and the engines are at the back. Besides, you would feel the ship slow down if that were the case. I think that someone is taking apart the counterfeit machine so they can take it out of the cargo hold before they destroy the ship."

"Really. We couldn't have been down here that long. We should have several hours left before we get close enough to land for them to get off the ship."

Winston thought for a moment before he connected the dots.

"Land, that's it. That's their plan. They are going to get off the ship when the captain makes his not-so-secret stop at Isle Royale tonight. Then they can row the machine to the island and wait out the storm."

"So how long does that leave us to escape?"

"I would say it moves the time up about three hours, leaving us with about six hours to find a way to escape."

"That's not much time," Catherine said dejectedly.

"Okay. Let's work on the parts of the escape plan we can right now. Namely, what we are going to do once we get out of the cargo hold."

Catherine perked up a bit as she had something constructive to fill her mind. "We need to get off the ship as soon as possible."

"Yes and no. We need to be careful. With the winter conditions, we do not want to be in the water at all. We would freeze to death in minutes. We also don't want to be in a small boat for too long as there is a great risk of capsizing with the waves."

"So what is the answer?"

"We need to get out of here and find the rowboat that they are going to use to meet the Indian Gitchie Manito. We will hide aboard it and let them lower us over the side with it. Once in the water, we cut the lines and row for the island. Even if they saw us at that point, it would take too long for them to launch another rowboat to chase us."

"How can we hide on a small rowboat? They will see us."

"No, they won't. I have already hidden on one of the lifeboats while you were holding my briefcase for me. It is deep enough between the ribs that we can lay down and throw a tarp over us."

"So we will need to find a tarp as well during our escape."

"Right. Don't let me forget that."

"We will also need a knife to cut the ropes."

"Good thinking. Don't let me forget that either!"

"So what is the plan after we get to Isle Royale?"

"We hunker down and wait for the opportune time to leave."

"Hunker down where?"

"We will have to find a shelter or a cave to hide in."

"Okay, let's say we find a place to hunker down, then what? How long do we wait? Where will we go once we leave the island? Back to Owen Sound? Back to Minnesota to be near my dear old dad or to your old stomping grounds?"

"Ah, I see your point. I guess we can go anywhere we want. Start over. Somewhere new. It will be an adventure."

"That's the '*they lived happily ever after*' stuff your boss said was a lie. You will be out of a job, and I will have no family money to fall back on."

"Okay, if you could choose, where would you want to live?"

Catherine thought for a moment. "I suppose somewhere warm, where no one knew me, and I could feel safe. A small town just outside a larger city so that it's quaint but not isolated nor overcrowded, somewhere where I never have to get on a ship again."

"That sounds pretty good to me. Mind if I join you?"

In the darkness, Catherine smiled and blushed at the same time. "It was a nice thought," she whispered.

Winston was quiet for a moment, thinking about how to say what was in his heart. He finally said, "Why does it have to end there? What's stopping us from running away together to some place wonderful like you described?"

"Besides being trapped on this death ship, you mean?"

"Yes, obviously. I promised you we would get out of here alive, and we will."

"Okay. Let's get real for a minute. Let's just say we get off this ship alive and want to settle down. What about getting justice against my father for killing your parents? Where does that fit in to our idyllic future? You told me that was something you couldn't let go. I don't even know if I can let that go."

Winston didn't know how to reply to that, so he just squeezed her hand in the darkness. After a few moments of silence, he whispered, "Those are just details that we can work out when the time comes."

*****

"Archer. Git th' crates open in th' room upby. Sae we kin stairt loading th' bits in thaim."

Archer nodded and climbed the ladder to room above to make sure the crates were still there. Then he climbed back down and told McDuff that they were ready to go."

"Weel then stairt hauling th' bits up th' ladder, while ah tak' apairt th' rest o' th' machine."

An hour later, all the parts had been brought up to the room. Archer was exhausted and sitting on the edge of the bed when McDuff came up the ladder.

"How fur come th' pieces ur nae in th' crates, 'n' how come urr ye sittin' doon?"

Even though he was tired of going up and down the twenty-foot ladder fifty times or more, he would not admit that to McDuff. Instead, he said, "I was thinking about getting to have fun with the woman we kidnapped."

McDuff didn't say a word. He just began to pack the crates himself. He knew better that to start an argument now, as time was of the essence, and he would need Archer's help later to load the boat and to help row it against the storm.

"While ah git thae crates loaded, ye gang 'n' fin' a lifeboat fur us tae pat thaim in."

Archer got up and left to do as he was told. McDuff locked the door behind him after he was gone to make sure no one accidentally walked in and saw what was going on.

*****

"Ralston, what is the latest weather report?" the captain asked as he made his way back to the bridge.

"Captain, the barometer has fallen to 991.1, wind still coming from the east with twenty-five- mile-an-hour gusts with twenty-foot waves, and it has now begun to snow. What does this all mean?"

"It means that we are sailing into an unprecedented winter hurricane."

"I thought that only happened in the oceans, not in the Great Lakes."

"That's why it is unprecedented. What's our current location?"

"I have us on course seventy-eight miles northwest of White Fish Point. Fifty-four miles to the west of Copper Harbor, Michigan. That leaves us one hundred and twenty-two miles to Port Arthur, and eighty-two miles until we clear Isle Royale's north end. We are making due at nineteen knots."

"Very well, I resume control of the ship. You are relieved."

Immediately, the captain began to plot a course for the middle of Isle Royale and not the safe passage around the north end. He still had a stop to make.

"By my calculations, we should be at our unscheduled stop at two o'clock in the morning. Which is perfect, because all the passengers will be asleep," the captain mumbled to himself.

*****

Crigger and Tibbs had carefully made their way down to the brig. As far as they knew, that was the base of operations for McDuff and Archer. They had come up with a plan for Tibbs to call for them to come over to where he was by the stairwell. Then Crigger would sneak out from behind the stairwell. Once they passed by and from behind, he would hold the chloroform over their face until they fell unconscious. They called their plan operation dentist. For it to succeed, they needed to make sure both McDuff and Archer were not together when they attempted this.

Both men looked at each other and took a deep breath as they reached the corner where they hoped this would work as planned. Crigger took out a rag and poured some chloroform on it. Then he snuck behind the staircase to wait for Tibbs to do his part. Tibbs waited for him to get into his spot, then took a deep breath and walk out around the corner where he was visible to the brig. To his surprise, it was empty. He slowly walked up to it and looked around. There was no one around, so he walked back to Crigger and told him they struck out. Crigger was upset.

"Where could they be?" he wondered out loud as he took the rag and stuffed it into his pocket. "Let's keep moving. Once we find them, we will work out a new plan. You go on in front so if you get seen, I can still sneak up behind them."

Tibbs agreed and started walking toward the engine room. Crigger followed about twenty-five feet behind, trying to stay out of sight. When Tibbs got close to the engine-room door, he glanced back and saw Crigger trying to get his attention, so he walked back to where he was.

"What's up? I was about to search the engine room."

"And then what? What if they were in there, how would I be able to sneak up on them? It's too tight in there. They would see me coming for sure."

"So what are we going to do, skip the engine room?"

"No! Give me a few minutes to work my way around to the door on the other side of the room. Then you can go in and walk toward me. If they are in there, get them to come out the back door, and I can get them there."

"Good thinking…and I will give a signal if they are with me when I get to the back door. I will say, 'Some weather we're having, huh?'"

"Okay, whatever. Just give me two minutes before you enter." Then Crigger left to make his way around the engine room to the back door.

Once he left, Tibbs began to count. He wished he had a pocket watch, but it wouldn't have mattered as he couldn't read one anyway. After he felt the appropriate amount of time had passed, he opened the door to the engine room and went in.

Just as soon as he did, the first engineer, Niklas's boss, yelled, "What in the tarnation are you doing here? Get out. Authorized personnel only! It is too dangerous in here with these waves tossing us about. You could fall into one of these machines and gum up the whole works. I don't need that kind of mess on my hands."

Tibbs turned and left the engine room, closing the door behind him. Not knowing what else to do, he made his way around to the back door where Crigger was waiting for him. Crigger saw him approach and threw his arms up in despair.

"What are you doing? You were supposed to go through the engine room, not around it, you dolt."

"Tried, got kicked out as soon as I entered. Said I would fall into one of the engines and make a mess of things."

"Well, we can't stay here…you know, that is a stroke of luck. If it's too dangerous for us, it will be too dangerous for them as well. Let's search elsewhere and come back if we need to later. Let's search the cargo hold up to the middle bulkhead wall. Then we will have to go up to the second deck, go to the front of the ship, and go back down to the cargo hold, and work our way back to the bulkhead wall on the other side."

Tibbs took the lead again. It didn't take long to enter the cargo hold. He didn't like it in there under the current conditions. It was beginning to become difficult to walk normal because the waves were bouncing the ship up and down. Not only that, but the cargo was groaning and creaking against the chains that were securing it to the floor. He looked at the cargo. It was a bunch of train stuff. Iron rails and train wheels was what he could mostly see. The path between was narrow, and he was getting bruises from being knocked between them as he passed through. He didn't stop until he reached the bulkhead wall. Then he waited for Crigger to catch up. He turned to see where he was at, but he saw no one. He waited another minute, but still no one came. So he yelled out over the noise of the waves hitting the ship.

"Crigger. Where are you? No one is up here."

There was no reply, so Tibbs started working his way back out of the cargo hold.

*****

On the other side of the wall, Winston heard the voice faintly over the noise of the storm. He craned his ear to hear more, but could not. He woke up Catherine, who had fallen asleep against his arm.

"I heard a voice behind the back wall. It sounded like someone was looking for someone. Perhaps it is us?"

"What did they say?" she said as she shivered from the cold.

"I couldn't make out the words, but I am sure they were searching for something or someone. Why else would they be in the cargo hold?"

"Maybe the storm shifted the cargo, and they needed to resecure it?"

"No, I only heard one person talking, not a bunch of men."

"This storm is making me sick. I have never been in such conditions before. I am worried that this is going to be my last moments on earth," she complained.

"We need to hang on to hope. Without that, everything is pointless."

"Hope in what? We still haven't figured out how to get out of this dark hole we are in."

Winston changed the subject. "How do you feel about dogs?"

"What are you talking about?"

"Do you like dogs?" he repeated.

"Yes, I like some dogs."

"What kind do you like?"

"Medium-sized ones. Not too big, not too small, I guess. I have not given the subject much thought."

"Great, so do I. I think we should get one right away once we get out of here."

"What are you talking about?"

"We will call it Goldie, short for Goldilocks. You know, because it's not too big or too small."

"Why do you want a dog? Don't we have a hundred other things to worry about right now?"

"Yup. That is the first thing we are going to get when we escape from this ship," he said as if oblivious to her question.

Her heart stopped when she heard that. "First before what?" she said. In her heart, she was hoping for a certain answer, hoping he was on the same page as her for once.

Winston squeezed her hand in the darkness but did not answer her question.

Finally, after a silent pause, he answered. "It's kind of funny to think about, but not once in my adult life before today have I ever considered getting a puppy."

"I don't understand. What made you want one today then?"

"Don't you see what is happening? It's a miracle! It took this complete and utter darkness to help me see the light."

"What miracle? Your talking nonsense. Are you okay? Are you going to faint again?"

"All of my scars and the dullness of my heart are beginning to heal themselves, and you're responsible. Catherine, you have changed me in the short time we have known each other. I used to be a coward and run away from my problems. Now I am willing to fight to the death to protect you." He stopped and thought for a second. "You made me a fighter instead of a fainter." That made him chuckle. He continued, "I used to think I would never amount to anything, be anything, or have anything worthwhile. I was scared of life, scared of living, because all I saw was the bad and the darkness in the world. But you bring me confidence and inspire me to be a better man. You make my heart happy and light and filled with wonder. I see light instead of darkness, love and happiness instead of pain and suffering. And I have never met anyone who has turned my world upside down like you have."

Catherine blushed in the darkness. She started to say something, but Winston told her he needed to say the rest of what was on his heart.

"The problem is that I can't stop thinking about what will happen when we get off this ship. I don't want it to end. I don't want us to go our separate ways. I can't have this voyage be our only shared moment in life. I want to spend every minute of the rest of my life with you by my side. And if that is not a possibility, then I do not want to leave this dark hole on this ship, because even the light of day would not be able to cheer me up or replace the hole in my heart that would remain there until I die. In fact, I decided I would rather die today on this ship than face the future alone without you."

There was silence in the room for a moment before Winston continued. He didn't know it was because Catherine was softly crying and had tears of joy running down her face. He didn't notice that her hands were trembling slightly.

"I know this is probably the worst time and place to say this, but I am going to say it anyway. Catherine, I want…no, I need you to be my wife. Will you do me the great honor of marrying me?"

Catherine smiled into the darkness so bright, it would have lit up the room if possible.

"Yes, a thousand times yes. I would be honored to be Mrs. Catherine Hawes."

*****

Tibbs finally made it back to the beginning of the cargo hold. Crigger was waiting for him.

"What took you so long?"

"It ain't so easy walking through all that stuff with the ship bouncing so hard. Got bruises all over from it."

"Well, if you would've gone faster, you would've gotten less bruises."

Tibbs just shook his head. "Let's head to the other side. They weren't in the aft cargo holds."

"Are you sure?"

"You can be my guest and double-check if you would like."

"Can't. I have the chloroform. Can't sneak up from in front."

With that both men turned and made their way back toward the engine room. When they got to the back door, Crigger suggested that they try to search it again. This time in reverse order. Tibbs agreed, so Crigger went on ahead to where the front door was. Tibbs did his best to count out two minutes, then opened the door to the engine room. To his surprise, there was no one there to immediately challenge him. He stepped inside and closed the door behind him. He saw men feverously working in the hot and sweaty room. No one had time to pay attention to him, so he quickly started walking up the center aisle looking for McDuff or Archer. About halfway through the engine room, the head engineer saw him again and marched straight over to him.

"Are you mad? What is so blasted important that you are risking not only your own life and limb, but the safety of the entire ship to be here?"

Tibbs knew he needed to think of a quick answer, so he blurted out the first thing that came to his mind.

"Captain sent me down to make sure everything was still shipshape."

"Did he now? And why would he send you and not Niklas, the second engineer? That is the standard procedure."

Tibbs was in a dilemma. Before he knew what happened, he said. "Niklas was unavailable."

"And just what does that mean? Why is he unavailable?"

"He, ah, he fell down the stairs from the bouncing ship and got banged up real good. He is resting his injuries in the crew's quarters."

"Why wasn't I informed of this? I need to go see him immediately."

"You can't right now. That is why the captain sent me. He wants you to know that you will have to work Niklas's shift as well until we reach Port Arthur." Then he added, "And what is your reply about being shipshape?"

The first engineer stared at Tibbs, looking to see if the man was lying for some reason. Finally, he decided that no one would make up a story like that.

"Tell the captain the message was received, and we have no mechanical issues at this time. And we shall do our best under these circumstances." Then he took the huge wrench in his hand and pushed it into Tibb's chest. "And as for yourself, if I find out that you have been lying to me, you will wish you hadn't."

Tibbs took the message and hightailed for the front door. Once he passed through, he met Crigger again.

"Let's keep going. I will catch you up when we get to the front of the ship."

"Catch me up on what?"

But Tibbs didn't hear as he had already left.

*****

Tibbs climbed the stairwell up to the top deck. He stopped as he reached the top stair as he could hear McDuff and Archer talking in the distance. He motioned for Crigger to be quiet and pointed around the corner so he would understand. Crigger quietly stopped alongside Tibbs and strained to listen to the voices above the sound of the wind and waves. A few minutes later the voices had disappeared. Tibbs slowly glanced around the corner to see if they were still there, but the deck was empty.

"No one there," he said out loud.

"Well, where could they have gone? They didn't have time to walk all the way to the stern of the ship without us seeing them, and they didn't come back toward us."

"Better question would be, what were they doing up on deck? Do you think they threw someone overboard?"

"I hope not. Let's go check it out."

CHAPTER 9

Into the Dark

It was time to regain control of the situation. Fear needed its place, while hope needed to be snuffed out like an extinguished candle. Once fear replaced hope, everything else would fall into place.

—McDuff

Captain Thomas walked over to the door on the bridge and went outside, over to the railing. He needed to get some fresh air. The night had been a stressful one, considering everything that was going on at the same time. He questioned the sanity of his decision to continue on with the pickup off Isle Royale. The southeast winds were going to push his ship toward the island and its deadly rocks as they attempted the exchange. But he knew that it would be several months before he could make another attempt, as winter would make the voyage impossible, and he was worried that McDuff was on to him. He also knew that he had no way to stop the Indian Gitchie Manito from rowing out to meet them. If he didn't show up, it would surely mean he would capsize and drown in this storm. Then he would have to find another person to fill his vital role in this business venture. No, he would have to continue on. The die had been cast. He just had to hope for the best. Thomas was not a religious man, but he prayed that the eastern winds would let up long enough for him to get in and out of the area safely. Thomas felt the coldness in the air as the snow fell lightly out of the skies. There were no stars to look at, as the storm clouds had blotted them out of existence for the time being. He took out his pipe, and after preparing it, he began to puff on it. It was comforting to him, relaxing his muscles and taking the edge off his tension.

What a life, he thought. He always dreamt of being the captain of a large ship, and he had spent his entire life working toward that end. The rugged and stoic aura of a captain had always appealed to him, along with the high regard they held in society. The ability to sail from one civilization to another and to test your mettle, courage, and toughness against nature and come out successful was a challenge that he had always relished. To be in total command of everything that came in your path—be it crew, passengers, or the seas themselves—made him feel important and, to a degree, invincible. There were times that he wished he was captain on one of those whalers chasing after giant beasts. But he had never left the Great Lakes. He knew them like the back of his hand, especially Lake Superior.

By all definitions, it was an inland sea, not a lake. More than a thousand feet deep in places, with dangerous shoals and rocky outcroppings submerged around islands that crossed his path near both ends and the middle of his journey. There were stories about waves that had reached up to forty feet tall in the past, retold in saloons by those fortunate enough to have survived the encounter. Most dismissed them as embellished tales, but Thomas believed. He also believed that Superior deserved a name grander than one starting with the word *lake*, which brought to mind pictures of men fishing out of canoes, catching walleye at the rise of dawn in some tranquil setting. No, this was not that lake, and anyone who thought so would learn from their harsh experience real quick. He leaned against the railing and soaked up the moment. He truly only felt alive and in control at times like these. He stayed there lost in his thoughts until his pipe went out. Instead of relighting it, he made up his mind to head back inside. As he did so, he perceived that the winds were subtly starting to change directions. His body told him that it was getting colder in front of him. If that were true, then his prayers would be answered. He had hoped that the winds would come out of the northwest. That would make the island a natural windbreak when they stopped, which would make the seas calmer and safer. But it also meant that it would bring the bone-chilling cold out of northern Canada into their path.

*****

At midnight, First Mate Ralston returned to the bridge for his shift. Captain Thomas updated him with the speed and direction they were headed."

Ralston went to the map and plotted out the course.

"Captain, by my calculations we are off course and headed directly for Isle Royale. We need to make a course correction immediately."

"You are correct, Mr. Ralston. The pressure has continued to drop and is now at 990. I feel it is too much to try to sail into the full face of the storm going around the north end of the island as scheduled. It will be calmer to wait it out until morning on the leeward side of the island, which will shelter us from the ferocity of this storm."

"Captain, is this the right decision? If the wind picks up in intensity and becomes one of those Nor' Easters we all fear, it would push us straight into the rocks of Isle Royale."

"I am convinced that by the time we get close, the wind will be in our face and not at our backs."

"Really, sir, how can you be sure?"

"Here is a learning moment for you. As a future captain, you will need to make educated decisions based not only on current facts but also on experience and gut feelings. We can't always wait for proof before we decide, a porter can do that! Instead, we are expected to trust our instincts and act upon them. What-ifs will always lead to indecision and inaction, which never lead to a good outcome."

"No disrespect meant, Captain, but what if your hunch is wrong?"

Captain Thomas did not take offense. He was teaching a young man how to become a great captain like himself, to follow in his footsteps. He knew it would be a source of pride for him when his sailing days are over to know that one of his protégés was still out there living large on the seas.

"Plan for the best and prepare for the worst is a motto we must live by every day. As such, I have considered this and plan to stop no closer than one mile out from the island. We can anchor there if necessary. There is a firm bottom at that depth, and our sea anchors will hold us off the rocks in the event of a Nor' Easter."

"Yes, Captain. I shall remember this valuable lesson."

"Mr. Ralston, you have the bridge. Keep the ship on the course I have charted. By my calculations, we will be in calmer waters around two o'clock this morning, where we will wait it out until the storm passes. I will return to the bridge at one thirty promptly."

With that, the captain left the bridge and went to make sure everything was ready for their unscheduled stop.

*****

Crigger and Tibbs made their way up the port side deck where they had heard McDuff and Archer talking. They stopped about a quarter of the way down and looked over the rail. They knew it was hopeless to even look, but they felt compelled to see if anyone had been thrown overboard. All they saw were angry seas.

"They were here for at least ten minutes. There had to be a purpose. It's too treacherous to be out here without a reason. I mean look, we are the only other souls out here. The captain has ordered everyone to stay in their rooms. The only reason the crew would be out here would be to take down the sails," said Tibbs.

Crigger looked up at the sails. They were still up and had not been taken down yet. He wondered why that was. Usually, the sails came down in storms like this. As he looked back over to the water, he noticed the tarp was loose on the life boat above them.

"Tibbs, look! The tarp is loose on the lifeboat. They must have snuck inside."

"What for? They could freeze to death in there."

"Go on, take a look. It's the only way we will know for sure."

Reluctantly, Tibbs climbed up on the stanchion that suspended the lifeboat in place above the deck and lifted the edge of the tarp ever so slightly to peek inside. Then he climbed back down.

"Well?"

"They are not in it, but it has been loaded with some crates."

"Crates of what?"

"How do I know? I didn't open them."

"Move out of the way. I am going to take a look for myself." Then Crigger climbed up and peeked under the tarp. Looking back at Tibbs, he said, "Keep watch, I will be right back." Then he loosened the tarp some more and crawled under it into the lifeboat.

Tibbs was nervous standing on the deck by himself with no answer to give on why he was there if someone had happened by. He wished Crigger would hurry. Just then he saw a sailor coming his way as Crigger started making noises in the boat above him.

"Got company," he said to Crigger. "Be quiet."

But Crigger didn't stop. He must not have heard him. No time to say it again, he needed a plan. So he put his arms on the railing and threw his head over the side and made loud noises like he was puking.

Halverson, the other sailor who had approached, looked at Tibbs and laughed as he slowly passed by.

"Crigger was right, my poor friend. You really are a land lubber." Then he continued walking past him and out of sight, laughing the whole time.

Once he was sure he was gone, Tibbs stopped pretending that he was throwing up. He was mad, not sick.

"Crigger, get out of there right now!" he demanded.

Crigger came out of the lifeboat a few seconds later and climbed back down to the deck.

"Good thinking about pretending to toss your cookies."

"Never mind that. How does he know about my nickname L. L. Tibbs? That was just between us."

"It was?" Crigger said in a surprised tone. "I told everyone about it, as I assumed you told everyone I was B. R. Crigger."

Tibbs just glared at him for a few seconds. Then he said, "Well, I will now. You can count on that. Everyone will know you are a barge rat."

"Fine, but we have more important things to worry about. I know what they hid in the lifeboat. The boxes are full of machine parts. I think they are going to smuggle it off of the ship."

"It must be valuable then."

"The bigger picture is that they don't know that we know about it," added Crigger.

"Yeh, that's true. And if it's valuable, that means that they will have to return here at some point to lower the lifeboat and make their getaway."

"So we can wait nearby and sneak up on them when they do!"

"What is it with you and the dentist thing. I've got a better plan than that," said Tibbs with a devilish grin on his face. "Follow me, we need to get a few things."

"Where we going?"

"Just follow me."

Crigger didn't press the issue. He knew that Tibbs had a darker side to him. He just nodded and followed behind as Tibbs led the way.

A few minutes later, they were back near the engine room. Tibbs opened up the locker that stored all of the tools on the ship. He started to rummage through, looking for a specific item, when he heard a voice in the distance from inside the closed engine room. He quickly closed the locker and spun around just as the door opened.

The first engineer looked at Tibbs and said, "How is Niklas doing?"

Crigger was dumbfounded, his mouth hanging open in confusion.

"I'm afraid, sir, that there has been no change. I shall notify you at once if he shows any signs of getting better," Tibbs replied. "You have my word on that."

"Very well. Are there any more instructions from the captain?"

Crigger was watching this conversation, not sure of what was going on.

"No, sir. He just sent me to tell you to keep up the good work."

"Did he now? It feels good that your work is appreciated," he replied as he turned and went back into the engine room with a smile on his face.

Once the door was closed, Crigger said, "What haven't you told me?"

"I had to think fast, as he caught me going through the engine room the second time. So I told him that Niklas had taken a bad injury falling down the stairs in the storm and is recuperating in the bunks."

"That was pretty quick thinking on your part, but what if he goes to check?"

"He can't. I told him the captain ordered him to stay in the engine room till we reach port. Now keep watch while I retrieve what I'm looking for."

Crigger kept watch. It took a few minutes, but Tibbs finally found what he wanted in the back of the locker. Once he saw what it was, he smiled the same devilish grin that Tibbs had.

Tibbs said, "You take this stuff to the lifeboat, and I will meet you there. I need to stop by the kitchen first. We need one more thing."

Crigger didn't even ask what at this point. He just took the stuff and headed to the lifeboat.

*****

"What kind of wedding are we going to have?" asked Catherine.

"That is an excellent question. I guess it depends on how many guests we are going to invite."

"Oh, yeah. I guess that will be a problem," said Catherine as she thought out the logical conclusion. "Well, we cannot obviously invite our parents, and neither of us have brothers or sisters… I guess that is a work in progress. Perhaps we should figure out where we want to get married first."

"I guess there are three options," Winston replied. "Church, courthouse, or outdoors."

"Hmm, every girl always dreams of a big church wedding looking like a princess in front of everyone she knows, showing off her man in his tuxedo to the whole world."

"I agree, church wedding it is then."

"But that costs money, and we are going to be dirt poor."

"If that is what you want, I will find a way to make it happen," he said with his best bravado.

"You know, you truly are my knight in shining armor."

"Speaking of that, as pleasant as this conversation is, we probably need to discuss our escape plan first."

"You're right, of course. What have you come up with?"

"Let's review what we know. We know that McDuff is playing both sides against themselves. And both sides want the ship sunk, so that will probably happen. There is no other conclusion that can be made. But we also know that we are still alive because McDuff needs the counterfeit plates and he needs them before he sinks the ship. So we have some leverage with him."

"Go on, what else do we know?"

"He needs the counterfeit machine as well as the plates, so he has to get that off the ship as well."

"I bet those were the noises we heard a while ago. They have already taken apart the machine and hidden it," Catherine interjected.

"Very clever," Winston said. "We know that the captain is going to stop the ship near Isle Royale so he can meet the Indian Gitchie Manito and lower the lifeboat to meet him. We also know with a fair degree of certainty that this is when McDuff is going to blow up the ship, as he can escape to the Isle…" Winston was lost in his thoughts for a moment. "Which means, that he probably has arranged means of transportation off of the Island as well."

"Of course. That makes perfect sense. He would have had time to plan it out."

"No, on second thought, that is not true. I was the one who told him about the captain's secret stop after we were on the ship. So he would not have had a way to communicate to have someone meet him on the island. However, that is a vulnerability in his plan."

"Too bad. I was hoping we could use that transportation for ourselves if we made it to the island."

"Yes, that is unfortunate. But we also know that he plans to sell the counterfeit machine to your father, in exchange to cut you out of the will and take your place…So if we can stop that from happening, perhaps you will be left in the will."

"My dad would just find another opportunity to cut me out at some point in the future. I'm afraid McDuff is right on that account. My dad doesn't think I am smart enough or ruthless enough to run his business. And besides, I don't want to have anything to do with him after this."

"But McDuff doesn't know that. Perhaps we can convince him that we plan to sell those plates to him ourselves and cut McDuff out of the will."

"What good would that do?"

"It would give him something to think about that he hasn't considered. It might confuse him enough to give us an opportunity to escape."

*****

After waiting in the shadows for a few minutes, Crigger finally saw Tibbs arrive near the lifeboat.

"What on earth did you need from the kitchen?"

"I remembered that the cook kept a drawer full of used wine corks. It was his little collection. Liked to sniff them, I think. So I took a handful of them."

"So what's the plan?"

"We are going to use the brace to drill holes in the bottom of the lifeboat. Then we are going to shove the corks into the holes very carefully so that they will pop back out once the ship hits the water. The paint is so we can paint the cork the same color as the underside of the lifeboat and keep it from being discovered until it is too late."

"Brilliant. In these seas, they won't stand a chance…blup, blup, blup, they will go all the way to the bottom."

"Thanks, I thought so. Now let's get started before we are discovered. Go stand watch."

Crigger stood watch as Tibbs began drilling holes in the bottom of the lifeboat. Before too long he had made ten different holes along the bottom. He reached in his pocket and began to put a cork in each one while Crigger went behind and painted each cork. Everything went perfectly until Tibbs ran out of corks after only eight holes.

"You dolt. Didn't you count the corks before you made the holes?" Crigger admonished him. "I can't believe our luck. Now what are we going to do?"

"I can go back and get two more."

"No time. We might get discovered before then."

"Why am I the one coming up with all the solutions. Why can't the barge rat figure it out for once?" Tibbs said in self-defense.

Crigger thought for a moment and then said "Fine. Give me all your chewing tobacco."

"What for?"

"For my solution to your problem."

Reluctantly, Tibbs handed over the pouch, which was his most prized possession. Crigger immediately put a big chaw in his mouth and slipped the pouch into his coat pocket.

"How is you using all my tobacco going to help with the hole problem?"

Crigger just looked at him. After getting it all moistened up inside his mouth, he pulled it out and stuck some in each hole, effectively plugging them. Then he dabbed it with his paintbrush and said "Ta-da," as he threw the paint can and brush over the side of the ship.

"What about the rest of my tobacco?"

"I used it all."

"No, you didn't. That was a brand-new pouch. I saw you stick it in your pocket."

Just then McDuff and Archer appear in the distance and yelled at the men.

Startled, Crigger and Tibbs swing their heads around to see the villains off in the distance.

Crigger whispered to Tibbs, "Throw the brace over the side before they get too close."

Tibbs turned and did his best puking imitation over the rail, but instead of tossing his cookies, the brace came out and made its way to the bottom of the lake. As he looked down, he noticed some wood shavings on the deck from where he had cut the holes. Quickly, he put his boot over it, just as the leprechaun and his goon arrived.

"Well, noo. Whit urr ye twa sailors daein' oan th' deck?"

Crigger answered, "My buddy was feeling a bit sick below, so we came up to get him some fresh air, but as you can see, he is still losing his lunch over the railing."

Archer said, "Is he the one they call the land lubber?"

Tibbs scowled, but Crigger smiled and said, "Yes, it is. But he doesn't like being called that too much."

"Weel, it fits him perfectly," replied McDuff. "He shuid git used tae it. Noo git back tae yer stations afore ah report ye tae th' captain."

Both men thanked the man for not turning them in. As Tibbs started to leave, he pretended to slip, causing the toe of his boot to slide toward the railing. He was hoping that he could slide the wood chips over the side without being noticed. In the effort, he fell forward onto the deck.

Archer started laughing. "The bloke can't even stand up. Is this his first voyage?"

"A've ne'er seen a worse sailor."

As Tibbs got back up to his feet, he scooped up another wood chip with his hand as he pushed off the floor. Then he hightailed it after Crigger, who was several steps in front. When they got out of sight, Crigger stopped him.

"What was that all about?"

Tibbs opened his hand and showed him the wood chips. "There were several of these on the deck. I saw it when I pretended to throw up. I pushed some over the side with my boot as well."

Crigger was impressed. "You might not be the worst sailor after all," he goaded him.

"What I want to know is how did the two most evil men on the ship know my nickname? Did you write it on the bathroom walls?"

"Let it go, my friend. Sometimes these things just take on a life of their own."

*****

Meanwhile, back at the lifeboat, McDuff was still skeptical as to why they had been standing under the very lifeboat they had just loaded.

"Climb up 'n' check oor cargo. Ah git a funny feeling."

Archer did as he was told. He climbed up the side of the stanchion and lifted the tarp. He looked inside, which was dimly lit from the deck lights above, as the canvas had blocked most of the light out from the inside of the lifeboat.

"All the crates are right where we left 'em," he said after a few moments. Then he climbed back down and stood next to McDuff at the rail. "What's wrong. What are you looking at?"

"Do ye see ony puke oan th' railing?"

"No."

"Do ye detect ony odor o' puke at a'?"

"No. Why?"

"When wis th' lest time ye saw a sailor puke 'n' nae git it oan his-sel 'n' th' deck?"

"Maybe land lubbers are better at puking than sailors?"

"Or mibbie thay wis up tae something. Unload th' crates. We ur aff tae pick a different lifeboat."

Archer just nodded. He knew nothing would change McDuff's mind once it was made up. He climbed back up the stanchion and got into the lifeboat.

An hour later, they had moved all the crates to a lifeboat closer to the front of the ship.

*****

Crigger and Tibbs resumed their search, but this time it was for Winston and Catherine, as they already had made preparations for the demise of the leprechaun and his goon. They decided to resume their search where they had left off, the forward cargo holds. This time both men went together as they had no need to pull the dentist ploy, which meant they didn't need to be stealthy either.

"Really, how does everyone know about my nickname?"

"Beats me. Now let's focus on finding those two poor souls."

Tibbs stopped and called out with a loud voice. "Winston! Catherine?"

They stopped to listen but got no response. So they went a little farther into the cargo hold and yelled their names again. All they heard was the sound of the cargo creaking with the rolling of the ship.

"I think I am getting sick for real," exclaimed Tibbs. "I think all that fake vomiting did something to me."

"Pull it together, man."

"You go on, I need to lean against this box for a moment."

Crigger gave him a look, like really? But he went farther in to the hold by himself. Five minutes later, he reached the bulkhead wall.

"Hey, Tibbs, nothing here. We need to go back," he yelled.

Just as he turned to leave, he heard banging from behind the wall. He put his ear to the wall to listen. Then he heard muffled voices.

"Can you hear me? I can hear you," he yelled through the wall.

Inside the secret hold, Winston and Catherine were overwhelmed. They both yelled.

Winston yelled the loudest. "Help us. We are between the bulkhead walls."

"How is that possible?" Crigger yelled back.

"There is a secret entrance in room number 71, in the closet floor."

"Hold on. I am coming to get you."

Then Crigger ran back to where Tibbs was still leaning against the crate.

"What is that awful smell?" then he realized what Tibbs had been doing. "Really, you seriously tossed your cookies?"

Tibbs was embarrassed and used his sleeve to wipe his mouth. "I wouldn't step any farther to the left if I were you."

"Never mind. I know where the man and lady are."

"That's great. Where are they?"

"Between the walls. Now shut up and follow me."

*****

It was one o'clock in the morning, and the captain made his way back to the bridge thirty minutes earlier than expected.

"Mr. Ralston, what is our position?"

"Sir, we are on course as plotted. But I'm afraid we lost some of our speed as the winds have been changing and the sails are working against us. Right now we are only making twelve knots."

"How far are we from the Isle?"

"I calculate it at thirty-two miles ahead."

The captain ran the numbers through his head. That meant they were going to be in position at four o'clock instead of two o'clock in the morning. No matter, the Indian knew to wait on shore in bad weather until he heard the steam whistle from the ship.

"Have the crew take in the sails. Perhaps it will increase our speed."

"Yes, sir. Right away, sir."

"What is the weather report?"

"Pressure has dropped to 985.6 millibars. Wind is gusting up to thirty miles per hour, with twenty-five-foot seas. I am glad you made the decision to wait on the east side of the island. Your hunch was right about the wind changing direction."

"If this storm keeps intensifying, it won't matter. We will capsize before we get there. Now tell the engine room I need all the power she can muster."

"Aye, Captain."

Silently, Thomas was enjoying the challenge. If they survive this, he will be one of only a handful of captains to ever do so. He was sure that this storm was going to sink ships on the Great Lakes tonight. And he was confident that it wouldn't be his.

"Keep a sharp eye for other ships in the area. Other captains might have the same idea of waiting out the storm on the leeward side of the island."

"Aye, Captain," came the reply.

*****

Tibbs was following behind as fast as he could go. It seemed like Crigger was running faster than humanly possible on this sea-tossed deck. Up ahead, he watched him stop beside a cabin and unlock it with the master key ring he found under the mattress. When he finally caught up, he saw him prying up the floor in the closet.

"Close the door, you fool," was all he said as he entered the room.

Once the secret entrance had been removed, he peered into the darkness below. He could not see the bottom, but he could hear Winston and Catherine talking excitedly that they had been found. He looked around the closet and found the light switch. He pushed it in and the space below flooded with light. He quickly climbed down to the bottom. Tibbs followed behind.

"We are so glad you are here to rescue us," said Winston.

"We need to hurry. McDuff might come back at any moment," Catherine said in a panicked voice. "Besides, it is freezing down here."

Crigger untied Catherine while Tibbs untied Winston.

Once free, Winston shook Tibbs hand. "We need to find a safe place, and then we need to tell you what we know. Everyone is in danger."

"Say no more," replied Crigger as he climbed up the ladder.

Once they were all safely in room 71, Tibbs put the closet floor back in place and turned out the light.

Crigger motioned for everyone to be quiet while he checked the hallway. He opened the door a crack and saw and heard nothing.

"Okay. Here's the plan. I have a master key to every room on the ship. We are going to go down two cabins to number 75 and hide out there until we can figure out what is going on. Any questions?"

Catherine said, "Let's go down four cabins. I will feel safer talking then."

"Okay, cabin 79 it is. Let's go."

Crigger nodded and checked the door once more. Then he walked out into the hallway and went straight to cabin 79 and unlocked the door. He checked to make sure it was empty and then waved for everyone to follow. Quickly, everyone made their way to the room and closed the door.

Once the door closed, everyone started talking at once. Crigger got their attention and spoke first.

"We are going to help you because they killed our friend Niklas and we are out for revenge."

"And we weren't going to let them do the same to you," Tibbs added.

Catherine said "I'm sorry" and "Thank you" to both men, who didn't know how to respond back.

"We have worse news for you, I'm afraid," said Winston. "McDuff and Archer are going to sink the ship. We think they are going to do it when we stop near Isle Royale tonight."

Then Winston took the next few minutes filling them in on what they knew. He told them everything except the location of the plates.

Tibbs let out a low whistle. "Sounds like we saved our own lives by rescuing you. Better still, we now know why they loaded the lifeboat with those crates and when they plan to lower it into the lake."

Crigger let out a little snicker. "Too bad we sabotaged the lifeboat. It will sink like a rock once it hits the water."

"That's great," said Winston. "But we need to stop them from sinking the ship. Otherwise, good people are going to die."

Tibbs agreed. "You're absolutely right about that. But how?"

"We need to come up with a plan, but before we can do that, we need to know how many people we are up against," said Crigger.

"Well, we better do it in a hurry, because we only have an hour or two left before we get to Isle Royale, by our calculations," replied Catherine.

"It would also help if we knew how they were going to sink the ship. Then we would know what they were planning," said Tibbs.

Winston took charge. "Okay. It sounds like we are all like-minded on this. Everyone that is willing to do what it takes to stop McDuff and anyone else from sinking this ship say, 'Aye.'"

All four of them agreed without hesitation.

"And we can't all be doing our own thing so we need one person in charge of this, to give us our best shot at success. Are there any volunteers to be in charge?" asked Winston.

No one spoke up and volunteered, so Winston said, "I will if no one else objects."

Catherine quickly agreed with Winston and gave him her vote. Crigger and Tibbs followed suit. So it was settled.

"All right, but Crigger is second in charge. If something happens to me, it will be on you to finish what we started. Now here's what we need to do first. Crigger, find out exactly how long we have until we get to Isle Royale but be discreet. It is still a secret as far as the captain knows. Tibbs, I want you to quietly find the lifeboat that they plan to lower to meet the Indian. That is going to be the escape plan for the four of us off this ship in case we can't stop them. Catherine and I are going to go get the counterfeit plates. We might need them later to trade our lives for them."

Everyone nodded in agreement.

"We will meet back in this very room as soon as possible, understood?"

Again, everyone nodded in eager anticipation.

"One last thing. I need the set of master keys. The plates are in a locked room."

Crigger handed the keys to Winston. "For Niklas!" he said.

"For Niklas!" everyone repeated.

Crigger and Tibbs left the room first.

Winston looked at Catherine and said, "I need you to stay here and let everyone back in the room. Besides, where I am going is too dangerous, and if it goes bad, I don't want us both captured."

Deep down, Catherine knew he was right, but it was hard to let go of him.

"I am worried. Are we able to pull this off, stop these horrible people from sinking this ship?"

"What kind of people would we be if we didn't try?" he softly answered. "I don't want that hanging over our heads for the rest of our lives."

"I know you are right. I am just worried that I am going to lose you now that I just found you. I couldn't live with that either."

He squeezed her hand and said it will be all right. Then he left the room before she could say anything else.

*****

Bryson met the captain in his quarters at the predetermined time.

"Sir, I have lifeboat number 1 on the aft port side loaded with the money for the exchange as we had discussed."

"Anyone see you?"

"No, sir. I made sure of it."

"What about our storage place for the silver, is it ready to go?"

"Yes, sir. I have made a concealed place in the galley."

"Very well. Head up on deck and watch Duncan and Halverson take down the sails. It will take time in this storm as there are two masts and will allow you to watch our lifeboat to make sure no one tampers with it."

"Aye, Captain."

Then Bryson left the bridge and went to the main deck. There he found that Halverson had already climbed up the first mast with a few other sailors and was fighting the wind to get the sail furled while Duncan was manning the ropes below. Bryson was glad that it was not his job to climb up there. It looked really dangerous and scary from where he was standing. As he watched the men do their dance with the sails, he kept glancing over at the lifeboat to make sure everything was still good. He kept turning back and forth to keep the wind off his face. Finally, he decided to move so he could watch both with the wind at his back. That helped quite a bit.

Unknown to him, when he turned his back to the wind, it gave Tibbs an opportunity to watch what was happening without fear of being seen. He carefully watched Bryson as he kept moving his head from watching the sailors to looking back at the lifeboats. Tibbs knew that the lifeboat being used was now at the back of the ship. It would just be a matter of looking at a few different ones, once the sails were down to confirm the correct boat.

*****

Meanwhile, Winston had snuck into the captain's quarters to recover the counterfeit plates. As he went to close the door behind him, he saw McDuff turn the corner and start down the hallway. Quickly, he closed and locked the door. Then he ran to the captain's private bathroom, closing that door as well.

Moments later, he heard the hallway door open and close. He knew that McDuff was here searching for the plates since he had told him the captain had them in his possession. He could only hope that McDuff would not search the bathroom, or all would be lost. Moments later, he heard the door open and close again. He wondered why McDuff would have left so quickly. No, that wasn't it. He decided to wait quietly to see what was going on. His hunch was a good one, as he heard McDuff speak quietly to another person in the room.

"Tear this room apairt if ye hae tae. We ur dane bein' sneaky!"

"Sounds good to me," answered Archer. "I like making a mess."

Archer started to trash the room in his search while McDuff stood back and looked around with a careful eye. Looking for any place where the captain might have hidden the plates. His eye finally came to rest on the painting of Ponce De Leon. He walked over and removed the painting from the wall. Behind it he found a small wall safe.

"Archer, stoap. Whit yer dae in' 'n' git ower here."

Archer stopped right after he finished turning the captain's desk over. He looked and saw the wall safe.

"Looks like you found the hiding spot."

McDuff stood on the couch and pulled on the handle to see if it was unlocked. Unfortunately, it wasn't going to be that easy. "See if ye kin git it open."

Archer immediately went and moved the leather couch out of his way. Then he put his ear up to the safe and listened for the tumblers as he spun the dial. "This isn't a high-quality safe. I should be able to get it open in no time at all."

"Weel, git tae it."

Archer began to spin the dial slowly until he heard the first click from inside the dial. Then he spun it back the other direction until he heard another click. Finally, he spun it back again the first direction until he heard the third click. Then he stood back, smiled, and pulled the handle down. However, it didn't open.

"Whit happened? How come did it nae open?"

"Maybe it goes in the other direction. Let me try again."

Archer did the same thing, but this time he started by spinning the knob to the right, instead of the left. After three clicks, he pulled on the handle again. It still didn't open. Now Archer was getting mad.

"I heard of a safe that had four clicks before. Let me try that."

So he went back and turned the dial to the left, then the right, then the left and finally back to the right. He pulled on the handle. Nothing! So he did the four clicks in the opposite direction, right, then left, then right, then left again. But the safe still did not open.

"Ah thought ye said ye cuid dae this. Whit's neist, five clicks, then six? Wur wasting oor time. Let's gang git th' captain 'n' force him tae open it."

Archer just shrugged his shoulders. This was the first safe he couldn't crack. He looked at the safe and punched it out of frustration. To his amazement, it cracked and fell off the wall.

McDuff just stared at it lying on the ground. It wasn't a safe at all. Just a thin metal plate with a dial. There was no opening in the wall behind it.

"That captain is mair clever than we've given him credit fur. Let's gang, tis nae in his affice. He haes a better hiding steid than that."

Archer bent down and picked it up. He looked at both sides of it, making sure it wasn't some magic trick. Then he threw it across the room in disgust. He watched it fly until it lodged itself in the giant globe next to the desk. He wasn't sure, but he thought South America took a direct hit. He looked around the room, satisfied with the amount of carnage he created, and followed McDuff out into the hallway.

*****

On the other side of the wall, Winston had heard the whole thing and had been doing his best not to laugh. After he was sure the room was empty, Winston took a peek outside the bathroom and saw the damage that had been done. The only thing not turned over was the globe that was hiding the plates. He looked at the piece of metal protruding from its side. It made him wonder why the captain had a fake wall safe behind a gigantic painting in his office. His inner monologue told him to figure it out later, as he needed to get out of the room before someone else came in. Quickly, he lifted the base of the globe enough to pull the plates out from underneath. Sticking them under his jacket, he left the room with haste.

*****

On the deck above him, Crigger was trying to eavesdrop on the conversation in the bridge. He was outside the door swabbing the deck. He had only been there a few minutes when the captain suddenly opened the door to go smoke his pipe again. He took a good look a Crigger swabbing the deck in the middle of a storm with snow falling and waves crashing over the bow of the ship and leaving water all over the deck every time it did so.

"Do you really think this is the proper time to wash the deck?" the captain asked in a semipolite voice. He was too amused and taken aback to yell yet.

Crigger stopped and looked the captain in the eye, feverishly trying to come up with a quick answer. Before he could say anything, the captain continued mocking him.

"Perhaps its soap and not snow falling from the sky! Is that what you think is happening here?"

"No, Captain. I didn't even know that was possible."

"Then what in the blazes are you doing?"

"I wanted to make sure that everything was proper and ship-shape, sir."

"A dirty deck is your only concern at this time, sailor?"

Finally, a light went on inside Crigger's brain. "No, Captain, I knew that you liked to come out here and smoke your pipe, and I saw the freezing weather and the waves, so I went and got hot water to make sure no ice formed here to keep you from falling."

The captain just stared at him for a full minute. "You're an idiot. Did anyone ever tell you that before? Now get back below decks and make sure the cargo is properly stowed and secured."

"Yes, Captain. Right away, Captain."

And with that, Crigger got out of there as fast as he could. He made a beeline to room 79. Instead of opening the door, he stopped and pretended to tie his shoe. This gave him an opportunity to make sure he wasn't followed. Then he entered the room to wait for the others. To his surprise, everyone else was already there waiting on him.

Winston was the first to say something. "What did you find out?"

"Nothing important, only that the captain believes I am an idiot." Then he explained to them what happened.

Catherine started laughing at the thought of seeing that happen firsthand.

"I wish I could have seen his face," she said while still laughing, which in turn made everyone else start laughing.

Once it had run its course, Winston slapped Crigger on the back.

"You may have struck out on uncovering any vital information, but you did manage to lift the tension in the room, even if for only a few minutes. So thank you for that."

Crigger said thanks, not sure if he was still being made fun of or not. "What did the rest of you discover?"

Tibbs answered immediately, "I almost discovered the lifeboat."

This made Catherine laugh all over again. "How could you almost find something? Either you did or you didn't."

"Well, I have it narrowed down to just a couple of boats," he said defensively. "It won't take long to check when the time comes."

Catherine, realizing that she had hurt his feelings, decided she better put on some charm to smooth it over.

"Both of you are the funniest men I have ever met in my life. I feel like you both are the brothers I never had."

Tibbs, not wanting to let it go that easy, said, "How could we be like brothers you never had? Either you did or you didn't have brothers."

Crigger elbowed him so he would shut up. "He meant no disrespect. He just doesn't know how to talk all proper and such."

Winston jumped in to get them refocused. "Well, I have something to show you," he said as he pulled the counterfeit plates out from under his coat for all to see. "Now, we are running out of time. Let's go back and determine which of the lifeboats it is exactly. With the storm, I am sure they already have it prepped to meet Gitchie Manito. Once we find it, we will hide the plates on it. That way it is not with us if we are captured, and it will already be in our escape vessel when the time comes."

*****

McDuff and Archer decided it was time to go get frisky with Catherine so Winston would give them the plates. He knew more than what he was telling. McDuff was sure of that. After leaving the captain's office, they made a beeline to room number 71. Once they got into the room, Archer pulled a quarter out of his pocket.

"Do you want heads or tails?"

McDuff slapped the quarter out of his hand. "Open th' trap door. We wull flip th' quarter wi' thaim peepin'. It wull hae a dramatic effect."

Archer let out an evil laugh, opened the trapdoor in the floor, turned on the light, and made his way to the bottom of the hold. When he got there, he looked around twice, not believing what he saw. By the time he realized that they were not there, McDuff was standing next to him shaking in anger.

"I don't get it. How does that scrawny reporter keep getting one up on us?"

"Ah guarantee that wisth' lest time. Gang cut th' power taeth' ship's lights. Tis time tae stairt th' end game."

*****

Back on the main deck, the crew had gotten the sails down off the first mast and were climbing up the second mast to do the same. Bryson was frozen to the bone, and he had to hang on to the railing to keep from falling and being washed overboard from the waves that were pounding the ship. He couldn't imagine anything worse. That's when the lights on the ship went out, leaving him and the other crew stuck in utter darkness. There was no light from the moon, as the storm clouds had blotted it out of existence as well. Above him, he could hear men yelling and shouting at each other, trying to climb down the rope ladders in the darkness without falling, or making someone else fall to their death. Without his sight, the waves were beginning to make Bryson's stomach flutter. He couldn't see the waves coming, so he could balance himself properly to withstand them. Several times he hit his ribs hard into the railing as the boat seemed to roll more violently in the darkness. Then he lost his footing when the next wave slammed into the ship. He hung on to the railing for all he was worth. Trying to stand up, but for some unknown reason, it was a task he was not able to accomplish. He yelled for help, but in the chaos, his voice blended into the background, not loud enough or distinct enough to be noticed. He worried how long he was going to have to hang on, hoping the lights would come back on quickly so someone would see him. But his hope quickly faded as the next wave pounded into the ship, washing the freezing water and spray over the deck once more. When the wave finally passed, Bryson heard the ship from a distance, then he was no more.

CHAPTER 10

The Sinking of the Algoma

It was November, and we found ourselves sailing in the midst of a blizzard upon the deadliest and coldest of the Great Lakes. Visibility was so slight that we could barely see over the bow of the ship. Waves up to thirty feet high were crashing into the ship unmercifully. The winter storm was packing hurricane force winds.

—Capt. Thomas Ericson, *SS Algoma*

In the engine room, the chief engineer was making his way through the darkness over to the mechanical room, just outside the engine room where all the circuit breakers were housed. He was yelling, "Make way," as he was trying to navigate from memory in the pitch black. Twice he fell because of the ship rolling to its side in the waves. The last time causing a sharp pain in his left knee. He pushed on, knowing it was on him to get the lights working again if possible. He also knew that the captain was now sailing blind without the lights on the ship illuminating the seas in front of them.

That was why they were probably rolling so much in the darkness, he thought.

The captain can't see the waves, to hit them straight on, and he was steering by feel. As he continued on his quest, he began to wonder what kind of mechanical issue could have caused them to go out. He hoped it was something simple because he wasn't sure if he knew enough about them to fix it anyway. After all, electric lights on ships were cutting-edge technology. He finally got to the front door of the engine room. He spun the watertight handle and pulled on the latch. The door opened effortlessly, and he stepped through and began to feel his way past the tool lockers to the next door on his right, which was the mechanical room. He stopped at the last locker and took a match out of his pocket and lit it. In the faint light, he saw what he was looking for. He opened the door to the locker and retrieved the oil lantern he remembered was there. The match in his hand went out, so he took another match out of his pocket to light the wick. The lantern flickered a small steady light, which he used to locate the door to the mechanical room. Once inside, he moved toward the wall until he could see the handle to reset the circuit breakers.

That's odd, he thought. The handle was down into the Off position. He grabbed it, said a prayer, and pushed it up, hoping for the best. Immediately, the lights flickered and came back to life. Satisfied with his accomplishment, he blew out the lantern and put it back in the last storage locker. That way he knew where it was. Then he made his way back to the engine room to see if any damage had been done.

*****

Back on deck, the men stopped climbing when the lights returned. They looked around trying to determine if they should climb back up and get the last sail down. After a few moments, while everyone was looking back and forth at each other, Halverson took matters into his own hands and began to climb back up. Soon after, the other men followed. They knew it was the right decision. To leave the sail up would risk capsizing the ship in these conditions. Everyone was too busy to notice that Bryson was no longer with them.

*****

Catherine had moved over and hugged Winston in the darkness. It made her feel safe. When the lights came back on, she saw that Crigger and Tibbs were looking at the embrace, so she let go and said, "Now, what were we talking about?"

Crigger ignored her question and offered one of his own. "What do you think it means?"

Winston replied, "I think it was a signal of some sort. Perhaps that it is time to end things."

Everyone was quiet, silently hoping that wasn't true.

"I think we need to move up our plans as well," said Tibbs. "We need to hide you and Catherine in the lifeboat now, with the plates."

"I agree. I estimate that the longest you would have to wait there would be an hour. But if it happens sooner, we will not have to worry about sneaking you onboard with all the commotion," Crigger stated.

After a robust conversation, Winston finally agreed and simply said thank you to Crigger and Tibbs. Then he grabbed the blanket off the bed and gave it to Catherine. "We need to keep you warm."

"What are you going to do while we hide out?"

"We have a score to settle with the leprechaun and the bear. We have to avenge Niklas."

"Okay, I get that," said Winston. "But once you're done with that, how are you going to get off the ship?"

"We was kinda hoping to hijack your rowboat and help you get to shore. If that is all right with the lady," Tibbs said very politely, trying to show he did have manners.

"Absolutely," said Catherine. "I wouldn't have it any other way."

With that, the four of them left the safety of room 79 and began to sneak their way to the back of the ship. Once there, they stopped at the aft stairwell, listening for signs of people. Tibbs told everyone to remain there while he went topside and located the correct lifeboat. Then he left, not waiting for an answer. He climbed the stairs and peeked around the corner. No one was at the back of the ship; however, there were several sailors amid ship working high up on the sails. He knew that they could see him if they happened to look down in his direction. He took the chance anyway and quickly darted to the first lifeboat and ran underneath it. That would eliminate the threat of being seen from above. Then he climbed the rear stanchion so that the lifeboat was between himself and the view of the sailors. He lifted the tarp and peeked inside. It was too dark to see anything, so he had no other choice but to crawl inside and search it with his hands. It took about five minutes for him to make that happen, but he was glad he did, as he discovered that this was the very lifeboat that they were going to use to meet the Indian Gitchie Manito. Slowly, he climbed back out of the boat and retraced his steps back to the others.

"Did you find the right one this time?" Crigger asked.

Tibbs shot him a look. "Yes! Now we will go one at a time. I will take Miss Catherine first and get her inside. Then I will come back and get Winston."

Catherine objected, "I don't want to be split up from Winston again. We need to do this together."

Tibbs looked at Winston. His face showed that he agreed with Catherine. So he shrugged his shoulders and said, "Okay then, follow me."

It took about fifteen minutes, but finally, both Winston and Catherine were safely aboard the lifeboat. Tibbs had pulled the tarp back down over the edge, leaving them completely alone.

Winston felt around the bottom of the lifeboat and found two soft bags. He positioned them as pillows and got Catherine as comfortable as possible. Grabbing the only lifejacket he found, he made her put it on, then he pulled the blanket over her to help keep her warm. He lay down next to her, feeling helpless and vulnerable. He hoped everything was going to work out like they had planned.

*****

On the bridge, the captain was barking rapid fire orders to anyone within earshot.

"Get me a status report on the engines! Find out why the lights went out! Did we get the sails down properly? Did we take on any water on that last roll? Do we have any damage? Where's my weather report!"

All around men were jumping to action in the chaos, trying to get the captain the answers to his questions.

Then the captain got on the loudspeaker.

"Attention, attention, this is your captain speaking. The storm system we are sailing through has intensified to unprecedented levels. For the safety of all passengers, I ask that you remain in your cabins until we dock at Port Arthur in the morning. I will send the porter, Mr. Bryson, around to each of your cabins to address any concerns you might have. That will be all."

Just then Halverson entered the bridge, out of breath and soaking wet.

"Captain, the sails are down. Only minor damage to them to report at this time."

The captain nodded to him, then turned to First Mate Ralston. "Replot our position and determine if we are off course."

"Aye, Captain, right away, as soon as I can see the stars again. I do have the weather update, if you want that first, sir."

As he finished speaking, another sailor entered the bridge.

"Captain, happy to report that the engine room reports no damage. The first engineer was the man who restored the lights said the breaker handle was in the Off position for some reason."

The captain didn't acknowledge the sailor. Instead, he kept staring at First Mate Ralston. Ralston knew what this meant, so he gave him the updated weather report.

Then another sailor entered the bridge. "Captain, sir, the cargo holds are dry, and the cargo is still safely secured."

The captain didn't acknowledge him either. Instead, he looked out the window into the violent seas. This was his defining moment as a captain. He knew it. He was confident he could beat the weather, but he was beginning to wonder if that was going to be enough. He began to think that maybe McDuff had sabotaged the lights for some reason. Perhaps he was going to do more? Perhaps he was after more than just the counterfeit plates? Did he learn of my secrets? Does he know about the silver mine and the exchange? Only one person could have told him. Then the captain made another message over the loudspeaker, calling Bryson to the captain's quarters immediately.

"Mr. Ralston, what is our position? Are we still on course or not?"

"Sir, to the best of my abilities, I have determined that we are still on course."

"Very well, keep us on them! You have the bridge for the next few minutes." Then the captain left and made his way to his quarters.

When he got there, he couldn't believe his eyes. His office was destroyed. Nothing remained untouched. At first, he thought it had occurred when the ship rolled violently, but then he saw the fake safe door embedded in his globe. Then he knew McDuff was responsible. As he waited for Bryson, he determined that he was going to have to rid himself of that little man after all. He set his mind to thinking of how he was going to do it. He knew the storm would give him the perfect cover. He just needed an opportunity. He made his way to where his desk had been. Then he got down on his hands and knees and pulled back the rug to reveal a floor safe. He opened it and retrieved his pistol and tucked it inside his uniform, out of sight. Then he concealed the floor safe again.

*****

McDuff and Archer were hiding near the mechanical room. McDuff had counted how long it would take for the crew to get the lights back on. Surprisingly, it was faster than he anticipated.

"Six minutes," he said. "It teuk thaim ainlie six minutes. Th' neist time thay wull dae it even quicker. That leaves us aboot five minutes tae safely dae oor deed in th' mirk."

"That engineer made his way out here pretty fast. That's for sure."

"Too fest."

"When are you going to tell me the plan?" asked Archer.

McDuff's face got a devilish grin on it. "Sae 'ere it's. While a'm cutting th' power taeth' lights. Yer aff tae gang doon tae th' secret cargo haud whaur we hud tied up Winston 'n' Catherine 'n' light th' fuse taeth' bomb ah hae hidden thare. Then yer aff tae catch up wi' me 'ere at th' lifeboat we stored th' cargo oan. Then we lower th' lifeboat 'n' mak' oor wey taeth' island whaur we wull capture th' Indian whin he returns 'n' force him tae tak' us taeth' silver mines."

Archer's eyes lit up. "So how long do we need?"

"Twa times that lang. Bit lea that tae me. Ah hae anither idea aboot that."

"When are we going to do this?"

"Whinth' captain stops tae catch up wi'th' Indian. Then we cut th' lights 'n' lit th' bomb."

"How will I be able to light it in the dark?"

"Fur, yer aff tae be doon in th' haud afore the lights gang oot. Haudin' th' fuse in one haun 'n' th' match in th' ither. That's how fur."

"Then I climb up the ladder and run in the darkness down the hallway to the staircase and climb it to the main deck and meet you at the lifeboat?"

"Ye git it doon cauld."

"Can't I have a lantern? I could take the one the engineer used from that locker. Then I am not doing everything in the dark."

"If ye mist."

Archer immediately went to the locker and took the lantern. Then he closed the door back and returned to McDuff a few feet away.

*****

"Where in the blazes is Bryson?" the captain yelled into his office. He decided he could wait no longer and made his way back to the bridge. He knew that Bryson would finish the job tonight as discussed. Besides he had more important things to worry about. When he entered the bridge, he relieved Ralston.

"Sir, I show us getting very close to our destination. However, the wind and waves have not subsided yet."

"What is our position exactly?"

Ralston was glad that the stars had shown through long enough to give him a reading.

"Eight miles out from the Isle, sir. No more than thirty minutes at this speed."

"Very well. Slow our speed to ten knots and post two lookouts with spyglasses. Tell them to watch for the island and shout out as soon as they see anything."

The captain lit his pipe, this time inside the bridge.

I bet that's where Bryson is, thought the captain. He is getting ready to lower the lifeboat as planned. Good old Bryson. He is more reliable than I imagined.

*****

Crigger and Tibbs had made their way back down to the second deck after getting Winston and Catherine safely into the lifeboat. They were heading back toward room 79, when they saw Archer come out of the middle hallway and turn in front and away from them. He walked to room 71, opened the door, and made his way inside.

Tibbs pushed his elbow into Crigger's ribs and whispered, "Here's our chance. We have him alone and cornered. Let's get our revenge."

Both men carefully made their way to the room. They put their ear to the door but didn't hear anything. They knew that this was because he was down below in the secret cargo hold.

Crigger whispered, "Let's trap him in the room below. He will not be able to escape."

Tibbs smiled. "Agreed! Let's do this while we can." Then he took the master key and unlocked the door.

They were right, that trap door was open, and the light was on below. Tibbs got on his belly and crawled over to the opening and looked over the edge. Below him was Archer looking under all the stacks of supplies for something. He motioned to Crigger, and they picked up the trapdoor and quickly placed it back over the hole. As soon as they did, they heard Archer yell from below. Crigger told Tibbs to stand on the trapdoor, while he went to push the dresser into the closet. Tibbs could hear Archer climbing the ladder quickly.

"Hurry! He's coming."

Crigger manhandled the dresser and tipped it over in the closet, so it fell on top of the door. Luckily, Tibbs had room to jump to the side out of the way. Then he climbed over the dresser and got out of the closet. They could hear Archer banging against the door, swearing up a storm. But he was not able to budge the door open. Satisfied, the men left the room and locked the door behind them.

*****

Meanwhile, Archer was standing on the twenty-foot-tall ladder and pushing against the door with all his might. He could feel it budge a little every time. But not enough for him to get his fingers underneath. He climbed back down the ladder and looked around the room for some tool or piece of wood or metal that he could use to pry the door open. He knew he had to hurry. All he saw was the supplies of ink and paper for the counterfeit machine. He sat down on a stack of paper and stared at the floor. Then it came to him. The ladder was made out of metal, and so were the rungs. He didn't need the bottom rung. He got back up and went over to the ladder and began to stomp on the bottom rung. It didn't budge. So he climbed up the ladder a couple of rungs and jumped down to the bottom rung, hoping his body weight would help loosen it. He did this several times. Finally, he heard the metal weld let loose as he hit it with all of his force as he jumped down on it. As it snapped free, he landed awkwardly on his left ankle and heard it snap as well. He let out a roar of pain and frustration.

*****

Duncan and Halverson were each in a crow's nest, located near the top of each mast, some fifty feet above the deck. Both had a spyglass and were scanning the horizon in search of the island. Luckily for them, the clouds had thinned slightly, which was letting just a faint amount of moonlight to brighten the stormy sky. By their estimation, they could see about a half to three quarters of a mile out into the distance. They were both finding it difficult to keep looking through the narrow lens, as the waves were moving the men side to side several feet with every wave, like a giant upside-down pendulum. The thirty-mile-an-hour wind was driving the biting cold deep into their bones. Luckily, they were high enough to not get wet from the spray of the waves crashing into the boat. That was the only advantage they had in their favor. Even though they had only been up there twenty minutes, it felt like it had been hours.

Duncan yelled over to Halverson, "See anything yet?"

"Nothing at all. It will be hard to see the island with these massive waves."

"Let's split up the horizon. Each search half. It will make us more efficient."

"Okay. I will go from twelve o'clock to six o'clock, and you go from six o'clock to twelve o'clock."

"Agreed," came the reply.

A few moments later, Halverson yelled to Duncan. "Put your scope at one o'clock. What do you see?"

Duncan refocused his spyglass. "You found the island."

Halverson signaled down to the man on the deck that they see the island three quarters of a mile out, bearing 260 degrees.

The man on the deck ran to the bridge. "Captain, Isle Royal spotted, bearing 260 degrees, three quarters of a mile out."

The captain immediately signaled the engine room for a full stop.

"Turn the ship to face north," he told the helmsman.

"But, Captain, the waves will be broadside."

"Yes, but it will take a few moments to slow to a stop, and I do not want to get closer to the island and the deadly rocks that surround her. So turn the ship to the north!"

"Aye, Captain."

Then he blew the foghorn to signal to Gitchie Manito that he was there and as a warning of danger to the crew and passengers.

*****

In the secret hold, Archer could feel the ship slow down and begin the roll more from side to side. Hearing the foghorn, he lit the lantern, knowing that McDuff was going to cut the lights at any moment. Then he grabbed the metal rung he knocked loose and tucked it in his waistband. Using mostly his arms, he pulled himself back up the ladder, stopping near the top and bracing himself with his good leg. He only had a few minutes, if that, to get the door open. He pushed against it with his shoulder and tried to pry the metal rung under the trap door. He almost had it. Just a little more. With one hand hanging on to the ladder, he used the other to push the makeshift tool into the miniscule space between the frame and door. Eventually, he got just enough to get the rung wedged in place. He stopped and looked at the rung stuck into the opening he created. He grabbed the rung and began to pull down on it, forcing the trapdoor to rise ever so slightly. Then he pushed with his shoulder, while pushing down with his forearm arm on the bar. That's when the unthinkable happened. The bar slipped out of the opening and fell to the floor, landing directly on the lantern, which knocked it over and started a small fire. Archer quickly slid down the ladder and tried to put the fire out, but he knew it was useless with all the dry paper in the room. He broke open the barrels of ink so he could put out the fire, but it burned a thick black smoke that made him feel nauseous. Then his mind shifted to the bomb.

*****

McDuff also heard the foghorn and felt the ship slow down. That was his signal to cut the lights. First, he went over to the watertight door to the engine room and wedged a mop handle against the mechanism so it couldn't turn open. Then he went to the mechanical room and cut the lights. As soon as he did, he made his way to the stairwell and began to climb to the top deck. From below, he could hear the sailors yelling in panic. He laughed and finished his ascent to the top deck. He grabbed the railing in his right hand. He began to run to the front of the ship. In no time, he was at the lifeboat, waiting for Archer to show up. Seconds later, the ship jumped out of the water with a loud explosion. Then it fell back into the water, bent in half, with the middle of the ship lower than either end. McDuff fell to the deck. Instantly, he knew that the plan had went all wrong. He hoped that Archer had gotten far enough away from the explosion.

*****

Inside the engine room, there was total darkness. Men were screaming that water was coming in the ship. The first engineer was already at the door trying with all of his might to open it up, but it was no use. Quickly, he turned around and started to head to the door at the aft end of the engine room. He yelled for his crew to shut down the engines and bleed off the pressure in the boilers. He knew it was only a matter of time before the cold sea water would explode the hot boilers. He also knew that men would die tonight.

*****

Crigger and Tibbs were surprised by the explosion. They figured they had prevented it when they locked Archer down below. They picked themselves up off the floor and made their way back to the lifeboat. Only thing to do now was to get to safety with Winston and Catherine.

*****

Captain Thomas, at first, thought they had run aground; but he knew that the rocks didn't come out that far. Then his ringing ears let him know what had happened. They had been sabotaged by McDuff. He tore out of the bridge as quickly as he could. Looking down, he saw McDuff standing by a lifeboat. He pulled the pistol out from under his uniform and took aim. He fired right at McDuff's head, but with the ship rolling in the waves, he was lucky to have hit him in the forearm. He thought about firing again but decided against it.

*****

Duncan and Halverson were still in the crow's nest. They could see all the carnage below. The ship was going to sink, no doubt. It was nearly cut in half by the force of the blow. In fact, the two crow's nests were leaning dangerously close to each other. Duncan was in the forward one, which was now leaning aft, while Halverson was in the aft one, which was now leaning forward. Getting down now was almost an impossibility with the angle of the mast and the ship rolling side to side.

"We need to get to a lifeboat. It is our only option," yelled Duncan over the raging storm.

Halverson looked around at the scene below them. He saw McDuff sitting on the front starboard side deck, holding his blood-soaked arm with the other. He saw the captain standing on the deck beside the bridge with a gun in his hand. He saw the ship had been turned toward the north, which meant the starboard side was now facing the sea and not the island.

"We need to get to one on the port side of the ship, or else we will need to row around the ship to get to land…and let's head to the back of the ship. I don't like what I am seeing up front."

*****

Winston lifted the edge of the tarp to see what in the world was going on. All he saw was chaos in the dim moonlight. All the lights were off, people were yelling and screaming, and the ship was bending in to the middle. He knew he needed to lower the lifeboat to have a chance at saving Catherine, but he decided to wait for a moment, hoping that Crigger and Tibbs would show up and escape with them.

He lowered the tarp and whispered to Catherine, "Everything is going to be okay. We are in the safest spot possible. Soon Crigger and Tibbs will join us and we will all row to the island."

*****

Gitchie Manito heard the explosion and rowed on with all his might to get to the ship. This would now be a rescue operation. He knew he was risking his life in this storm, but he had learned to conquer fear as a young Indian, so he remained calm and was not afraid. He was thankful for another opportunity to gain favor with the white people, which was his plan for survival. The missionary man, who befriended him several years ago and taught him English, helped him come to the conclusion that they weren't going away and that the way of his ancestors was coming to an end. He quickly decided to continue to the predetermined meeting spot at the back of the ship, to see if the lifeboat had been lowered. Every time he crested a wave, he recalculated his progress.

*****

When the Captain walked back into the bridge, everyone was staring at him. He grabbed the intercom and said, "Abandon ship, abandon ship. This is not a drill." Then he instructed his crew to drop anchor and go to their emergency stations to assist the passengers into the lifeboats. Meanwhile, he left the bridge to go finish McDuff off in person. He wanted the satisfaction of seeing him die for ruining his one shot at sea captain glory and for destroying his office.

*****

Tigger and Cribbs finally reached the lifeboat. Tibbs poked his head under the tarp.

"Am I interrupting anything?" he said with a tinge of humor.

"Thank God you are here," replied Catherine. "Let's get this boat in the water and make our escape while we still can."

Tibbs didn't reply. Instead, he pulled his head out from under the tarp and told Crigger to get on the other side of the rowboat and help him lower it into the ocean. Both men knew it required two men to lower a lifeboat, and that if they were going to be on it, they would need to climb down the ropes after it was in the water. Slowly, they swung the davit until it had the rowboat hanging over the side of the ship. Then both men began to use the pulleys to lower the boat toward the angry sea.

*****

Back in the engine room, the first engineer had made it to the aft door. It was higher up than the rest of the engine room, because the middle of the ship was sinking first. Even so, he was standing in a foot of water. As the door opened, the other sailors followed the engineer out of the engine room. He made his way to the aft stairwell and began to climb up to safety, away from the water.

*****

Duncan and Halverson froze as they heard loud cracking sounds from below. It wasn't metal, but wood. They looked down just in time to see the masts start to split apart from the strain on them.

"They're going to break in half!" yelled Duncan.

"We are going to have to ride it down and jump off at the last second, before it crashes into the deck," replied a fearful Halverson.

Duncan nodded. Too scared to speak, he looked down to watch and wait for the moment to jump. A few seconds later, he heard another loud crack, then he was falling. Before he knew what had happened, he slammed into the deck. There was a bright flash of light, immense pain, and then nothing.

*****

Crigger yelled, "Look out!" as he saw the mast falling in their direction. He jumped back, hoping Tibbs did the same. The mast fell straight where the lifeboat had been just a few seconds before, hitting the deck and railing, breaking the davits free and sending them over the side. He got back on his feet and rushed to the edge and looked over to see what happened to Winston and Catherine. The lifeboat was nowhere to be seen. To his horror, he realized that the davit must have fallen on the lifeboat and put it straight to the bottom of the lake. Before it could register in his brain that they were gone, he heard Tibbs yell out in pain.

"Help me get this crap off my leg," he shouted as he was pinned under the wreckage, not realizing the full extent of what had just happened.

*****

Halverson had better luck. He timed his jump perfectly and landed on the deck beside the bridge just before the mast landed on the bridge, smashing it to pieces. As he struggled to get back to his feet, he realized that his shoulder was all busted up. Fortunately, everything else seemed to work okay. He looked around and saw the captain approaching. He was preparing to say something as the captain stopped to see how he was, but the captain walked past, not noticing the man. His eyes were focused on someone else.

*****

"McDuff! You destroyed my ship!" Captain Thomas yelled as he approached the man. "Now I am going to destroy you."

"Your ship. Ah think nae. It belongs taeth' CPR."

"Wrong. When it is on a voyage, it is mine. I am responsible for it."

"Yerricht. A'm sure ye wull be held responsible fur this, na doubt."

"Too bad you're not going to be around to find out."

"Sae urr ye aff tae shoot me again? Or urr ye aff tae huv a go, tae best me lik' a real jimmy?"

"I don't need a gun to kill you," Thomas replied. Then he squared off with the leprechaun, and the fight began.

*****

Winston realized that the lifeboat was upside down and sinking under the water. There was a small pocket of air trapped inside. He pulled Catherine so that her head was above the water in the underside of the boat. She was barely conscious, shivering and mumbling incoherently. Pinching her nose shut, he closed her mouth and took a big gulp of air. Then he pulled her down under the boat and out from underneath it and swam with her toward the surface. He could see the light from the surface just a few feet away when he was stopped. His leg was tangled in the rigging from the mast that crashed over the edge of the ship. He struggled with it but couldn't break free. He had to make the toughest decision of his life and pushed Catherine toward the surface, alone. Then he turned to get his leg untangled before he drowned. As he did so, all he could think was that death was still pursuing him.

*****

Gitchie Manito had seen the lifeboat get sunk by the falling debris just as he crested the last wave. He continued on, being only a few yards away, when he saw a woman pop up to the surface as he crested the next. Good thing she had a lifejacket on. He skillfully moved his boat closer to her and then, after a few attempts, hauled her aboard his boat. She was unconscious, probably from the shock of the cold water. He turned the boat around and headed back to shore. There might be others to save, but she needed a fire to get warm quickly, or she would die of exposure.

*****

Crigger had finally gotten Tibbs free of the debris he was trapped under. Tibbs was able to stand, but his left leg was pretty busted up. They both went back to the edge and looked over. They saw nothing but waves. The island was less than a half mile away and seemed to be getting closer.

"We need to get into another lifeboat and search for Winston and Catherine!" Crigger said in desperation.

Tibbs looked around at the carnage. "We are not going to get any of the others on this side of the ship launched with that mast fouling everything up. We will need to get one on the other side."

Crigger agreed and helped Tibbs hobble over to the starboard side of the ship. When they got there, they grabbed the first lifeboat they came across. As they prepared to lower it, they saw the engineer and a few sailors from the engine room come up the steps. After explaining that they were on a rescue mission, the sailors agreed to lower the boat with them in it. After all, there was another lifeboat twenty feet away for them to use for themselves. Once they were in the boat and almost at the water's edge, Crigger realized that this was the boat they had sabotaged. He motioned for the sailors to stop, but they didn't understand and completed their task. Crigger then slapped Tibbs out of frustration.

"What was that for?"

"You had to go and drill holes in a lifeboat, and now we're in that boat!"

Tibbs gulped and immediately looked down at the bottom of the boat. "No water!" he exclaimed in relief.

Crigger looked down in disbelief. "How is that even possible?"

"I guess the pressure of the water is forcing the corks tighter into the holes. Luckily, we pushed the corks in from the underside."

"You, sir, are a terrible saboteur. And I am extremely happy about that. Now let's go rescue Winston and Catherine before our luck runs out."

*****

Thomas struck first and landed a blow to the injured arm of McDuff, who was unable to move it out of the way.

"Is that a' ye git? Mah grandmother hits harder than that."

Thomas took the bait and wound up for a bigger punch. Before he unleashed it, McDuff counter punched, hitting the captain square in the gut, which doubled him over for a second. Thomas took a step backward so he could regain his breathing before McDuff could hit him again.

"Juist as ah thought, a' bluster 'n' na muster. Ah will tell ye whit, ah will battle wi' yin arm behind mah back. Na hauld yer horses, ye aw ready seen tae that." McDuff laughed as he continued to taunt the captain.

Thomas picked up a piece of broken timber off the deck. "Come here, little boy, and I will muster your head clean off your shoulders!"

He swung the weapon and missed as McDuff lunged and tackled the captain, pinning him against the deck. He landed blow after blow on his face. That's when Duncan saw the captain and ran to his defense. He kicked the leprechaun in the side of the head, knocking him off the captain for a moment. Then a few other sailors saw the commotion.

*****

Crigger and Tibbs had finally gotten the rowboat around the back of the ship and to the spot where Winston and Catherine had been. Tibbs took off his shirt, grabbed a rope, and tied it around his waist.

"What are you planning on doing with that?"

"Hold this end of the rope, and I'll show you." Then Tibbs jumped out of the boat and sunk beneath the waves.

Crigger couldn't believe his eyes. That was a suicide mission. He was going to freeze to death, and all he was going to find was dead bodies, if he found anything. He waited for Tibbs to tug on the rope so he could pull the fool aboard. He kept waiting. Then he became worried that Tibbs wouldn't tug on the rope at all. That's when he surfaced on the opposite side of the boat.

"What are you doing looking for me over there? Hurry up and pull me in. I'm freezing."

Crigger quickly pulled him onboard and handed him his shirt. "What did you find?"

Tibbs had a sad expression on his face, even though he was shivering uncontrollably. "I saw the lifeboat at the bottom several feet below where I could get to. It definitely sunk. I'm afraid they're both gone."

Without saying another word, both men started to row to the shoreline. Thirty yards in, they heard and felt another explosion as the boilers met their fate. The ship was completely split in half now, and both pieces were drifting away from each other in an arc. Perhaps they were swinging on their anchors now that they were separated.

During the melee, Thomas's gun had fallen out on the deck. McDuff quickly picked it up and pointed it at Thomas as he backed up to the lifeboat.

"Ah wid shoot ye, bit ah wull let th' storm tak' ye instead. Dinnae waan ta' body saying thare wis a mutiny oanboord. Noo hae yer, sailor laddies, lower this boat fur me or ah wull stairt shooting."

The sailors looked at the beaten-up captain, then they lowered the lifeboat as ordered into the water. From below, they heard McDuff yell one more insult.

"If ye dinnae see the bottom, dinnae wade."

That was the last lifeboat that was able to leave the *Algoma*. The debris from the second explosion destroyed the remaining ones. So the sailors turned their attention to the back half of the ship and watched as it began to sink beneath the waves. They looked on in horror at the bodies of people trying to swim in the water against the waves. Ten minutes later, there was only those on the front half of the ship left.

CHAPTER 11

Land at Last

The winter hurricane of ice and snow was too much. In the darkness, I couldn't see anything, and I was cold beyond comprehension. Waves kept pounding me into rocks. I gave up, ready to die, when my feet hit solid ground.

—Unknown survivor of the *SS Algoma*

Gitchie Manito safely landed his boat back on Isle Royale. He picked up the frozen and lifeless body he had pulled from the storm and quickly made way to a hidden cave system he knew about. In no time, he had a fire roaring that was concealed to everyone else. He left the woman by the fire and made his way back out of the cave and returned sometime later with his wife, Ahsubbi, and some furs to wrap the woman in, to warm her up. Ahsubbi looked at the woman and then began to make a medicinal compound whose aroma has healing properties when burnt.

*****

Crigger and Tibbs were struggling to row against the storm. The boat had developed small leaks in the bottom, which were getting worse by the minute, and they still had only covered half of the distance to shore. Crigger out of the corner of his eye saw another lifeboat cresting in the waves every so often off to his right, which was farther north. He was unable to see how many were in it, but he hoped that it would make it to land. He pointed it out to Tibbs.

"I think that must be full of people. It is sitting low in the water like it has a heavy load."

"I hope it's people," said Crigger as a new thought popped into his head. "Maybe it is the leprechaun making his escape with the cargo?"

"Then I hope it sinks," replied Tibbs.

"Speaking of sinking, we better row harder before we sink. Can't believe we've made it this far in this boat you turned into Swiss cheese."

As they doubled down on rowing, the waves were pushing them to the northwest, away from the *Algoma*, which was all but invisible to them now in the dim moonlight. After what seemed like an eternity, they saw rocks under their boat, which meant the shore was not too far away. A few moments later the ship grounded to a stop, and both men tumbled out after a wave flipped the boat over. They quickly made their way to shore and got their bearings. They soon discovered they landed on a small barrier island just off Isle Royale, so they made their way north to a narrow crossing point to the island and crossed over there. Then they built a fire to warm up. Because of the terrain, it wasn't visible to the south, being protected by the rugged and steep landscape.

*****

Back on the ship, the men discovered that the front half of the ship had run aground on a large rock and was not in danger of sinking unless the waves pushed them off. With this discovery, the men changed their mindset from escaping to survival on the ship, until help would come. Surely, the rising sun in a few hours would bring help their way. With the bridge and the cabins above deck destroyed, the men hunkered down on the stairwell to the decks below. This kept them out of the fierce wind, and the spray from the waves. The captain was so badly beaten that he was carried by the others off the deck and out of the storm.

*****

After sitting around the fire for the better part of an hour, Tibbs felt the warmth return to his bones.

"Let's go find that rowboat to the north. If it is survivors, they could use our help, and if it is the leprechaun, we still have a score to settle for Niklas."

"Not just Niklas, my friend. For everyone that has died on that ship at his hands," replied Crigger.

They set out walking the shoreline to the north, pretty soon their campfire was not visible to them. Every few steps, Tibbs would stop and listen for the sound of people as he rested his busted leg. They walked for twenty minutes that way until Crigger spotted a rowboat beached up ahead. Immediately, both men dropped to the ground and crawled over to some brush for cover.

"It's from the *Algoma*," stated Crigger.

"I don't see anyone near it."

"Doesn't mean they haven't found a place to hide from the storm."

"Agreed. Let's split up. You work your way inland and around to the north, and I will take a straight approach along the shoreline from the south," said Tibbs. "I will give you a five-minute head start."

"You know you can't count that high," teased Crigger.

"Now's not the time," Tibbs rebuked the man.

With that, Crigger started out on his five-minute head start.

*****

Back in the cave, Catherine began to wake up. Slowly at first, as she saw the flames dancing off the rock walls. It made her think she was dreaming. Then she saw the two Indians.

"Are you real?" she asked.

Ahsubbi moved closer to her and took her hand. "Yes, we are just as real as you are."

"Oh, I thought I was dreaming. Where am I?"

"You are safe, on Isle Royale. You were in a shipwreck, and my husband pulled you out of the water."

Then Catherine remembered, and she sat upright. "Where's Winston?"

Gitchie Manito spoke. "You were the only one I saw."

Then Catherine cried hysterically. "No, there was a man with me. You must find him. You must save him. I love him."

Ahsubbi said something to Gitchie Manito in her native dialect, and then he left.

"You will be all right, my child. If your man is alive, my husband will bring him to you." Then she started to sing and sooth Catherine until she finally fell back asleep out of exhaustion.

*****

In the distance, Crigger could hear men talking. He drew closer and listened. Then he walked out into the open.

"Glad you made it safe," he said to the engineer and three of the sailors from the engine room.

Just then Tibbs jumped out of the shadows hollering, all ready for a fight. Quickly realizing what was going on, he apologized. "Sorry, thought you were someone else."

The men just looked at him, not knowing what to say.

"Come follow us, we have a good campsite down the beach and have a fire going. Let's get you men warm."

The men agreed and followed them back to the campsite.

"Did you ever find the people you went looking for?" asked the first engineer.

"No. Their lifeboat was sunk. They both drowned."

"Sorry to hear that, mate. I am sure a lot of people lost their life tonight."

"What happened?" asked one of the sailors.

Crigger and Tibbs took the rest of the night filling them in on what McDuff had done to Niklas.

*****

The rising sun was met by a relatively calm day. The fierceness of the storm from the past day and night had lost its teeth. A local fisherman headed down to the beach to get his nets ready when he spotted wreckage washed up on shore. At first, he was puzzled by the sight of the beached dressers and mattresses. Then he saw a mangled body and realized what it meant and ran to get the others. Soon all the other fishermen were at the beach looking at the damage. Then one of them spotted the *Algoma* way off in the distance.

"Men, we need to get out to that ship!"

They ran back to camp and decided to take the biggest of their fishing boats. If there were survivors, it would be able to bring them back to land. Three fishermen jumped in the boat and started the voyage out of the Moskey Basin and through the Middle Island Passage that leads to Lake Superior.

*****

Onboard the *Algoma*, a sailor who was keeping watch saw the ship headed their way.

"A ship! Everyone, wake up. There is a ship coming from the island!" he yelled.

It didn't take long for most of the crew to get back up on deck. In all, there were seven sailors besides the captain still on the *Algoma*. Two of whom helped the captain to the top deck. The men all waved and whistled to the ship, but it didn't matter, as the ship had already seen them.

Two hours later, they were all back at the fishing camp, relieved that their ordeal was over.

*****

Catherine woke back up and looked around the cave. The fire was out, and both Indians were sitting cross-legged on the floor watching her.

"You're back. Where's Winston? Did you find him?"

Gitchie Manito put his hand out to signal to slow down and be patient. Then he pointed over to the back of the cave. In the darkness, she saw the figure of a man slumped over in the dirt, covered with a blanket to keep him warm."

"What's wrong with him? Is he dead?" she asked with a panicked voice, trying to get up and go see him.

"Not dead! Just recovering from injuries. He lost a lot of blood," answered Gitchie Manito. "Let him rest."

A flood of relief washed over Catherine as she settled back down. "Thank you so much! How can I ever repay you?"

Gitchie Manito didn't answer. Instead, he got up and left the cave.

"Where's he going? Did I say something to offend him?"

"No. He's going to get food for us. You must eat to get your strength back," said Ahsubbi.

With that, Ahsubbi moved next to Catherine and began to rub her arms and legs to get the circulation going again in them. Catherine smiled at her.

"What does your name mean. It is such a pretty name."

"It means 'Net.' My husband changed my name because he said I must have used a net to catch him when we were young." She smiled at the memory. "He was the best and bravest of the Indians. So I guess I was lucky to have caught him at all. Every squaw was after him."

"Well, he certainly is brave. I will give you that."

"What is your name?"

"Oh, goodness. I forgot to tell you mine. It is Catherine. It means 'pure,' or so I was told…"

Catherine's sentence died on her lips as she looked up and saw pure evil standing in front of them with a knife in his hand.

"Weel, noo, lookie whit we hae 'ere," McDuff said with a sneer on his face. "Looks lik' ye 'n' ah survived, bit yer boyfriend did nae."

Catherine was too astonished to say anything. Her mind was whirling. The Indian must have confused McDuff with Winston. Does that mean Winston is dead? She felt like she was going to die a thousand deaths, the weight of her burdened heart felt as if it were about to burst open.

Ahsubbi quickly stood to her feet.

"Sit back doon afore ah mak' ye."

But Ahsubbi refused.

"Mibbie she doesn't know whit a'm saying, sae ye tell her fur me."

Catherine got up and stood beside Ahsubbi, so she could whisper into her ear. It was also an excuse to get up. "This man is very bad. He has killed many people. Please be careful."

Ahsubbi nodded, but remained standing, taking a step to her right, toward the back of the cave. She grabbed Catherine's hand and pulled her with her. This made McDuff turn to face the back of the cave so he could keep them directly in front of him.

"Ye kin stoap noo. Thar eis nae anythin' back thare tae hulp ye. Thare is na wey oot back thare."

McDuff stepped closer to the women.

"A'm aff tae let ye decide who dies first. Who knows, if ye pick th' Indian, mibbie we kin come tae some arrangement."

Catherine stared back at him, using her defiant silent approach.

"Sae tis up tae me then."

McDuff grabbed Ahsubbi and held the knife to her throat as he pulled her closer to him.

"Looks lik' ye lost."

"No. You did," she said defiantly. "My husband will track you down and kill you like the dog you are."

"Brave lest wurds. Ah will gie ye that."

Catherine could no longer hold back all the emotion and agony in her heart as her hope that Winston was alive once again was turned to disbelief. She stepped closer to McDuff so she was just inches from his face. She no longer cared that he had a knife and wanted to kill her; she was going to give him a piece of her mind first.

"You are the most vile, disgusting, greedy human being on the earth," she screamed. "And that's saying something. It wasn't enough that you had conned the railroad and my father into making you rich. You had to have more. So in exchange for our lives, we told you about the captain's get-rich plan that you could take over. But that wasn't enough. You refused to let us go, contrary to your promise you gave us, and still required the counterfeit plates. You murdered everyone who came across your path in your unquenchable thirst for riches and almost lost your own life in the process. I hope you rot for all eternity, you piece of filth! You killed the only man I ever loved!"

McDuff at first was taken aback. No one had dared talk to him like that for many, many years. In fact, he couldn't remember the last time someone had done so. But that only lasted for a second as a sneer reappeared on his face.

"Oh, boo hoo. Lef isn't fair. I'm a spoiled rich lass, wha is juist finding oot that ye hae tae tak' whit yi'll waant in lef, unless ye hae a rich daddy that wull gie ye whitevur ye want."

"You're a monster. You take what belongs to others. The fruit of their labor and hard work. Their dreams and hopes. Their loved ones and even their very own lives."

"Sic a sel righteous, young lass. Ye ne'er teuk something that wasn't yers? Ye ne'er dashed someone's hawp?"

"Never!" Catherine retorted with distain.

"Howfur mony men's hearts did ye crush, whin ye refused thair offer o' marriage?"

"That's different. They were assuming something that wasn't promised. I never had professed my love to any of those men. Their hearts turned out to be as greedy as yours."

"Saeyer saying that mibbie we hae a future th' gither, is that it?"

Ahsubbi lean back just a bit to keep the knife from pressing so tight to her neck.

McDuff looked in her direction for a moment. "Wis ah pressing it tae solid?"

Ahsubbi relaxed and said something in Ojibwe. "Gigawaabamin wayiiba gaakamine." (Translated to English, it means, "I will see you soon die suddenly.)

McDuff laughed and replied, "Dinnae ye ken that a sneeze is a ill omen. Mah ma used tae say,

> Sneeze oan Monday, sneeze fur danger.
> Sneeze oan Tuesday, winch a stranger.
> Sneeze oan Wensday, sneeze fur a letter.
> Sneeze oan Thursday, something better.
> Sneeze oan end eh the week, sneeze fur woe.
> Sneeze oan Seturday, a journey tae go.
> Sneeze oan Sunday, yer safety seek?
> Fur de' il wull hae ye fur th' rest o' th' week!"

Then he looked back at Catherine.

"Ye ken whit day it's? Tis Seturday. This means we need tae gang oan a wee journey."

"I'm not going anywhere with you, monster! You have already destroyed my life, my future! What are you waiting for, kill me now and get it over with." With that, she dropped to her knees and lowered her head.

As she did so, Ahsubbi grabbed McDuff's wounded arm and twisted it as hard as she could. As a result, McDuff lost his grip on the knife and dropped it to the ground, allowing Ahsubbi to take a few steps backward.

McDuff growled in pain at her. "Yer aff tae regret daein' that."

And those were the last words ever uttered by McDuff as an arrow flew into the cave and pierced his heart. Then a second one hit him in the neck as he fell to the ground as dead as a stone.

Ahsubbi looked over at her husband standing in the opening of the cave. She knew he never missed. In one hand was his bow; at his feet was the rabbit he went to get for breakfast.

Catherine screamed as she saw McDuff fall dead to the earth right next to where she had kneeled. She stared at him to make sure he was really dead, then she spit in his face, then pounded her fists into him.

Ahsubbi helped Catherine back to her feet and then walked over and gave her husband a big hug. Gitchie Manito entered the cave, dropped the rabbits by the fire, and left. He had never once let Ahsubbi down. It was always a mystery to her why he chose her and was always there to protect her. That is why she named him Gitchie Manito when they were married. It means "Great mystery."

Catherine was grateful for everything they had done for her, but her heart wasn't in a good place. She needed to know what became of Winston. The thought of him dying was too much to handle, and she found herself coping by rocking back and forth, with her arms wrapped around herself, like she was giving herself a hug.

Ahsubbi helped her sit back down in the soft dirt and wrapped her back in the furs. "You rest, while I make breakfast."

Catherine remained quiet, hugging herself. It felt like it was the only thing to keep her from falling apart.

When breakfast was served, she was unable to eat. Instead, she was eager to get out of the cave and figure out what to do with her life. She followed Ahsubbi, as she followed Gitchie Manito down the trail. She did not know where they were going, nor did she care. After a half hour of walking, she let out a scream into the air.

The Indians stopped and looked at her.

"Come," Gitchie Manito said.

"Sorry. Just had to get that frustration out of my system. Life isn't fair, and even though I saw justice come to fruition with McDuff's death, I have no hope for the future. My hope died today. And I just realized that Winston was right. 'They got what they deserved' is the greatest ending ever written. McDuff got what he deserved, but I will add that even though justice was sweet, life is still empty without hope. You can learn to live without justice, but not without hope. Life cheated me on what I deserved—Winston." She stopped talking as she looked up and saw them staring back at her.

"Come," he said again.

So she started walking along, not sure of where they were going or why.

A while later, they stopped walking, so she stopped. She was still staring at the ground, feeling lost and lonely, when she heard Ahsubbi speak.

"Gitchie Nini," she said as she pointed down the path in front of them. "Gitchie Nini."

Catherine didn't have a clue what that meant. But she looked down the path, and that's when she saw Winston sitting against a tree near a fire. She took off running and fell and hugged his neck.

"Your alive. I was so worried. How?" were the first words that came out of her mouth. He was still very cold to the touch, and she realized that his skin was still slightly blue.

"Gitchie Manito found me laying on the beach. Half in and half out of the water. I was pretty much dead when he found me."

She squeezed him tighter just to make sure it was real and not a dream. Then she turned to look at the Indians and jumped up to give them both a big hug.

"Thank you both! I can never repay you for the kindness you have shown us."

"Friends don't need to repay kindness," answered Ahsubbi.

"You are so sweet. Yes, of course, we shall always be friends. By the way, what does that word Gitchie Nini mean?"

"It is Ojibwe for 'great man.' It is the name we have given him."

Catherine was dumbfounded. "I am curious why you gave him that particular name."

"Because he was strong enough to survive being in the Great Lake during its most powerful storm. It truly takes a great man to beat the Great Lake. Why? Do you not like it?"

Winston spoke before Catherine could answer. "It's perfect! I always thought that Winston was a bit too stuffy and formal. I like the ring to it. Gitchie Nini it is."

Catherine laughed hearing Winston say it.

"And we have named you as well. We now call you Apenimo. It means 'hope,'" said Ahsubbi.

Catherine and Winston stayed on the island with Gitchie Manito and his wife Ahsubbi for the next few weeks while they recovered and made plans for their future and how to start their lives over with new identities, now that they were listed among the dead off the *Algoma* shipwreck.

Before they departed their newfound friends, they were married with an outdoor wedding among the natives of the island, which is the last wedding to occur on the island to this very day.

I would like to tell you Winston and Catherine lived happily ever after, but that's a fairy tale and this story is not. Instead, I can assure you that they both got what they deserved—each other.

EPILOGUE

It had been several months since the sinking of the Algoma. Enough time had passed to let loved ones grieve for the lost. Now it was time to set the record straight. To make sure those responsible paid for their wicked and immoral conduct.

—Gitchie Nini and Apenimo, spring 1886

It was a beautiful Saturday morning in Tennessee. Spring had arrived, bringing its magic touch. Everywhere one looked, evidence of new life was visible. The sun was warm, and everything was fresh and green and growing. If you listened close enough, you could imagine dogs barking and kids playing in their yards.

Mr. and Mrs. Owen were sitting on their porch swing, having their morning coffee. They lived on a small farm, in a beautiful old farmhouse on the outskirts of a small and charming town they had fallen in love with and the Southern hospitality it offered. The gentle breeze smelled of pine trees, as it whispered past them, reminding them of the Northern clime where they had met and fallen in love. When they looked past the trees, they could see the hilly landscape turn into grand mountains rising off in the distance, reminding them of how small and insignificant their lives were in the grand scheme of things and how fortunate they were to be able to appreciate the beauty that the world offered.

"Where did that dog get off to?"

"Probably harassing the squirrels again. You know that is her favorite sport."

The woman nodded.

Nothing else was said as they continued to gently swing back and forth.

After a while. Mrs. Owen went inside to fetch some iced tea and cookies. When she came back out, she asked, "Do you think they printed your letter?"

"Only one way to find out. We should probably stroll into town and buy a newspaper. See for ourselves," answered Gin, which is what people call him even though he uses the initials G. N. It is easier to say that way.

Hearing a bark in the distance, Mo got up and whistled once for her dog.

"Good girl, Goldie," she exclaimed as the dog ran to her side. "Did you catch any of those squirrels?" She patted the dog on the head. "We're headed out, so you watch the place until we get back."

Gin got up and took Mo's hand. They walked through the gate, closing it behind them. After walking in companionable silence for a few moments, thinking about what they were about to discover, Mo started flirting with Gin by pretending to kiss his cheek but stopping short. Then she ran a few steps ahead, laughing, causing Gin to speed up to catch her. Then the race was on. Before they got too far down the road, where they could be seen by the townsfolk, she let him catch her and give her a proper kiss. Then they walked respectably into town, with smiles etched on their faces.

They said good morning to everyone they came across as they walked over to the five-and-dime store to buy a paper. When they got there, only a few papers were left for sale, which was unusual. Gin picked up one of the last copies and put it under his arm as he got some money out of his pocket to pay for it.

"I think you're going to enjoy reading that one," said Mr. Bacon, the owner of Bacon's Sundries, the town's most trusted supply store.

"Why's that?" Gin asked.

"Someone named Gitchie Nini wrote an article about a shipwreck a last year. Must be a made-up name, like Mark Twain. Anyhow, according to him, it was sunk intentionally."

"Why on earth would someone do that?"

"Claims it had to do with the Canadian railroad and counterfeit American money."

"That is going to be an interesting read."

"The best part is that he named names of those he said was responsible."

"Well, if it is true, then I hope they are brought to justice."

"Agreed. He even mentioned a few folks who were killed, trying to stop it from happening. He called them heroes, protectors of society."

"I like the ring to that. They must have been really special people."

"The rumor is that there are some people from this very town that were on that ship that night."

"Oh, really." Gin said, dismissing the possibility. "I find that to be highly unlikely." Then he paid for the paper and said goodbye. "Thanks for the paper. See you in church tomorrow."

Once they had left the building, Mo nudged him. "Let's go see them."

Gin turned and headed back toward home. Once they reached their property, they headed past their farmhouse and over to the far side of the farm. A few minutes later, they came across a small barn containing several chickencoops.

"Anyone home?" Mo said loudly.

Two men stopped what they were doing and looked up. They were covered in scratches from head to toe and smelled faintly of chicken poo.

"Well, lookie who came to visit us," said the first man.

The second man walked over to them and attempted to shake Gin's hand, except he didn't offer his hand in return.

"No telling what is on that hand, my friend." Gin said with a smile.

"How's the chicken farming going?" asked Mo with a chuckle.

"It's safer than our last job, that's for sure."

"Yeah, none of the chickens have kidnapped anyone or tried to blow anyone up yet!"

"Well, I am glad it's working out for you. We are both proud of you for sticking with it."

Crigger and Tibbs exchanged a glance.

"We was wanting to thank you again for getting us started and giving us jobs working on your farm."

"And for fixing up the old servants quarters for us to live in!"

"Don't mention it. That's what friends do. Besides, we still had some of the Canadian money from the lifeboat that Gitchie Manito found and gave to us as a wedding present."

"We've been talking about that and decided to pay you back with free eggs, as many and as often as you want from us."

Mo muttered under her breath, "How kind of you to give us free eggs from our own chickens…"

Gin interrupted her before she could be overheard. "As a matter of fact, we would like you both to come to the house for dinner tonight. Talk about old times…"

"Great, we was wanting to talk to you about your newspaper article anyways."

"You've already read it?" Gin and Mo glanced uneasily at each other.

"Of course. You know we get up with the chickens!" Tibbs said as he started laughing at his own joke.

"See you at six, after you finish your chores," said Mo with a warm smile.

AUTHOR'S NOTES

For those of you interested in my thought process for developing this story, please read on.

Not only did I want to create realistic characters with quirks and flaws, I also wanted to carry two themes throughout the development of the characters and the progression of the storyline. Those two themes are hope and justice. I brought this out early with Mr. Fontaine asking what was the greatest ending to a story. Most of us, like Winston, would at first think that it is "that they lived happily ever after." But in reality, life is never that clean; and the absences of challenges and difficulties are, at best, temporary and the exception, not the rule.

I settled on hope and justice because these tenets are central to a healthy society and a healthy life. We can see too often today that people that lose hope become depressed, despondent, and, eventually, if unresolved, violent toward others or themselves. If you find yourself without hope for a better future or have nothing substantial or good to place your hope in, you're not alone. Don't give up, I will share some good news with you that can change your life if you will let it.

Even though life in this world can become overwhelming, cruel, unsafe, lonely and unfair, *our life in this world is not the end of our story!* Just like Winston, who tried to run away from his problems in an attempt to find a place without troubles, we can eventually go to a place just like that. A place called heaven, which is perfect. A place with no sorrow or tears, no regret or remorse, no pain or suffering. And the best news of all is that it will last forever, for all eternity without measure, and anyone who desires to go there, can freely *choose* to go there. Sounds too good to be true, doesn't it? Before you tune me out, thinking I am going to talk about religion, I am not, because religion is defined as mankind's attempt to reach God. I am instead going to talk about God's attempt to reach you. Bear with me for just a little bit.

When God created this world, it was perfect, just like heaven. He created the first man and woman and gave the entire world to them to live in and rule over. *God only had one rule for them to follow.* Can you imagine life with only one rule? The rule was, "*You must not eat from the tree of the knowledge of good and evil. For when you eat from it you will certainly die.*" We find this written in the Bible in Genesis 2:17. Well, we all know what happened. Both Adam and Eve broke the only rule God had given them. And death entered into the equation for the first time in human history. Not just physical death, but also spiritual death. Our spiritual nature, connection to God, died; and it happened immediately. God calls our disobedience sin. This spiritual death separated us from God, because God hates sin and will not allow it in His perfect presence. Romans 3:23 tells us that "*all have sinned and fall short of the glory of God.*" That means that both you and I are sinners and have been separated from God because of our own actions and choices.

But God didn't let our story end that way. Romans 6:23 tell us that "*the wages of sin is death, but the gift of God is eternal life in Christ Jesus our Lord.*" This is where the amazing part happens. Before I go any further, let me ask you a question that rocked my world many years ago: *why did Jesus have to die?*

Jesus left the glory of heaven, humbled Himself by becoming a human being, and lived on this earth for thirty-three years for one purpose! To take our punishment for us. He refused to give up on us. He refused to leave us destitute and without hope. He refused to leave heaven off-limits to us. How did He do that? He became a man and lived a perfect life. Not one sin, not even once. That means that He was not under the death curse that all of mankind is. And He willingly offered His life as a substitute for ours. That's the gift of God mentioned in Romans 6:23. He took our punishment (God's wrath) upon Himself so that those of us who believe in Jesus and accept Him as our Lord are no longer under God's wrath, because it was satisfied by Jesus's actions. Not only did Jesus willingly die, but He rose from the grave three days later! He conquered death! And because He did that, He can offer us life everlasting. You have probably heard or seen John 3:16 before. It says, *"For God so loved the world (us) the He gave His one and only Son, that whoever believes in Him will not perish but have eternal life."*

This is how Jesus saves us from our sins and why He alone is called our Savior. Acts 4:12 says, *"Nor is there salvation in any other, for there is no other name under heaven given among men by which we must be saved."*

So the next question is, *What must I do to be saved?*

Romans 10:9–10 tell us that *"if you confess with your mouth the Lord Jesus and believe in your heart that God has raised him from the dead, you will be saved. For with the heart one believes unto righteousness, and with the mouth confession is made unto salvation."*

Simply put, humble yourself before God. Commit to God that you no longer want to live a disobedient, sinful lifestyle. Acknowledge your sins, and ask Him for forgiveness, believing in your heart that Jesus is the Son of God.

If this is a decision you have made today, rejoice, your name is written in the book of life! Find someone to share it with.

The second theme is justice. We are all born with a sense of fairness. We want people who break the rules to be caught and appropriately punished. In America, we believe that nobody is above the law. Unfortunately, this process can get distorted because of the sinfulness of mankind as well. Sometimes the bad guys get away, or even get away with it. Life isn't always fair. Maybe today there are some people who feel they are above the law.

Do you know what the good news is to the unfairness and injustice of life. God is the ultimate judge, and He shows no favor or partiality toward anyone. He cannot be bought off, bribed, or lied to. He knows everything, and He will judge everything.

Here are a few verses that tell us about God as a judge:

> But the Lord shall endure forever; He has prepared His throne for judgement. He shall judge the world in righteousness. (Psalm 9:7–8)

> God shall judge the righteous and the wicked. (Ecclesiastes 3:17)

> For God will bring every work into judgement, including every secret thing, whether good or evil. (Ecclesiastes 12:14)

> If one man sins against another, God will judge him. (1 Samuel 2:25)

As Catherine said at the end of the book, "I realize that I can live without justice, but not without hope." Injustices do happen in this world. My prayer is that you do not let that keep you from placing your hope and trust in Jesus Christ.

ABOUT THE AUTHOR

Steven Persen has enjoyed a successful career in business management, working for both small- family and multibillion-dollar businesses. He has been married for over thirty-five years to his first love, Sherri. They have two children and three grandchildren, which provide them countless joy.

After a career of conquering business while living in several different states (Minnesota, Ohio, Kentucky, and Florida), he has returned to his beloved Ohio and turned his creative and analytical mind toward his love of history and writing.

Printed in the USA
CPSIA information can be obtained
at www.ICGtesting.com
LVHW092346081024
793245LV00001B/191